SOLDIER DOLL

KAREN MCKIBBIN

For Mum

PROLOGUE

They walk from the city centre, following the bus route home, her arm linked through his.

'Wait,' she says, stopping suddenly. 'I can't walk another inch in these friggin' things.' She leans against him for support as she pulls her shoes off swollen feet. She touches her heel and winces. 'Blister.'

'Come on,' he says, offering her his back. 'I'll carry you.' He puffs with the effort. After a hundred yards he sets her down.

She sways and topples against him. 'Oops.' She giggles.

'I told you to go easy on the rum and cokes.'

An armoured vehicle turns into the street. He holds her upright as he catches his breath. The vehicle slows then rumbles past.

'Wankers,' he mutters.

'Good craic tonight, wasn't it?'

He nods.

She looks at her watch. 'Christ, is that the time? My ma will tan my hide. Come on,' she says, tugging at his arm.

They set off, her in stockinged feet.

They turn into a dark, terraced street, its lights smashed long ago.

'Nearly home,' he says when he sees the chip shop.

The odour of fried batter hangs in the air. There is another smell; she knows it but can't place it.

'What's that?' he says.

'What's what?'

Her eyes are on the pavement littered with empty wrappers and cigarette stubs. She watches out for anything sharp. She sniffs the air again. Paint? Yes, that's what the smell is.

He nudges her. 'Over there. Look!'

They peer at the lamp post in front of the chip shop. Something – a rag doll, or a scarecrow – is tethered to it. The head is black. It's been charred in a fire. The stuffing has come loose.

They edge closer.

'Shit! It's moving.' She puts her hand to her throat. 'Oh, Jesus!' She takes in the paint and feathers, the shorn hair. 'That poor girl.' She looks up and down the street. The house lights are off. No sign of anyone watching. She takes a step forward. 'We should do something.'

He holds her back. 'Don't get involved.'

Out of the darkness looms a bloodied brute of a man. He has a knife.

They back away.

The man staggers past. He stops at the lamp post.

The girl twists, trying to free herself. She wants to cry out but her voice is muted.

'Sshh,' the man says. He saws furiously at the rope. He cuts her free.

The girl slumps into his arms.

The man gently removes the tape covering her mouth.

'Daddy,' she sobs, clinging tightly to him.

'It's alright, love,' he says. 'I'm here now.'

ONE

November 1971

I t was one of those days when the sun shone bright in a clear, blue sky but the cold could flay you. Brenda cupped her hands to her mouth and blew. Her breath escaped in wisps and hung white in the air.

The older women had dressed sensibly in thick woollen coats. Some wore furry hats that nestled on top of stiffly permed hair; others covered their heads with shawls. Handbags hooked over arms, they listened earnestly to the speaker on the steps of Belfast City Hall. Brenda hopped from one foot to the other and willed her to wrap up her speech. A crow flapped across the roof of the building. It circled the crowd once, cawing loudly. The first heckler; she was sure it wouldn't be the last.

A young mother next to her balanced a small, rosy-cheeked child on her hip. An impressive river of mucus flowed down the child's face and into the corner of its mouth. In the name of god, could she not just get a hanky and wipe its nose? Brenda was beginning to wonder why she'd come. Her dad would think she was mad to stand around here for hours. He'd laughed when she first mentioned the peace group. He couldn't see what a bunch of Christian women were going to do.

'Do they honestly think they can change things with a few prayers?'

'There's nothin' wrong with praying, Jimmy,' her mum had scolded. 'You should give it a go.'

Of all people, she had thought her dad would understand.

He had a knack for soothing ruffled feathers, was always the first to step in and break up a scrap. Before long he'd have both parties shaking hands, each believing they'd won. 'More listenin' and less shoutin' is all it takes,' he'd say. 'It's something our politicians should learn.'

'There's more to the peace group than you think,' Brenda had tried to explain. 'At least they're trying to do something.'

But her dad was having none of it.

It was midday now. The women were beginning to attract the attention of the Saturday shoppers. A man approached the police and army cordon and demanded to know what was going on.

'Peace rally,' was the clipped response.

'A what?' The man looked the women up and down. He squinted at the messages on their placards and mouthed the words. 'Women Together?'

The policeman shrugged.

The man sauntered back to his group of friends. A young lad, who looked like his son, caught Brenda staring. He nudged the others. They put their hands together in mock prayer then dissolved into fits of laughter. Brenda turned back to the crowd. Her face was burning.

'Stupid gobshites,' whispered a voice in her ear. A girl had moved into the spot beside her. She grinned at Brenda. 'Just ignore them.'

A permed head swivelled round and tutted. The woman's face was make-up-free apart for a dab of coral lipstick, which had obviously been applied to pursed lips. Brenda giggled.

'Want a Polo?' asked the girl, reaching into her bag. 'I'm Hazel, by the way.'

Brenda fumbled as she tried to extract a mint from the top of the packet. 'This is my first rally,' she said.

'I hope it won't be your last.'

'I'm not goin' to be put off,' Brenda lowered her voice, 'by arses like those men over there, if that's what you mean.' She jerked her head in their direction.

'Good on ye.'

'Mind you. I thought there'd be a bigger turnout.' Brenda did a quick calculation. Fewer than two hundred she reckoned.

The evening paper had written a feature about the women, praising them for the work they were doing. It had inspired her to come along today. She thought more would have felt the same. But then it was one thing to wish the killing would stop; it was another thing to actually try to make it stop.

There was a ripple of applause. The speaker paused for a moment to soak up the crowd's appreciation then turned to a fresh page of notes.

'She does go on a bit.'

Hazel rolled her eyes. 'Count yourself lucky. You're not the one who has to live with her.'

'Huh?'

'She's my mum.'

Brenda thought of her own mum. She might sound supportive of the women but she'd never be seen in a crowd like this. Brenda's mum believed in avoiding trouble, in keeping to herself, although it didn't stop her wanting to know everybody else's business.

'If mine knew I was here she'd…'

'Troops out,' yelled a man from the back of the crowd.

Hazel's mum dropped a page of her notes.

'Brit lovers!' came the shrill voice of a woman.

A small group had unfurled a banner. As the group began to chant loudly Hazel's mum fell silent. A large space opened up as the peace women sidled away from the protestors. Brenda braced herself, ready for the moment it would all kick off.

Someone tried to snatch the banner. A scuffle broke out. Elbows dug into Brenda's ribs. A boot stomped on her toes; she yelped in pain.

'Move!' shouted a soldier. He cleared the way for two policemen dragging one of the protestors towards the security cordon, and shoved Brenda on the shoulder. She staggered backwards.

'There's no need for that,' Brenda yelled after the soldier. She was shaking as she turned to Hazel. 'I've a good mind to report him.'

'Why? Sure he's only doin' his job.'

'Yeah well, they're always throwin' their weight around.'

When the soldiers had first arrived, they'd been sent to

protect Catholic communities like hers. She'd welcomed them then thinking they'd only stay for a few months. Now they seemed to cause as many problems as they solved.

Hazel's mum had recovered her composure and finished her speech to loud applause. She made her way towards them.

'How did I do?' she beamed.

'Really well,' said Brenda. 'Shame about the interruption.'

'It happens. You learn to live with it.' The woman turned to her daughter. 'I need to catch up with the others. Why don't you take a dander into town for a while?'

'How long is a while, Mum?'

'I don't know – say a couple of hours.' She smiled at Brenda. 'Nice to meet you, dear. It's good to see we're attracting some young ones.'

'Hang on a minute. Where will I find you?' asked Hazel, but her mum was already weaving through the crowd.

'Come on,' said Brenda. 'I'll go with you. I need a hot drink inside me. It's Baltic out here.'

———

The coffee shop smelt of cinnamon and freshly baked scones. Brenda ordered a slice of the lemon meringue pie she'd spotted on the way in. The girls chatted as they waited for their food to arrive. It turned out they were both in their first year at Queen's University.

'Have you tried the cafe on Stranmillis Road?' asked Brenda.

'No, not yet.'

'I must take you some time. The food's a lot better than that muck they serve up in the Student's Union.' Brenda thought for a moment. 'Well, most of the time.'

Talk turned to Women Together.

'Mum's organising a meeting for next week. Fancy going?'

'I don't know,' said Brenda. 'Maybe.'

'We could go together.'

'Alright then, you're on.'

The waitress brought two steaming mugs of hot chocolate, each topped with a generous swirl of whipped cream. Brenda took a couple of spoonfuls of cream then tilted the mug to her lips. Her meringue pie failed to arrive. The waitresses had stopped serving. Instead, they were working their way round the tables telling people they needed to leave the premises.

'Ah, Jesus.' Brenda looked longingly at the sweet trolley. 'Typical of my luck.'

'It's probably another scare.'

A policeman stuck his head round the door to reinforce the urgency of the bomb warning. The waitresses herded customers towards the door. Brenda and Hazel grabbed their coats and followed them out. The top of the street had been taped off. The bomb-disposal squad had arrived.

They looked at one another.

'Let's get out of here,' said Brenda.

They scurried away. A few minutes later the dull crump of an explosion reverberated in their chests.

TWO

Brenda yelped. The water from the hot tap had turned to ice.

'Mum,' she hollered. 'Are you fillin' the kettle?'

It was an annoying quirk of their forty-year-old plumbing that every time someone turned the taps on downstairs, the hot water upstairs ran cold. Her dad kept promising to fix it.

'Sorry,' shouted her mum. 'Finished now.'

'Ok, thanks ... Shit!' The water had switched to boiling. Brenda inspected her hands. It was a wonder she hadn't lost a layer of skin.

Her mum would be off to Mass soon. She'd have made herself a cup of tea, peeled and chopped the vegetables for Sunday lunch and had a quick whizz round with the hoover. Brenda heard the key turn in the back door and her mother's footsteps in the yard. By the time she had made her way downstairs, her mum had pegged a full wash of clothes to the line. Her dad's overalls, shirts and vests looked huge as they flapped in the breeze next to her mum's slips, skirts and blouses.

Brenda poured herself a bowl of cereal.

'Get off you stupid thing,' came a voice from outside.

Her mum was making her way back into the house with the empty clothes basket. Next-door's cat followed, weaving in and out of her legs. She gave it a boot with her toe. The cat shot in through the open door and ran under the kitchen table. Brenda filled a saucer with milk and placed it on the floor.

'Don't be encouragin' that ball of fleas,' said her mum. She made a grab for the scruff of its neck but the cat arched its back and dug its claws into her legs.

Her mum let out a cry just as Brenda's dad wandered into the kitchen. He looked at his wife's ripped hosiery and the little beads of blood that had formed on her shins, then burst out laughing.

Brenda's mum fired tiny daggers in his direction. 'I'm goin' to have to change these now,' she said. A few minutes later she popped her head round the door. 'I'm off.'

'Bye, love.' Mr MacRae planted a kiss on his wife's lips.

'Get off me, you big lump.' She pushed him away. 'That's prickly.'

He rubbed his unshaven face, grinned and reached for her again. Brenda's mum made her escape.

'I'm starved,' he said once she was out of the house. He opened the oven door and peered inside. There was usually a full Irish breakfast being kept warm for him.

'She didn't have time,' said Brenda.

Her dad shut the oven door with a sigh.

'I can make you a fry if you want?'

'You're alright, love. Cornflakes will do me too.'

Brenda was relieved. She hated the way the lard spat and jumped from the pan.

Her dad proceeded to eat his cornflakes with one hand and turn the pages of the Sunday paper with the other. Occasionally he'd shake his head and mumble something about keeping it in your trousers.

'What's the big scandal this week?' asked Brenda.

'Ach, it's the same old thing ... someone cheatin' on their wife ... that actor fella who just got married. You know the one.'

'Let me see.' Brenda pulled the paper towards her and checked out the photograph. 'I don't get it,' she said, shaking her head. 'His wife's far nicer lookin' than her. What does he see in this one?'

'Maybe she goes like a train?'

'Daddy!'

'I'm only sayin'.'

'Well, she looks like a right minger to me.'

'Who does?' Brenda's sister, Clare, had finally made an appearance, nursing a fierce hangover, if the pinched look on her face was anything to go by.

'They seemed a really nice couple.' Brenda pointed to the picture in the paper.

'It just goes to show,' said Clare. 'You can't trust any man.'

Mr MacRae cleared his throat.

'She wasn't talkin' about you. You're different.'

Brenda meant what she said. Her dad wasn't at all like the other men around here. He was a mountain of a man – big hands, big feet, big heart. Yet when he spoke it was with a soft Scottish brogue. He was as commanding a presence in Brenda's life as the tall gantry crane that straddled the Harland and Wolff dockyard and dominated the skyline of

East Belfast.

'For cryin' out loud, Brenda. Did you not think to bring the washing in?'

Brenda stared out the window. It had started to rain. 'I'll do it then, will I?'

Clare ran out in her dressing gown and slippers and began to strip the clothing from the line. Brenda was close behind her. Together they unpegged the washing and dashed back into the kitchen.

'Come here a minute, Brenda.' Her dad beckoned her over. He pointed to the paper, which lay open at a double-page spread. 'If I didn't know any better, I'd say that was you.'

Brenda stared at the black-and-white evidence. 'Um...'

'What do you mean it's her? Let me see,' said Clare. 'So it is!' She furrowed her brow as she took in the scene. 'Where is this? Who are all those people?'

'A peace rally at the City Hall.'

'What were *you* doin' there?'

'Showin' my support.' Brenda looked to her dad for his reaction, but he was still focused on the paper. 'Anyway, I'm glad I went. They've invited me to a meeting.'

Clare snorted. 'You're not goin' to go, are you?'

'I'm thinkin' about it.'

'Catch yourself on.'

Brenda gave her sister a sharp look. 'Do you even know the first thing about Women Together?'

'It says here,' said Mr MacRae, drawing their attention back to the paper, 'that there was a disturbance.'

'Some people were protestin' about the troops.' Brenda

noted the concern on his face. 'A bit of a skirmish, Dad. Nothin' serious. The Army moved them on.'

Clare's face darkened. 'I bet they did.'

'It was meant to be a peace rally. They were turnin' it into something else.'

'For fuck's sake, Brenda. Whose side are you on?'

Mr MacRae scowled. 'Clare, just because your mum's not here doesn't mean you can use language like that in the house.'

'It's not *about* takin' sides,' said Brenda. 'That's the whole point.'

'Oh yeah? What are your precious peace women goin' to do when those Orange bastards start burnin' us out, eh? I'll tell you ... Nothing!'

Brenda threw her hands up. 'There's no talkin' to you when you get like this.'

'That's because you know I'm right.'

'Pack it in, the pair of you. Can a man not enjoy a bit of peace and quiet in his own home?'

'I'm only tellin' it as it is,' said Clare.

'Aye well, we've heard enough.'

Clare looked at her dad then back to Brenda. 'In that case I'll leave you to yourselves. I'm away to get dressed.'

'You're not annoyed with me, are you?' said Brenda once her sister had made her way upstairs. 'For goin' to the rally, I mean?'

'You can go to as many rallies as you like.'

Brenda smiled. But her relief was short-lived when he added, 'I just hope you know what you're getting into.'

'I'm not goin' to do anything stupid, if that's what you mean.'

'Good, because I wouldn't want to see you gettin' caught up in any trouble.'

Brenda couldn't help laughing. 'This is Belfast, Dad. You can't avoid trouble.'

His face remained serious, and Brenda knew he was only looking out for her, but she had already made up her mind. She needed to find out more about these women and what they did, because, despite what her dad said, it felt exactly like the sort of thing she should be getting into.

THREE

No need for street names. The painted kerbs told her whose territory she was in. Red, white and blue. Prod colours. In Brenda's street they were daubed green, white and orange. Different turf, different flags.

She passed a giant mural of a man on a white horse. His hair was long and curly, like a cocker spaniel's ears. He wore a red and gold jacket. One hand was on the reins of his horse, the other brandished a sword. *1690* declared the date painted on the wall. *No surrender* read the slogan. King Billy mustering his troops for the battle that would rout the Catholics once and for all.

Brenda glanced over at her friend. It was alright for her. She was among her own kind.

'Don't worry,' said Hazel. 'We're nearly there.'

'Thank god.'

'Just don't be sayin' any Hail Marys.'

'Fuck off!' said Brenda, laughing at the very idea of it.

'By the way, I promised Mum we'd give her a hand to set up. Hope that's ok?'

Hazel's mum had arranged for tonight's meeting to take place in the Presbyterian church hall not far from where she lived. Women Together groups from all over Belfast were coming to a sewing circle.

It was Mrs Kennedy who'd first suggested making the quilt. She said it would be a great way to bring everyone together, a chance to get to know one another better. The quilt would be a symbol of their shared hopes. If that's what they thought then good on them, but quilting was for grannies. Brenda wanted action, not a new hobby. Besides, the last time she'd sewn anything was in school – a square of embroidery she'd somehow managed to stitch to her skirt. When she'd lifted the piece up to show the class, her skirt had lifted with it giving everyone a full flash of her knickers.

Hazel's mum was switching lights on when the girls got there. She greeted them briefly before darting into the small kitchen to put a couple of bottles of milk in the fridge. The walls of the room were lined with stacks of chairs and bare wooden trestle tables.

'Give me a hand with these radiators, girls,' she said, reappearing from the kitchen. 'It's brass monkeys in here.'

There was no sophisticated control system. The radiators were either on or off. Brenda and Hazel set them all to on. They pulled the chairs down from their stacks and placed them around the tables, which they had dragged into the centre of the room to form one large rectangle.

Women began to arrive shortly after seven o'clock, carrying sewing baskets stuffed with brightly patterned swatches of cloth, spools of threads in a rainbow of colours, pins and needles. They brought with them offerings of food, mostly sandwiches and filled rolls, which they handed to Hazel's mum through the kitchen hatch.

'We're not goin' to be hungry, that's for sure,' said Brenda. 'There's enough food here to feed half of Belfast, as long as you like sandwich spread and sliced pan.' She pulled a face. The combination made her stomach turn.

The women formed themselves into clusters around the table, each group working on its allocated section of the quilt. It felt odd to be sitting among people she'd never normally mix with. Brenda could count on one hand the number of Protestants she'd spent any length of time with and two of those were Hazel and her mum.

———

Already the windows had misted up. Brenda tugged at the neck of her jumper. The sweat was lashing off her.

'Is anyone else hot?' she asked, getting up from her seat. 'Mind if I open one of these?'

No, they weren't hot; it was nice as it was, thanks. Brenda sat down beside Hazel and her mum and continued to swelter and prickle.

'Now that I've had the chance to sleep on it...' said Ann Muldoon.

'Not literally Ann, I hope.' Joan Anderson gave her a wink.

'I've had second thoughts about the shamrock idea.'

The women had chosen symbols that represented their life in Belfast; these were to be stitched into the quilt.

'Who the hell picked a shamrock in the first place?' asked

the woman next to Mrs Muldoon. 'Might as well add a leprechaun for good measure.'

The women burst into laughter with the exception of Hazel's mum who looked as if she'd sat on her own pin cushion.

'I've been workin' on this all week,' she said, holding up a patch of green fabric.

'And that's, um... a lovely job you've made of it,' said Ann Muldoon, 'but maybe we should leave shamrocks for the souvenir shops.'

'We all agreed on the dove and the shamrock at the first meeting. If I remember rightly, everyone was happy enough with the choice at the time.'

'I don't remember having much say in it,' mumbled Ann Muldoon.

'What about something that represents the children?' someone suggested. 'All these riots and killings are ruinin' their lives.'

There was a murmur of approval. In the end they decided to ditch the shamrock and replace it with a symbol of two children holding hands.

Ann Muldoon got to work on cutting the new template. The women settled back into their sewing, catching up on the week's events and swapping stories. Brenda observed them at work and threaded needles on request ('Your eyesight's better than mine, love').

'All hell broke out on my street last night,' said Joan Anderson. 'Not that you'd know. There wasn't a word about it on the news this mornin'. I swear to god, there are times I think I've dreamed all this up.'

Brenda knew how she felt. There were nights her own

street turned into a battlefield. She'd lie in bed, listening to the rip of automatic weapons. It was incredible to think a raging gun battle could take place right outside her window and yet there'd be no record of it. Where did all those bullets go? Was no-one ever hit or injured? The empty cartridges littering the pavements the following morning told the real story.

'It's the men, with all their fightin' talk, that drag us into one disaster after another. Take my Billy...'

Ann Muldoon laughed. 'Can't say I'm tempted, Joan.'

'He says he'd rather die than give up Queen and country.'

'And would he?'

'If he had enough pints in him he'd fight anyone.'

There was a shared sigh of solidarity from the women.

Brenda's mum was thankful she only had daughters. She didn't have to answer a knock on the door and explain why her teenage son wasn't on the streets stoning soldiers like the rest of his mates. Her husband, with his Scottish roots, could just about be excused his impartiality on the grounds that he was foreign. A son born and bred in Belfast would be an entirely different matter. He'd be expected to support the 'Cause'.

It was a strange word – 'cause'. For Joan Anderson's husband, Billy, it meant fighting to remain part of the United Kingdom and to stay British. For many in Brenda's street, it was about fighting against the British occupation.

'It's gettin' worse, so it is. I'm scared for my boys. I've told them not to walk home on their own at night.' Ann Muldoon crossed herself. 'Not unless they want to be shot.'

A brief silence fell on the women. Groups of Protestant paramilitaries had taken to driving through Catholic areas on the lookout for a lone man. They'd open up with rifles then speed off leaving their target to die of his wounds.

'The halfwits ended up killin' one of their own the other night. A young lad. Only 17 years.' Ann Muldoon paused. 'Same age as my eldest.'

Brenda glanced at Mrs Anderson. Surely her Billy wouldn't be part of anything like that? Mrs Anderson was shaking her head in disgust, but Brenda caught a flicker of doubt in her eyes. She wondered if Billy knew his wife was here tonight. If he could see her now, what would he make of this bonding with the other side?

FOUR

Andy rubbed his eyes and groaned. His back ached from lying on his makeshift bed and, as usual, his mattress had provided little padding. A cockroach crept from beneath a blanket. With bleary eyes he watched it track its way along the edge of the bed. He shook the blanket and the cockroach dropped to the floor. It scuttled towards the skirting. Andy reached for one of his boots and brought it down hard. There was a satisfying crunch.

The old cotton mill was now his 'home', a temporary barracks, slap bang in the middle of the Catholic Falls and the Protestant Shankhill Roads. Andy's job was to keep the warring tribes apart. From the outside it looked like one of those tall, red-bricked buildings in a Lowry painting, belching smoke from its huge chimneys. But the chimneys of this mill no longer smoked and the building had been lying empty for years. Clattering spinning wheels and looms had been replaced with metal beds and the detritus of a hundred or more squaddies, all cramped together. Mess cans, packs, flak jackets, helmets and boots lay on the floor. A rifle was propped beside each bed. On the plastic chair that served as Andy's bedside table he had placed an alarm clock, his watch and a picture of him and his wife smiling happily from their wedding car.

Andy grabbed his wash kit. His squad was on the first patrol of the day. He checked the rest of his men were awake and moving. Dave still snored loudly. Andy kicked the metal frame of his bed. 'Rise and shine,' he bellowed. Dave didn't stir. Andy kicked a bit harder.

In the washroom they were passing around a newspaper.

'Take a look at the tits on that.'

A pretty girl, naked apart from a pair of scanty knickers, cupped two enormous breasts and smiled brightly.

'I wouldn't mind burying my face in those.'

'A little runt like you?' said Andy. 'You'd suffocate if you could find a stepladder.'

Andy had only arrived and already he couldn't wait to get out of the place. He could live with the grimy windows, mouldy walls, peeling paint, even the cockroaches. It was the smell of sweat and cold grease he found hardest to deal with. He breathed the rancid smell in, day and night. It seeped into his clothes and his bedding; it clung to his hair. No matter how hard he tried, he never felt he got rid of it.

He dressed and headed to the canteen where 'Taff' was cooking breakfast. 'One fried egg with that special burnt edge you do so well and two slices of bacon that have actually seen the pan, please.'

'Sod off,' replied Taff without looking up from the batch of fried bread he was tipping into a large aluminium serving tray.

Andy piled his plate with everything on offer, poured a

mug of strong tea, spooned in three sugars and took a large gulp. He spotted some of his men at a table in the far corner and went to join them. A small, wiry-looking soldier perched on the end of the bench. He shuffled up to make space when he saw Andy approach.

'Cheers, Smithy. How's it going?'

The entire table burst out laughing at the enquiry.

'He thought he'd drop in on the locals yesterday, sir. Pay them a surprise visit,' said one of the group.

'Oh, very fucking funny,' replied Smithy.

More sniggers.

'Fell through someone's front door,' continued the soldier. 'Landed on his bony arse right in the middle of their hallway.'

Smithy had been out on patrol. He'd stopped for a quick breather.

'I was squatting in a doorway and had my back pressed against the door. How was I to supposed to know it was on the latch?'

He'd fallen backwards and landed like an upturned turtle, gun flailing in the air.

'They weren't too happy to see me.'

There was another howl of laughter from the table.

Andy swiped the last of the egg off his plate with a chunk of bread. He shook his head. 'You twat.'

Back in his sleeping quarters he pulled on his flak jacket and slung his rifle over his shoulder. Then he wound his way down the dark, twisting stairs and clambered into one of the armoured vehicles. It was time to go to work. They were only a few hundred yards from the gate when the first brick ricocheted off the metal grille beside his head.

FIVE

Her mum thought it was a stupid idea. Why would Brenda want to live in a student house when she could easily travel in from home? Brenda sighed. Her bus route had been cancelled three times so far this month because of rioting. On one occasion the bus itself had been hijacked and set alight.

'It'll be easier to get to classes,' she said.

It wasn't just that. The area around the university was quieter. With its red brick buildings and leafy avenues, it was almost like being in a different country.

Clare's eyes had lit up at the mention of Brenda moving out.

'Does that mean I can have your bedroom?'

'No.'

'But it's bigger than mine. If you're not here, it'll only go to waste.'

'Keep out of it. I don't want you anywhere near my stuff.'

Clare sprinkled sugar over freshly buttered toast.

Brenda wrinkled her nose. 'You know what they say, don't you? Too much sugar gives you worms.'

Her sister bit into her toast. 'That's just an old wives' tale.'

Mrs MacRae wrapped a round of sandwiches in grease-proof paper and placed them on the table in front of Clare. 'There you go. Don't forget to take them with you this time.' She turned to Brenda. 'What about your Saturday job? Mrs Henderson will be sorry to lose you.'

'Oh, I'll still be back at weekends. I'm keepin' it on.'

Her mum gave her a tart look. 'Well, it's nice to know you're not totally desertin' us. Although I still can't think why you'd throw away good grant money on a room when you've got a perfectly fine one here.'

'Is Peter comin' round tonight?' asked Clare.

'Dunno. I hope not.'

Clare raised an eyebrow.

Brenda pushed her chair back. 'I better shift myself.'

Lately a distance had grown between her and Peter and neither was working to close it. The other evening, when they were together, she'd caught him staring into space and asked if he was alright. 'Of course I am,' he snapped. 'Why are you goin' on about it?'

'Be like that,' she told him. 'I won't ask again.' And she hadn't.

'Will you not take something to eat?' asked her mum. 'I can make you a bite of toast. It'll only take a second.'

'No time. I want to stop off at the bank first.' Brenda held a strand of hair between her fingers. 'And I need to give this mop of mine a wash before I go anywhere.' She looked across at Clare who was squeezing her mum's sandwiches into an already bulging schoolbag. 'I hope you left some hot water in the tank.'

Clare made a face. 'I only used a wee drop.'

Brenda left the house with her hair unwashed. She was making her way to the bus stop, silently cursing her sister, when Peter drove past in a blue Ford Escort. He pulled up outside the social club. Brenda lifted her hand to wave then dropped it. Two men had appeared from a side entrance; both got in. She took in the sallow face of the man now in the passenger seat and her heart sank. The man turned and spoke briefly. Peter nodded and sped off.

She was still thinking of Peter as she joined the queue for a cashier. It all fell into place – the reason he was always on edge, his reluctance to tell her what was on his mind. Peter had a decent job at Hanlon's garage. He was doing well for himself, bringing home a steady wage. She'd thought he had more sense than to get mixed up with McManus and his sidekick.

She sat through her lecture with a gnawing sickness in the pit of her stomach. It was the same with all her classes throughout the day – her mind kept skipping back to what she'd seen.

———

Later that afternoon she returned home to find Peter sitting in their kitchen. Clare had made him a cup of tea.

'I was on my way back from town. Thought I'd pop in to see if you fancied goin' for a drink later.'

Brenda filled the kettle. 'No, I don't.'

'I'll have some more, if you're makin' a fresh pot,' said

Clare. She nodded towards Peter's empty cup. 'Do you want another one, Peter?'

He didn't answer.

Brenda's back stiffened as she felt his gaze on her. 'That car you were drivin' this morning...' she said over her shoulder.

Clare nudged Peter's arm. 'I didn't know you'd bought a...'

'He hasn't.'

Brenda wheeled round, leaving the water in the kettle to bubble and steam behind her.

'Are you makin' tea or not?' asked Clare.

'Where did you get the car, Peter?'

'Did you nick it?' Clare looked excited at the prospect.

Brenda stood with her arms folded. 'Well?'

'It was a repair job at the garage. I offered to return it to the customer.'

'What, like your customer couldn't go to the garage and collect it himself?'

'I was doin' him a favour.'

'Yeah right. And those two men you picked up, they just went along for the ride, did they?'

Clare snickered. 'That was awful good of you, Peter. Goin' to all that trouble to return the customer's car. Did he realise it came with two free passengers?'

'Ha bloody ha.' Peter leant across and gave her a friendly cuff on the head.

Brenda remained stony faced. 'What were you doin' with McManus?'

Peter tensed at the mention of the name.

'McManus?' Clare's eyes widened. 'Playin' with the big boys now, I see.'

Peter got up and draped his arm around Brenda's shoulder. 'Trust me,' he said, with a hollow laugh. 'You didn't see anything.'

'Of course she didn't.' Clare tried to catch her sister's eye. 'Isn't that right, Brenda?'

Brenda prised Peter's arm off. 'I know what I saw.'

A key turned in the front door. 'Only me,' came a sing-song voice from the hallway.

'We're in here,' shouted Clare.

'Ah Jesus, it would founder you out there.' Mrs MacRae placed a cold hand on Clare's cheek. 'Here, feel that.'

Clare jumped. 'Wise up, Mum!'

'Hello Peter.' Mrs MacRae gave him her warmest smile. 'I didn't see you there.' Her smile quickly turned to a frown. 'I take it your dad's gone to the pub?'

'He said he wouldn't be long,' answered Clare.

Mrs MacRae muttered under her breath as she pulled a bag of potatoes from the pantry. 'Don't mind me,' she said, then proceeded to scalp one potato after another with a small knife. 'Are you stayin' for tea, Peter? I can add a few more to the pot. It's no bother.'

Peter grabbed his coat from the back of the chair. 'Actually, I should get goin', but thanks anyway.'

'I'll see you out,' said Brenda.

She put the front door on the snib and followed him on to the street. A frost was beginning to settle and already the pavement sparkled with a fine dusting of ice. Two doors down had put their Christmas tree up, the first in the street. It sat in the front window, its twinkling lights optimistically announcing the start of the festive season.

'Hello, Brenda. How's about ye?' It was Mr Donovan. He nodded to Peter on the way past. Suddenly he stopped and doubled back. 'Hey Peter,' he said. 'Did you hear about Alex?'

'I know he was pulled in for questioning.'

'And the rest.'

Peter frowned. 'I thought they'd let him go.'

'The hell they did.'

Locked up in the arsehole of nowhere, according to Mr Donovan. No charges worth a damn. No likelihood of a trial. There was no telling how long he would be held there.

'It's got to the stage where you get your door kicked in,' said Peter, 'and lifted for goin' to the wrong pub.'

Mr Donovan nodded. 'I know. It could be you or me the next time.' He gave Peter a searching look. 'And it's not like we've done anything.'

'Anyway,' said Peter, with a quick sideways glance at Brenda, 'thanks for lettin' me know.'

'Aye well, watch out for yourself.'

There was a brief flash of alarm on Peter's face but it was long enough for Brenda to spot.

'Good night, Brenda,' said Mr Donovan.

Peter lingered in front of the house. Eventually he spoke. 'So, are we goin' for that drink later or not?'

'No.'

'I see. It's like that, is it?'

'Listen Peter.' Brenda looked him straight in the eye. 'I know what you're gettin' into ... and I'm not goin' there.'

Peter looked at her, seemed about to say something then changed his mind. He turned to go.

'Peter, wait.' Brenda reached for his arm. 'It's not too late to stop.'

For a brief moment she thought her words had struck home.

'Thanks for the advice, Brenda,' he said with a mocking smile. 'I'll be sure to think on it.'

'I mean it, Peter,' she called after him, 'if you get involved, I don't want to see you again.'

He raised his arm and, without turning round, gave her a wave.

Clare had come to the door. 'What was all that about?

'What do you think?' Brenda pushed past her and went inside.

Her sister remained on the doorstep, her eyes glued on Peter as he made his way down the street.

SIX

Clare folded over her waistband and hitched up her skirt. Peter was looking good on it considering he'd just been dumped. She made straight for him. His uncle was none too pleased to see her. He and Peter were about to head into the pub.

'Hiya,' she said.

Peter grunted 'hello'. He was in his work overalls and smelt of oil and chamois leather. Clare liked garage smells. When she was at a petrol pump she'd roll the car window down to breathe in the fumes. The fumes left a delicious metallic taste at the back of her throat. Sometimes they made her head a little woozy. She liked that too.

'I'm sorry about you and Brenda.' She gave Peter a sympathetic smile.

'Don't be. I was about to finish with her anyway.'

Perhaps he had been about to break up with her. If so, it would be a first. Clare glowed inwardly at the thought. With her perfect skin and glossy auburn hair, Brenda always had boys tripping over themselves to ask her out. It had been like that at school. No doubt it was the same at university. She could just picture her walking into a lecture theatre and the lads shifting in their seats to get a better view of her. Or loitering by the door as she left, hoping for a chance to say hello.

A fine, persistent rain had been slowly seeping into Clare's school clothes. Her blazer smelt of damp wool. She tucked a wet strand of hair behind her ear. 'Mum misses havin' you around.'

'Send her my regards, will you.'

'I will.'

Her mum was still bewildered by the suddenness of the split. How come one minute everything had been fine between Brenda and Peter, the next it was all over? And he was such a nice lad too. She'd looked to Clare for an explanation.

'How would I know? It's Brenda you should be askin'.'

'The last time I tried, I got the nose bitten off me.'

Her dad had kept well out of it. His only comment on the matter was that he'd never taken to Peter.

It wasn't only her mum experiencing Brenda's short temper. Ever since she'd joined that peace group she'd had nothing good to say about the place she grew up in or the people in it: 'Why does everyone in this country have to be so narrow-minded?' 'Can't they at least *try* to be more tolerant of one another?' 'Things will never change if no-one's prepared to budge.' Brenda should try being a bit more tolerant herself, starting with her family, Clare thought. Peter too.

Peter was about to go.

'Listen, that whole thing about the car...'

He eyed her with suspicion. 'What about it?'

'I don't know why Brenda had to make such a big...' A bunch of girls from her school had gathered on the opposite side of the street. One of them shouted over.

'Hey, Clare, who's your friend?'

Clare did her best to ignore her.

'I wouldn't mind findin' him in my Christmas stocking.'

Peter grinned. 'Have you been a good girl?' he shouted back.

There was a lot of shaking of heads from the group, followed by a roar of laughter.

'Classmates?'

'No.' Clare grimaced. 'They're in the year below me.'

Peter's uncle shuffled his feet. 'I'm soaked standin' out here,' he said, as the girls moved on round the corner. He motioned with his hand for Clare to move on too. 'Don't you have some homework you need to be doin'?'

Clare glared at him. 'I'm on my way to the hairdressers for your information. And anyway, I've finished with all that now. Today's my last day.'

Peter gave her a quizzical look. 'A bit early for your Christmas break.'

'They get too much time off, if you ask me,' said the uncle. 'In my day...'

'Aye well, things have changed a bit since then,' said Clare. 'We've even stopped sendin' children up chimneys.'

Peter laughed.

'I mean I've left for good,' she continued. 'I've signed up for one of those typing courses they run at the tech. Dad's not happy. I think he was hoping I'd go to university, but I was never cut out for that.'

Brenda was the one who had always been set on going to university and their dad had encouraged it. He'd never broached the subject directly with Clare. Not that she'd have been interested, even if her grades had miraculously improved. Still, it would have been nice if he'd shown as much interest in her as he did in the brainbox.

'As soon as I finish the course I'm goin' to look for a job.'

'Sounds like a smart move to me,' said Peter. 'And just think: you'll be earnin' well before Brenda gets started.'

'Right enough. I never thought of it that way.'

His eyes rested on her skirt and legs. 'There's a group of us goin' to the social club on Sunday night. Maybe I'll see you there?'

'That'd be nice.'

'Come on,' urged the uncle. He held the pub door open. 'I'm gaggin' for a pint.'

'See you Sunday,' said Clare as the door swung shut.

———

The hairdresser was strictly for the Blue-Rinse Brigade. Any other time Clare wouldn't have been seen dead in the place but her split ends needed sorting out. They'd finished with her now and she was thumbing through a magazine as she waited for her mum. She glanced over at the line of dryers. Her mum had been sitting under one for the last twenty minutes. She was beetroot.

'Jesus, Mary and Joseph! I'm fryin' under here.' Mrs MacRae lifted the hood of the dryer and fanned her face with her hand. 'Am I not done by now, Bernie?'

Bernie was about to start on a full head of streaks. She excused herself and came over.

Brenda's mum tried to adjust the dial. 'No wonder I'm hot. The thing's been on high the whole time.'

Bernie patted her hand over Mrs MacRae's rollered head. 'A bit longer.' She turned the dryer up to full, snapped the hood back down and went back to her client.

Clare watched with fascination as she covered the woman's head with a tight rubber cap. The cap was perforated with small holes and Bernie began pulling sections of hair through each one with what looked like a crochet hook. Every now and then the hair caught and the woman let out a stream of expletives.

Clare could smell the peroxide paste from where she sat as Bernie applied it with a tint brush, to each section of hair. She wondered how long you'd have to train before you could be trusted to colour other peoples' hair.

'No, I don't see Peter at all these days,' said Mrs MacRae to one of the women under the dryers.

Clare's ears pricked up.

'I hear he's chasin' after one of Pat Keenan's daughters.'

'Which one?'

'The one with the chest,' said the woman with a cackle.

'Oh her.' Mrs MacRae gurned in mock disdain. 'Yes, I know the one you mean.'

'She likes to think he's interested,' said Clare but her comment fell on deaf ears. The women had moved on to a different topic of conversation.

'Is Brenda still involved with that peace group, Bridie?'

'Um...' Mrs MacRae struggled to find the right reply.

'Yes, she is and it's about time she packed it in. From

what I can see, they spend most of their time suckin' up to the security forces.'

Mrs MacRae shot her daughter a look.

'What? It's true.' Clare looked to the other women for backup.

'We all want an end to the fightin', Bridie, but...'

'Her heart's in the right place.'

'That might be so, but there's a lot of people around here who don't see it that way.'

'You see what I mean? It's not just me who–' Clare stopped talking and sniffed the air. A caustic smell filled her nostrils. 'Something's burnin'.'

Bernie glanced at her watch. 'Shit!' She dashed across to the full head of streaks she'd been working on earlier. 'Let's get that washed off,' she said, leading the alarmed client to the basin.

The woman's blonde streaks turned whiter with every rinse.

Mrs MacRae made wide eyes at her daughter as she tried to catch her attention. 'Christ! You'll not miss her in the dark!'

Clare didn't hear her. She was thinking of Peter's invitation. Sunday night couldn't roll round quick enough.

SEVEN

Mrs Irwin's peace meeting wasn't just about swapping stories and quilting. By the end of the night they had agreed a new press campaign, planned a leaflet distribution, reviewed where their support was most needed and how to action it. Brenda was impressed. Caught up in the moment, she'd volunteered to join her on today's house call, to a woman whose husband, an officer in the Royal Ulster Constabulary, had been killed. Now she was thinking she'd been too hasty.

'We won't stay long,' said Hazel's mum, clicking the gate shut behind them. 'We'll just pay our respects and go.'

Beds of winter pansies lined the path; a neatly trimmed cotoneaster bursting with red berries grew on a trellis by the front door. The downstairs curtains were pulled shut. What if the body was in the house? Some families did that – kept the dead person in the living room, with the coffin lid open, until the day of the funeral.

'Ready?'

Brenda gave a nervous lick of her lips. 'Yes.'

Hazel's mother rang the bell.

A voice inside said 'I'll get it, Mum.'

A young boy opened the door.

Mrs Irwin smiled. 'We're from Women Together.' The boy stared at her. 'We're here to see your mother.'

A woman with red-rimmed eyes appeared beside him.

'It's alright, love.' She pulled her son back gently from the doorway. 'You can let them in.' The woman took them through to the living room and told them to take a seat. 'I'll put the kettle on.'

'Please don't...' Mrs Irwin's voice tailed off as the woman went to the kitchen, leaving them to sit in the semi-gloom.

The only light was from a small candlestick table lamp and the glow of a well-stoked fire. A gleaming brass coal bucket sat on the hearth. To the right of the fireplace stood a tall, glass display cabinet that housed a collection of porcelain horses. Brenda counted up to thirty horses in various chestnut hues and poses – galloping, standing, rearing on hind legs, a foal sitting by its mother. Lots of sympathy cards dotted around the room. A vase of white lilies. No coffin.

'Are you here about my dad?' asked the boy.

Hazel's mother nodded. 'We've come to offer our condolences to your mother.'

The boy looked gravely at them.

'And to you too,' added Brenda.

'The funeral's tomorrow. Are youse goin'?'

'No,' said Mrs Irwin. 'We're just here to see you and your mum. We...'

'Tom,' the woman had returned with a tray, 'pull one of those tables over for me.'

The boy separated a nest of mahogany-coloured side

tables and slid one in front of them. The woman placed the tray down and poured two cups from the teapot.

'Aren't you having any, Mrs Docherty?' asked Hazel's mother.

'No. I've done nothing else for the last few days but drink tea.'

'We wouldn't have put you to any bother if we'd known you weren't having one too.'

'It gives me something to do.'

Mrs Docherty took a seat in the armchair next to the fire. No-one spoke. Brenda stared at the fireplace and sipped her tea, the cup clattering as she set it on the saucer. A lead crystal carriage clock ticked softly on the mantelpiece. Beside it sat a figurine of a girl. On the other side of the clock was a photograph of a man in a bottle-green uniform, gun in holster.

Mrs Docherty followed Brenda's gaze. 'That's John,' she said, with a wan smile. 'It was taken outside the RUC head-quarters. He's on duty there at the moment, or at least he was until...' Her voice cracked. She pulled out a tissue that was stuffed inside the cuff of her blouse. 'I thought he was safer there than out on the streets. Stupid. In the end he wasn't safe outside his own house.' Mrs Docherty dabbed her eyes with the tattered tissue.

Brenda reached into her bag for a fresh one and passed it to her.

'They must have been watchin' his movements. Followed him home. How else would they know which car was his?' Her eyes brimmed with anguish. 'What if one of the kids had been in the car?'

The boy remained silent. His face was drained of colour.

Mrs Docherty got up and reached for a note tucked behind the clock. 'The minister was here earlier,' she said, unfolding the piece of paper. 'He jotted down what he's going to say tomorrow at the service. He asked me to take a look and let him know if there is anything else I want to add.' She stared at the note then looked to Brenda. 'Should I tell him I begged John not to join the police but he went ahead anyway?'

'I, um...' stuttered Brenda.

'Or that we argued about it the morning he died?' She directed the question at Mrs Irwin.

'Every couple argues,' said Mrs Irwin. 'You're not alone in that respect.'

Mrs Docherty slid the note behind the clock. 'Yes, but if he hadn't left the house in a rage, he wouldn't have forgotten to check under the car. It's my fault he died.'

'Stop it! Stop it!' yelled the boy, clamping his hands over his ears.

'Oh, Tom, I'm sorry. I didn't mean for you to hear that.' She went to her son, tried to put her arms around him.

'I hate you!' He pummelled her chest with his fists.

She let go, her face full of hurt.

He kicked the side table over. The teapot landed on the carpet, its contents leaving a brown stain. Brenda bent down to pick it up.

Mrs Docherty out her hand out to stop her. 'Leave it.'

The boy stood with tightly bunched fists by his sides, his face contorted with anger.

His mother tried again to reach out to him. 'Tom, *please.*'

The boy shrank from her touch. 'Keep away!' He raised a

fist. He was trembling as he waved it in front of her face. Then he lowered his arm and ran from the room.

His mother stared after him. 'He really does hate me, doesn't he?'

'I've seen this before,' said Mrs Irwin. 'He doesn't mean it. The anger – it's all part of the grieving process.' She assured her that her son would come round.

'He was in the house at the time, getting ready for school. He saw it all. How can any child get over that?'

Mrs Irwin led the woman back to her chair. 'There's no such thing as getting over it. Of course there isn't, but given time, he'll find a way to deal with the memory.'

The woman shook her head.

'He will, Mrs Docherty.'

'Joan. My name's Joan.'

'I know you'll do everything you can, Joan, to help him.'

'I'm trying. God knows, I'm trying.'

After a few minutes she got to her feet.' I'd better check on him.'

'Do you want me to talk to him first?' asked Hazel's mum.

'Thank you, no. It needs to be me.' She took a long intake of breath. 'Do you mind seein' yourselves out?'

They gathered their things while the woman went upstairs to seek out her son. As they left the house they could hear the woman's placating voice followed by the heartrending sobs of the boy.

———

'God, that was fierce,' said Brenda. 'Is it always like that?'

'It's never easy.'

'I felt so sorry for the poor lad.' Brenda thought of his pale, shocked face. 'I don't know what his mother was thinking about, sayin' all that in front of the child.'

'I'm sure she didn't mean for it to come out that way.'

'No, but still...'

Hazel's mum could see how much the incident had upset Brenda. 'It's hard to watch something like that, especially when the grief is so raw,' she said, 'but you'll get used to it.'

Brenda's mouth tightened into a thin smile. 'I'm not sure I'm cut out for this, Mrs Irwin.'

'Don't be saying that.' She gave Brenda a reassuring pat on the arm. 'You did well today.'

It didn't feel that way to Brenda. If anything, it seemed their visit had only served to make things worse for the widow. A few days later, however, Mrs Docherty called the Women Together headquarters to thank them. She said it had been a relief to talk to people who didn't shy away from the stark realities of a killing.

Women who'd been caught up in violence didn't want to deal with the sensitivities of well-meaning people on top of their own grief. It was too exhausting. They craved straight talkers and practical advice. Mrs Irwin understood that. Now Brenda did too. She also realised that, in her own blundering way, she had helped the Dochertys after all.

EIGHT

On his first tour Andy hadn't known what to expect, only that it was a place where one side was shooting and bombing the other. He thought he'd be caught in the middle, hated by both. So he was confused when the people came out of their homes, all smiles, shaking his hand like he was some long-lost relative and offered him food and drink. He hadn't expected to be seen as a bit of a saviour.

'Here's a wee somethin' to keep you going.'

They said they were glad to see the soldiers.

'It makes us feel safer, so it does.'

Tray after tray would emerge, laden with plates of sandwiches, Marie biscuits, fruit loaf and slices of Victoria sponge cake. And there was tea. Lots of tea. Served up in china teacups and saucers. It felt odd to be sipping tea from their finest crockery, dressed in full army combat.

Last time round, the kids had been in thrall of him. They'd wanted to know what it felt like in all that gear. Was it heavy? Could they try his helmet on? Of course, they were most fascinated by his gun.

'Hey, mister, have you ever shot anyone with that?'

The enquiring boy's mother gave him a sharp cuff on the ear.

'I was only askin'.'

'Don't. It's rude.'

The boy was undeterred. 'Well, have ye, mister?'

Andy hadn't, although he wasn't about to let the boy know that. He took the magazine out of his SLR and let him have a closer look. The boy examined each of the parts; he smiled as he turned them over in his hands. He watched every step Andy took as he fitted them back together.

Things were different a year on. There was no way he'd let anyone touch his rifle now. Besides, the kids no longer asked to see it. They just stood at the side of the street and shouted abuse.

'Why don't youse fuck off back to England,' they yelled as his patrol walked by.

The women turned their faces from him. Mothers pulled their children close to their sides as if he was a contagion. He was no longer given tea and biscuits. Instead, the women greeted him with a cacophony of banging dustbin lids and whistles – their way of warning their men the soldiers were coming. They spat at him. He'd even had a soiled baby's nappy thrown at him.

'Sir.' Someone prodded him in the back. 'You need to move on.'

Christ! He was doing the very thing he warned his lads against – Don't be a standing target. Keep moving if you want to stay safe. He taught them to run across the street, not walk, to keep changing their positions. *Run, take cover, move* was the drill he hammered into them over and over again. At night, his knee joints hurt from the constant banging against a concrete pavement.

The patrol turned into a narrow, terraced street. The rain had eased off and the kids were playing outside, making the most of a watery sunshine. Andy heard the rhythmic thud of a football being kicked against a wall. As he got closer, the ball bounced into the road and skittered towards him. A boy scooped the ball up. He paused to look at Andy, gestured with two fingers and ran back to his friends.

A group of girls had set up a skipping game in an empty space between the parked cars. Two stood facing each other, with a loop of knotted elastic bands around their ankles. A third girl jumped in and out of the rectangle they had formed, to a chorus of:

'Peggy leggy in,

Peggy leggy out,

Peggy leggy in out,

Peggy leggy ON!'

They shrieked in unison as the girl completed her final move successfully. The rope of elastic bands was moved to knee height. The girl was halfway through her new jump sequence when one front door after another began to open. Mothers stepped into the street and hauled their children into the houses.

'Shit! They're taking the kids indoors,' said one of Andy's men.

An eerie silence descended on the street.

Andy felt the hairs on the back of his neck stand on end. 'Switch on,' he barked. 'Watch the rooflines.' He placed his thumb on the safety catch of his gun, ready to release it at the first sign of trouble.

The silence was broken by the crack of a gun being fired. 'Sniper.'

Andy ran in a zigzag back down the street, searching for the nearest cover. He dived behind a low wall, spread-eagled himself on the ground and propped his rifle on his arms. 'Keep your eyes on that tower block,' he yelled to his men. He looked through his rifle sights. Nobody on the rooftop. He scanned the building, searching for movement but the tower block was a grid of hundreds of windows. Another crack and shards of brick from the wall behind showered him.

The shooting stopped as suddenly as it started. Andy realised it was hopeless to attempt to track the sniper down. The gunman would already be gone. He'd be scurrying through the maze of back alleys on his way to a safe house. A bath of water would be ready for him to jump into and wash away any trace of cordite from his skin.

'Come on,' shouted Andy to one of his men who was still propped against a wall further up the street. 'Hurry up and get your arse out of there.'

Sam remained frozen in the same position. Andy was about to shout again until he noticed the pool of dark liquid. He ran to the soldier. There was a stain on the front of the lad's shirt.

Andy tore the shirt open. He could see the bullet hole but there was only a small trickle of blood coming from it. He shouted back to his signaller. 'Call in, Jim.' He turned Sam's body over, looking for the exit wound. 'Oh, Jesus Christ!'

There was a gaping hole with ragged edges, the size of a tennis ball, in the middle of his back. The flak jacket was a useless piece of shit; it had stopped nothing. Andy stuffed one of his field dressings into it. The dressing was immediately soaked.

'I need some more help here, damn it!' he yelled. 'JIM. Get on the radio. NOW.'

The young signaller stammered into his radio. 'Delta 4-zero ... Albert Street ... one casualty.'

The blood kept pumping out. It seeped through Andy's fingers and ran down his hands. It soaked his cuffs, turning the sage green of his uniform the colour of oxidised metal. Sam lay motionless. The only sound he made was a scarcely perceptible wheezing groan. Andy had heard that sound once before. A colleague had fallen from the top of a rope during a training exercise. He'd snapped his spine and as he lay in a crumpled heap, he emitted this same pitiful noise – like that of a badly wounded animal that had crawled into a hole to die.

Andy's stomach twisted into a tight knot. 'It's ok, Sam. The medics are on their way.'

An armoured patrol car, followed by a medical PIG, screeched into the street. Andy stepped aside and watched as the medical team stuffed more field dressings into the wound. The lad's face had turned grey.

'Come on, mate, stay with us,' they urged.

They stemmed the bleeding as best they could and loaded him on to a stretcher. The doors slammed shut and the PIG sped down the street. Andy made his way back to his men, leaving a trail of red boot prints on the pavement.

The young signalman hurried to his side. 'Is he going to make it, sir?'

'They're doing everything they can.'

'He's going to be alright, isn't he?' The signalman searched Andy's face for reassurance.

Suddenly a loud cheer went up from the direction of the tower block.

Andy stopped in his tracks. 'You fucking animals.'

He wanted to go back and grab the first man he saw. He wanted to smash his skull against a wall, to smash it over and over until it was pulp. He'd just lost one good man and these scumbags were whooping and hollering for joy.

———

Two of Andy's men packed the young soldier's kit. They stripped his bed, collected his clothes, gathered the family photographs, the cigarettes and personal oddments from his locker. His money was counted and recorded. Within a short space of time the only trace of Sam was a pile of kit stacked and labelled in a green metal cupboard in the orderly room, waiting to be shipped off. There was a procedure for dealing with death in the Army.

The debrief lasted hours, with Andy revisiting the exact details of the fatal incident again and again. He was emotionally and physically drained when he finally crawled into bed. That night he dreamed of a hooded figure at a window. Andy raised his gun and fired. One perfect shot. Contact made. The black hood became red. The window turned red then the concrete sides of the tower block and the pavements beneath it. A tide of red swept down the road until it reached Andy's feet. It rose to his knees, his chest and finally over his head. Andy was drowning in a thick, sticky ocean of blood. He woke with a pounding heart, gasping for breath.

NINE

The air inside the social club was thick with cigarette smoke. Clare stood for a moment, feeling unsure, before she spotted him through the fug. He was sitting at a table at the back of the room along with half a dozen other men. Clare walked over. The men were talking in hushed tones. She remained by the table, waiting to catch his eye.

'Are you lost?' asked one of the men.

'I'm here to see Peter.'

Peter looked up then frowned. 'Oh, you're here. I wasn't expectin' you so soon.'

'Why don't you buy your girl a drink while we finish our business,' said the man.

'Sorry about this.' Peter got up from the table. 'I won't be long,' he said, leading Clare towards the bar.

'I didn't mean to drag you away.' Clare glanced over at the table. The men had resumed their quiet talk. 'Not if it's important.'

'It's alright. We were more or less done.' He pulled out two barstools. 'What are you havin'?'

'Vodka and coke, thanks.'

'Who's with you?'

'No-one. I came alone.' She took in his surprise and wondered if she'd done the right thing. 'You said to drop in on you.' Clare gave a 'ta-da' gesture with her hands. 'Well, here I am.'

Peter placed an order at the bar, reached into his pocket and pulled out a packet of cigarettes. He offered one to Clare. 'You look nice.'

'Thanks.'

The barman was in the middle of bleeding a new keg of beer. The tap head sputtered and a cloudy foam filled the glass. He poured the top into a slop tray and offered the glass up again. After a few more tries the amber liquid ran clear.

'The figure's gone up,' he said. 'See.' He set a newspaper in front of Peter, along with his pint of beer. 'Fifteen dead now.'

Clare looked at the picture of the burnt-out pub. The bomb had gone off last Saturday night. It had ruptured a gas pipe, starting a fire.

'Here.' Peter folded the paper and handed it back to the barman. 'I've seen enough.'

'That was terrible,' said Clare. 'There were kids in that pub.'

She and her family had watched the live coverage on the ten o'clock news: locals forming a human chain, clawing at the rubble, searching for survivors.

'I know,' fumed Peter. 'The peelers tried to pin the blame on us. The Army too. They both know it was those UVF fuckers.'

He seemed convinced it was the work of the Ulster Volunteer Force. 'So, it was the UVF then?'

'Who else would it have been?' Peter held her gaze for a moment. 'Don't tell me you fell for their propaganda too?'

Clare's face grew warm. Reports following the bombing suggested it had been an Irish Republican Army device that had gone off by accident. Many believed it was true.

'You see? This is exactly what they're tryin' to do – plant doubt in people's minds, to get our own community to turn against us.'

'Well, it didn't work with me.'

'But I can tell you, there were none of our bombs there that night.'

Clare looked around the room. It was full of people out for a drink and a bit of craic. What if someone left a bomb here? She thought of her family – her mum, dad, Brenda. They had all drunk in here at some point.

'Those bastards are out to get us and the security forces aren't goin' to do anything about it,' said Peter. He took a mouthful of beer and leant towards her. 'That's why we need to protect ourselves.'

'Shit!' said Clare. The tip of his cigarette had caught her sleeve.

'Sorry. Did I burn you?'

Clare stared at the penny-shaped hole. 'No, but Brenda's goin' to kill me. This is her top.'

Peter laughed. 'That'll give her another reason to hate me.'

Clare had asked Brenda to lend her the top for the night. She'd refused, saying she'd just bought it. When she saw Clare's freshly applied make-up and blow-dried hair she'd asked her where she was off to, all dolled up, on a Sunday night.

'The social club. I'm meetin' Peter there.'

'My Peter?'

'He's not your Peter,' Clare told her. 'You don't own him.'

Peter reached for an ashtray and stubbed out his cigarette. He tilted his head back, looked up to the ceiling and slowly released the smoke from his last drag. It hung in the air above their heads. 'I hear your sister's been spoutin' off again,' he said. 'Tellin' the Provos to turn in their weapons.'

'The peace group people you mean?'

'Your sister's one of them.'

'Yeah, well I'm not, so don't have a go at me.'

'Tell her she needs to wind her neck in, if she knows what's good for her.'

'I'm not my sister's keeper.' She was about to take him to task but he seemed uneasy all of a sudden. It threw her.

'Just tell her,' he said in a quieter voice. 'I owe her that much.'

Clare shrugged. 'Fine.'

He relaxed a little, seemed satisfied with her response. Then he set his beer down, sat up straight and fixed his attention on her. 'Anyway, enough of your big sister,' he said. 'How's things with you?'

'Well,' Clare gave a proud smile, 'I signed up.'

Peter's gaze had drifted to Marie Keenan and her friends. It was only a matter of time before he spotted them. How could he not when everyone could hear the cackles of them long before they saw them?

Clare had clocked them straight away and had been doing

her utmost to blank them out, but their voices were getting louder. Every so often Marie would say something that would have them giggling and sneering and looking Clare's way.

'I signed up for that typing course.'

Peter gave her a blank look.

'The one I told you about. Remember?' She explained she'd have to do Pitman.

'What's Pitman?'

'Shorthand. I have to reach a certain speed before I can pass the course. I'm a bit worried about that. Honest to god, Peter, you want to see it. It looks like a bunch of squiggles.'

'That all sounds ... good.'

Marie had paid a visit to the ladies. She and her breasts were now making their way back to her table. Peter's eyes followed their progress.

'Sorry,' said Clare. 'Here's me blatherin' away about shorthand and I haven't asked you anything about your work at the garage.'

Marie nodded to Peter on the way past. 'How's about ye?'

Clare could see she'd had a quick tidy up – brushed her hair and reapplied her lipstick. It would be just like that fat arse to choose now to make her move on Peter.

'Better for seein' you.' Peter nodded in the direction of her friends. 'I see you've brought the Crazy Gang with you.'

'Peter,' yelled one of the girls. She patted the seat of an empty stool beside her. 'Come on over and say hello.'

'No, you're alright.'

Marie gave him a nudge with her elbow. 'Ach, come on. You can join us for one wee drink.'

'Not tonight.' Peter wrapped his arm around Clare's waist. 'I've got company.'

Marie made her way back to the table with a look on her face that could curdle milk.

Peter kept his arm entwined round Clare's waist. She melted into his hold. She hoped Marie and her friends were watching. It took all her resolve not to sneak a look at their table to check for herself.

'Hey, Peter.' One of the men sitting in the corner table indicated with his head that Peter was to rejoin them.

Peter released his hold. 'Looks like I'm wanted.'

'Aren't you goin' to finish that?' Clare pointed to his half-drunk pint.

'I've probably had enough. Best to keep a clear head.' He got up to leave. 'Nice seein' you, Clare.'

Clare watched him take his place at the table. He caught her eye and winked.

The barman removed Peter's glass from the counter. 'Looks like you've made an impression.'

Clare smiled. Tonight had gone better than she'd hoped and yet there was something poking at the back of her mind. When he'd said 'There were none of our bombs there that night' he'd sounded so sure. Did it mean what she thought?

TEN

Andy lifted the receiver and promptly set it down again. What should he tell her? He could pretend everything was fine. His wife wouldn't want to hear a gritty account of yesterday's events anyway. If he told her what had happened, she'd want to question him, ask him how he felt. He wasn't ready to discuss that with her. It shocked him that he felt so murderous, that he wrestled with a burning hatred for the people who had done this to one of his lads.

Best to stick to the everyday. He'd tell her that Taff's cooking had improved, that Robbie had become a father for the first time and was gutted to have missed the birth. All that sort of stuff was safe, neutral territory.

'Are you finished, sir?' asked someone in the queue behind him.

'No, I'm not.' Andy picked up the phone and dialled the number again. She answered straight away. 'How's it going?' he asked, trying to sound upbeat.

'You were supposed to call me last night.'

'I know but ...'

'I wish you wouldn't do that – say you're going to phone and then not bother.'

Andy bit his lip. He thought of the blood seeping through Sam's webbing and combat gear and how, despite everyone's frantic efforts, they had failed to save him. 'Sorry,' he said. 'I was ... knackered.'

When had he started to hold things back from her? They used to share everything. Now he felt he had to edit the bad news. He did it to stop her worrying about him. More recently, though, he sensed a distance in her. It was as if she was going through the motions of being a concerned wife but didn't really want to know.

'How's Stevie?' he asked.

'Fine. He's lost another front tooth. That was what he wanted to tell you last night. He jiggled it loose and pulled it out all by himself. He's put it in a matchbox; he's saving it for when you come home.'

'Tell him I'm impressed.'

'If you'd phoned when you promised, you could have told him yourself.'

Andy didn't have the energy to explain himself. 'So, how's things with you?' he asked after a brief silence.

'I'm fine.'

She talked about the humdrum of life at home. The electricity bill was getting bigger each quarter. They needed to do something about that electric heater; it was eating up money. Andy promised to sort it out when he was back. They'd missed their bin when they collected the rubbish and now it was overflowing; she was worried it would attract rats. Andy glanced at the soldier beside him. The soldier was cracking jokes; he looked happy he was able to grab precious time with his partner.

'Andy? Did you hear what I said?'

'Sorry, no. Run that by me again.'

'I was worried about rats.'

'We've got rats?'

'No. Oh forget it! I may as well be talking to myself.'

Andy latched on to another topic. 'How's your mum keeping?'

'Do you really want to know?'

He wanted to tell her that no, he didn't give a toss. 'Yes,' he said.

'She's actually very upset. I think Kate has pushed things too far this time.'

'It'll pass. Don't they always patch things up in the end?'

'This time is different.'

She proceeded to deliver a blow-by-blow account of what her sister thought about her mother and what her mother thought about her sister.

Was that all that mattered to Jenny? She must watch some of the news reports; she must see something of what he had to deal with. 'Oh, for fuck's sake,' he said.

'Sorry?'

'I'm not interested in who said what. Seriously, does it really matter?'

'It matters to me. I'm the one caught in the middle of it. Of course, if I'm boring you, I'll stop.'

'I lost Sam.' The words were out before he even knew he'd said them.

'Who's Sam?' Suddenly her voice was quiet, hesitant. 'What do you mean ... *lost* him?'

'Shot. They got him.'

Jenny gasped. 'Oh my god, that's awful.'

This last tour had been the toughest yet. Dealing with riots – being pelted with bricks and bottles or shot at by snipers – Andy had been prepared for that. He'd been trained for it, knew how to respond. But witnessing the bombing of soft targets? Ordinary people. Nothing could have prepared Andy for the first time he'd encountered dead or mutilated women and children. And now he'd lost a man. That was a first too.

'All these shootings and bombings,' she said, 'I don't understand what's going on over there.'

She made Northern Ireland sound separate and distant but it was only a ferry sailing away from her life with their son, on the mainland.

'Why is it getting worse? I thought the Army was supposed to be sorting things out.'

'I don't have the answers, Jenny. I just carry out my orders.'

How could he explain the senseless slaughter when he didn't understand it himself? All he knew was that it didn't help to think too deeply about it or question what his lads were doing. As for *sorting things out*, as she put it, Andy would leave that to the politicians.

'I wasn't having a go at you. It's hard to...'

'I know.' His voice was flat. 'Listen, Jenny, I've got to go. There's a queue of people waiting to use the phone.'

'Oh. Ok.'

'Send Stevie my love.'

'I will.'

'Bye.'

———

Later that evening Andy played pool with the lads. His way of unwinding before he hit the sack. He was normally a brisk, confident player, but tonight was different. He took longer to line up his shots. His men watched him miss one easy pot after another but no-one commented.

He was halfway through a game when someone turned on the television. A picture of Sam flashed up on the screen. The room fell silent as the details of his killing were read out. It took all of thirty seconds – name, regiment, age, killed by a sniper, relatives had been informed – before the newsreader moved on to a lighter topic to round off the programme.

Andy hurled the pool cue across the room. It bounced off the far wall. So that was it, was it? The young soldier had spent less than three months with the regiment defending ... what? On the day, his mates had been just been luckier than him. That's what it came down to. He left behind a shattered family but don't worry – that 30-second tribute on Ulster fucking Television meant it was all worthwhile. Someone picked the pool cue off the floor and handed it to him.

'Fancy another game, sir?'

Andy shook his head.

Back in his sleeping quarters he picked up his alarm clock, checked the setting and placed it on the plastic chair by his bed. He looked at the framed picture of his wife. That warm, smiley face didn't match the person he'd spoken to on the phone.

They'd been 19 years when they married. By 20 years, they'd had their son. At the time it hadn't seemed too young to be settling down and starting a family. It was part of Army life. The other lads had done the same. He realised now it had been a mistake.

They'd had no idea what it meant to have a child, thought Stevie would fit magically into their life. They didn't realise they would have to reorder their life to fit in with him. Nights had to be planned well ahead. They could no longer nip down to the pub together on a whim.

Andy hadn't helped. He'd taken up with his mates when he was back on leave, met up with them for drinks or gone to the snooker hall. It never crossed his mind to offer to look after Stevie for a night so Jenny could have a break.

They'd thought about having another kid a few years back. Or rather, Jenny had.

'I don't want Stevie to be an only child. I don't want him turning out selfish.'

Andy had studied her face to see if she was having a dig at him. He was an only child.

'We should try for a baby,' she'd said, as if it was a necessity.

'Is that what you want?' he'd asked.

'What do *you* want, Andy?'

He couldn't remember his exact response but it was something along the lines of he'd go with whatever she decided. From the way her jaw tightened he could tell it had been the wrong thing to say.

Andy took off his ring and set it on the chair; he turned over the picture and sank back into his pillow. Thoughts of what the next day might have in store for him tumbled through his head. He needed to put Sam's death aside, to move on. He had to consider the rest of his men. He felt the familiar sweat break on his brow and the footprint of fear pressing on his chest. His eyes stared, wide open, into darkness, seeing nothing.

ELEVEN

The double doors to the garage were pulled shut. Inside a radio was blaring. Clare could hear Rod Stewart's gravelly voice as he sang 'Stay With Me'. She entered through a small side opening. Peter was bent over the engine of a car, checking for oil and singing along to the track.

'Hiya.'

Peter looked up and caught the bonnet with his head.

'Fuck!' He rubbed his temple.

'I was just passin', said Clare.

'Were you now?'

She stood for a moment as Peter looked at her with teasing eyes.

'I wondered if you'd had any lunch yet?'

Peter picked up a rag and wiped the grease from his fingers. He turned the radio down. 'I haven't had time to think of it.'

A man who Clare took to be the garage owner walked in. He greeted her with a brief hello.

'I've got Mr Doyle on the phone. He wants to know when he can pick his car up.'

'Tell him it'll be ready this afternoon.'

'Sure?'

'Yes. He can come any time after three.'

The man slapped Peter on the back. 'Good lad,' he said then hurried back to the office.

'Looks like I've picked a bad day. I should leave you in peace.'

'Watch yourself!' Peter grabbed Clare's arm and pulled her towards him. 'I wouldn't want you breakin' an ankle.'

She hadn't seen the large pit in the floor behind her. The two oily planks placed on top of it barely covered it.

'Me neither,' she laughed.

'Sit here,' he said, pointing to a wooden chair, 'where you can't do any damage to yourself.'

Next to the chair was a two-barred electric heater, which made little difference to the temperature of the room.

'Christ, Peter, it's freezin' in here. How do you stick this all day?'

'It's better than nothing.'

In the corner of the workshop was a small stainless-steel sink. Peter washed his hands with a sliver of soap then shook them dry.

'My mum would tell you off if she saw you doin' that. She says you get chilblains if you don't dry your hands properly then go out in the cold.'

He held his hands for a moment in front of the heater. 'Happy now?'

Clare nodded.

'Right then. If it's a bite of food you're after, we'd better get goin'.' Peter pulled a woollen coat on over his overalls. 'But I can't stop for long.'

They were halfway to the door when the lunchtime news came on the radio.

'Hang on,' he said.

It was the same bulletin Clare had heard earlier that morning. 'That's the shootin' on the–'

'Sshh.' Peter turned the volume up.

'One soldier killed,' said the newsreader. 'Another seriously injured. The security forces were following a lead.'

Peter switched the radio off. 'C'mon. Let's get out of here.'

'Where do you want to go?' she asked.

'Dunno.' He lit a cigarette and took a drag, inhaling deeply.

On her way to the garage Clare had passed a small cafe. It had a few tables inside or they could get some sandwiches to take away if Peter was pressed for time.

'I thought we could try that place down the street,' she suggested.

'That'll do.'

Peter set off at breakneck speed. Clare wished she'd worn lower heels as she hobbled after him, struggling to keep up.

They walked past a row of soot-encrusted houses. A pushchair sat on the pavement. Strapped inside was a squirming toddler. His older brother was swinging on a rubber tyre fixed to a lamp post by a length of rope. The child clapped his hands in delight as the boy swung close whooping loudly. He tried to lift himself out of the pram. When he couldn't he began to cry.

'Marty!' thundered a voice from an upstairs window. 'Cut that out. You're tormentin' the life out of him.'

Marty looked up at his mother. 'I'm not. I'm just...'

The window slammed shut. Marty sat for a moment then resumed swinging.

Outside the end house a woman stood in her slippers, arms folded, talking to her neighbour. 'I told him I wasn't takin' any more of his nonsense.'

'Good for you,' said her neighbour. 'It's about time you gave it to him straight. Men. They're bloody useless at times.'

Peter greeted them on the way by. 'Afternoon, ladies.'

The women looked up in surprise. Peter made like he was doffing a cap. The women scowled then resumed their conversation.

'Cheeky bugger,' muttered one.

'I think your charm is wasted on those two.'

'Must be out of practice,' he laughed.

'I don't know about that.'

Peter lit another cigarette. By the time they'd reached the cafe, the cigarette was a stub. He threw it in the gutter. 'In you go,' he said as he held the door open for her. 'It's my treat.' He paid for a couple of ham sandwiches and two mugs of tea, which they had in the cafe.

'Your parents keepin' well, Clare?'

'They're both loaded with the cold at the moment. Mum blames Dad for passin' it on to her. Apart from that, they're grand.'

'A hot toddy last thing at night is the best cure. Sweats it out of you.'

'Dad would be all for that. Not sure Mum would approve of the whiskey.'

'Hot port works too.'

'Or that.'

Clare's mum never touched spirits. Apart from the time her dad had persuaded her to 'Try a wee dram' one Christmas Eve. It tasted better than she thought and after two or three more she went to bed in fine form. She woke up in the early hours and spent the rest of the night heaving into the toilet bowl. There was no turkey cooked that Christmas. Ever since then, the very smell of whiskey was enough to set her mum off.

'I hear Brenda's got herself some student digs.'

'Where did you hear that?'

'A mate of mine, a student at Queens's would you believe. You wouldn't know him.'

'Mum thinks it's a waste of money, but you know Brenda. Once she gets somethin' into her head...'

'Don't I know it.'

She couldn't tell if he was referring to Brenda's new digs, her decision to break up with him or her involvement with the peace group. She didn't want to ask.

'My typing course is going well.'

'That's great.'

'Yeah,' she said. 'I'm up to a good speed already.'

'You were worried about the shorthand the last time we met. Looked like squiggles, you said.'

'You remember?' That night in the social club she'd thought he wasn't taking in anything. 'It's not as bad as it looks. It's surprisin' how quickly you pick it up.'

'Dunno about that, Miss MacRae.' Peter leant back in his

chair and folded his arms. A smile crept on to his face. 'I suppose I'll have to start callin' you that when you become a secretary.'

Clare gave him a playful shove. 'Away on with you.'

'Miss MacRae, could you take some notes, please.'

'Stop it now.'

'Seriously though, it sounds as if you're makin' a good show of it.'

Clare blushed. 'Thanks. You seem very busy in the garage, Peter.'

'Too busy. My boss is really overloadin' me.'

'That's because you're the best mechanic he has.'

'I know but still.' Peter glanced at his watch. 'Sorry, Clare. As nice as it is to chat with you, I do need to get back.'

'That's fine. I understand.' Clare gathered up her things. 'I'll walk with you. Then I'll need to head on myself.'

They talked some more about Clare's course and what she wanted to do afterwards. She wasn't fussy; she'd take whatever was going. Peter told her he wanted to set up his own garage someday. If he was going to work this hard, he might as well get the benefit rather than line someone else's pocket.

'Too right,' said Clare.

She liked that they were sharing their dreams. It felt special.

As they neared the garage Peter grew quiet. His pace slowed to almost a stop. 'What do *they* want?'

Clare followed his gaze. Next to the garage sat an army Saracen.

'Dunno,' she said, throwing him an anxious look.

Peter gathered his pace again. He kept his head down and his hands in his pockets.

Clare's eyes were on the Saracen. The doors stayed shut. No-one got out.

'What are they doin'?' he asked.

'Nothing. Oh, wait!'

Peter gave a sharp intake of breath.

'It looks as if ... Yes, they're about to go.'

There was a throaty rumble as the vehicle moved on.

Peter heard it too. He looked up as the Saracen disappeared round the corner. 'Jesus, Clare.' He clutched his chest, feigning a heart attack. 'Don't do that to me.'

'Sorry,' she said, pulling a face. 'It's not you they're after then?'

'No.' He pulled the double doors of the garage back. 'And now,' he said, sounding more like himself, 'I really do need to get back to some work or the boss will be on my back.'

'Can't have that. I better go.' Clare's pounding heart calmed as she saw the colour return to his face.

'C'mere you.' Peter slid his hands inside her coat and locked them around her waist. 'Don't I get a kiss before you go?'

She was about to say 'yes', but he was already kissing her hard on the mouth. Clare closed her eyes and pressed her body tighter to his.

'Are you there, Peter?'

Another mechanic had popped his head round the door. Clare recognised him as one of Peter's drinking mates.

'Give me a hand, will you? I don't know what's wrong with this Cortina.' His eyes widened. 'Jesus, Peter, I see you're workin' your way through the whole MacRae family. At this rate, it'll be the mother next.'

'Fuck off!' said Peter.

Clare adjusted her clothes.

Peter looked at Clare. 'This time I've picked the right one.'

TWELVE

Mrs Henderson was obsessed with reading her stars. Every Saturday morning she'd make herself and Brenda a cup of tea and turn to the horoscope page in the paper. A positive reading cheered her up no end; a negative one was met with gloom. She was all smiles today.

'An unexpected windfall is coming your way,' she read. 'I wonder how much it'll be?'

'What does it say about Pisces?' asked Brenda. It was her birthday and she wanted to know if the stars predicted a happy one.

'It says...' Brenda crossed her fingers. '...a chance encounter could lead to romance.' Mrs Henderson winked. 'Looks like it's your lucky day, Brenda.'

Brenda liked Mrs Henderson despite her funny ways. She liked that she trusted her to run things when she wasn't there. That happened a lot as the woman was forever nipping out for messages. This morning was no exception. No sooner had she popped to the bakery for some bread rolls when Mrs

Brennan appeared with two of her brood in tow. Brenda's heart sank.

You could usually hear the Brennans before you saw them. One was always bawling from being on the receiving end of another's fist.

Brenda mustered up her broadest smile. 'What can I help you with today, Mrs Brennan?'

The toddler reached from his pushchair and made a grab for a rack of clothes. The other jabbed at a neatly stacked pile of cot clothes with a chocolate-stained finger.

'Shoes for this one.' The woman nodded towards the toddler.

Brenda led them to a plastic chair by the cash desk.

Mrs Brennan yanked her youngest out of the pushchair and plonked him on her knee. She wrapped her arms around him in a vice-like grip.

'Be a good boy for Mammy,' she said, as she looked over her shoulder to check on her other boy. 'Conor!'

Brenda jumped.

'Put that down. NOW!'

'I'll need to measure his feet.' Brenda bent down to unbuckle his right shoe.

Little Kieran screamed and kicked and tried to punch his way free of his mother's hold.

'Gimme that foot.' Mrs Brennan ripped the shoe off with such force Brenda feared she'd taken Kieran's foot with it. Brenda held the tape up to it and asked him to straighten his toes. He refused. Mrs Brennan unfurled them for him, none too gently. Kieran started to bawl.

'Sorry about this,' she said. She turned to her son. 'You do as the lady says or you'll see the rough end of my hand.'

Brenda offered up the measuring tape again, but the boy knocked it away.

'Right, that's it. I warned you.' Mrs Brennan swung her beefy arm and brought it down hard across the back of Kieran's legs. The slap made him cry louder. In the end, she gave up and dragged her boys out of the shop promising to return another time.

Brenda was surveying the damage when Mrs Henderson returned.

'What in All Saints happened here?'

'Your favourite customers were in.'

Together they tidied up the mess.

'I've a good mind to ban that family,' muttered Mrs Henderson.

Brenda knew she wouldn't dare. Why risk a brick through the window, or worse?

The remainder of the morning passed without incident and the shop ticked over with a steady stream of customers. There was no shortage of new babies to buy for and Tiny Tots did a good trade in matinee coats, bibs and babygrows. Brenda enjoyed talking to the other mothers and she was good with the kids, the Brennans being the exception. Mrs Henderson said she'd make a great mother one day. As far as Brenda was concerned that day was a long way off. She might like kids but she was in no rush to have one of her own.

Lunchtime came round quickly and Brenda headed off to catch the bus into town.

Her parents, on a shopping mission, were already there. She was to meet them at the Abercorn restaurant, just off Cornmarket for a bite to eat – their birthday treat to her.

There was a long queue at the security gate as people waited their turn to be called. A uniformed, gloved female security officer eventually beckoned Brenda forward. The woman tugged at the zip.

'It sticks a bit, said Brenda. 'Do you want me to...?'

'That won't be necessary.'

The woman gave the zip another tug and the bag burst open. She peered inside and pushed the contents around, had a go at closing the bag, failed, then handed it back. After a quick frisk by another female security officer Brenda was free to go.

Belfast city centre was packed with mums and dads, children in prams and young people, all enjoying a Saturday afternoon's shopping. Brenda joined the crowds and made her way towards Castle Street.

She felt the blast wave first. It was like being hit hard in the chest by a huge fist. There was an orange flash and a deafening bang. Everything went quiet. The unearthly silence seemed to hang in the air for ever. Then the screaming started. A young lad lay in a tangled heap on the ground, his legs twisted at an impossible angle to his body. Blood was everywhere, splattered over the street and up the sides of buildings. And ... what *was* that? It looked like ... The bile rose in her throat. It was bits of skin. Bits of people.

A woman staggered towards her. Only her eyes, wide with terror, were visible beneath her bloodied face. She held a small girl in her arms. The child's coat was singed; her hair and clothes were thick with dust. One foot was bare. On the other was a black patent shoe. It had a T-bar strap. A Clarks shoe. They sold that shoe in Mrs Henderson's shop.

———

Andy felt the sudden lowering of pressure. It was as if the sky was being dragged down and the air sucked out at the same time. A loud boom followed.

'That was a big one, sir.'

And right in the heart of the city, by the sounds of it.

A radio message confirmed it. He knew the restaurant; he'd eaten there himself. Christ! It was always full on a Saturday afternoon. The patrol was abandoned. His unit piled into armoured cars and raced towards the city centre.

———

Flames licked at the windows of the Abercorn. A soldier ran past. Brenda grabbed his arm and tried to yank him back. 'Stop! Please help me,' she yelled. 'My parents are in there.'

He offered some words of comfort then hurried on. Brenda sank to the ground and stared after him as he disappeared into the burning restaurant.

———

It was pitch-black inside the Abercorn building. Andy was met with the smell of smoke mixed with blood and burning flesh. It was thick and bitter. He could taste it in his mouth. A woman cried out in the darkness. Andy stumbled through the rubble, stepping over severed limbs, to reach her. He lifted her up. The lower half of one of her arms had been blown off. He carried her out on to the street. The woman's eyes were open, staring up at him. He held her as a medic wrapped a tourniquet around the stump of her arm. There was nothing more he could do for her. He left her with the medic, took a deep breath and hurried back into the smouldering, gruesome scene.

———

Brenda couldn't think what to do. Her head was fuzzy. She thought she heard someone call her name. Again she heard it. She glanced up to see her dad running towards her.

'Are you hurt?

'No,' she said as her dad helped her to her feet. 'Where's Mum?' Brenda looked frantically for her.

'She's ok.'

'I thought you were in there. I thought...' She threw her arms round him.

'We were late,' he said. 'I couldn't drag your mum out of Anderson and McAuley. She must have tried on every hat in the place.'

Her parents were off to a wedding next week; her mum had been looking for an outfit.

All around them was chaos. People were screaming and calling out names. Shop alarms rang. Mrs MacRae had been waiting just around the corner from the restaurant, still clutching her Anderson and McAuley carrier bag, praying her daughter was safe. She burst into tears the moment she saw her walk towards her.

They asked a policeman what they should do but he

seemed as confused as them. He told them to stay put. They looked at one another.

'Let's get out of here,' said her dad.

They picked their way through shards of glass and rubble until they made it back to the car.

There was no escape from the city centre. Her dad thumped the steering wheel and swore. The Army kept directing him away from the route he wanted to take. Roads that were familiar to them were now cordoned off. They were boxed in. All they could do was wait for the jam of cars to clear.

Ambulance and fire sirens blared from every direction. Images kept flashing into Brenda's mind – the woman whose arm had been ripped from her body, the child with the singed coat. Who would want to hurt a little girl? This was insanity. It had to stop! She squeezed her eyes shut but the images flared again.

THIRTEEN

I t didn't stop. Brenda watched with growing despair as one atrocity followed another. Yet life went on. Brenda still went to classes, still drank in the student bars and went to discos. At the back of her mind was the gnawing fear she and her friends could be the next target. She kept it tucked there, tried not to think about it. They all did.

Tonight it was as busy as she'd ever seen it. She'd literally had to push her way through to the counter dodging jutting elbows, sloshing pints of beer and the red-hot tips of cigarettes. Getting the drinks in was her penance for keeping Hazel waiting for three-quarters of an hour. She'd told her to go on in without her if she wasn't there but Hazel didn't like to. Mind you, neither did Brenda. They were the same when it came to things like that: both hated walking into bars and discos on their own.

A gap opened up in the crowd and Brenda dived in. The barman nodded to her.

'What can I get you?'

She was about to place her order when a male voice cut in. The bloke beside her had been waving a £10 note in the air and it was him the barman gave his full attention to. Brenda confronted the towering figure behind her.

'I was here first you know.' She glowered at him for a moment then turned away to catch the eye of another barman.

There was a tap on her shoulder.

Brenda spun round. 'What now?'

'I can add yours to mine,' said the bloke with the tenner. 'What are you having?'

He spoke with an English accent. Very good-looking, she realised, now she'd stopped glaring at him and most likely a squaddie.

'Well?'

'Um, thanks. Are you buyin'?'

He smiled and asked where she was sitting, said he'd bring it right over. Brenda returned to her table and, on seeing Hazel's disappointed face, promised her drinks were on the way. A few minutes later a tall frame emerged from the swarm of people carrying two glasses of vodka and coke. He introduced himself as Andy. 'And this,' he said, nodding to a short stocky bloke clutching two pints, 'is Paul. Mind if we join you?'

Paul, built like a Saracen personnel carrier in a shirt, had already set the glasses down and drawn up a stool next to Hazel. She threw Brenda a death stare that signalled she was in no way interested in Andy's mate. They had agreed tonight was about catching up and having a dance. They weren't out to be chatted up. Andy gave an apologetic shrug of his shoulders and waited for a response from Brenda. For a moment she considered saying they didn't want any company but she had already warmed to Andy's open smile. Brenda found herself telling him to take a seat. She hoped Hazel wouldn't be too pissed off with her.

They sorted it out in the ladies as they checked their make-up. Hazel would go along with it. She didn't fancy Paul, but she didn't mind chatting to him, especially as he was mug enough to keep buying her drinks. Andy, on the other hand, got a big thumbs-up – a rare seal of approval from Hazel.

Paul had finished off another pint by the time they returned to their seats. He patted the stool beside him.

'I've saved it for you, Hazel.'

Hazel forced a smile.

'You owe me,' she muttered to Brenda under her breath.

Brenda was surprised how easy it was to slip into a rolling conversation with Andy. They chatted about the music and the venue. He said it was his first time there.

'What do you think of it?'

'I like it.'

'Me too.' She asked him what type of music he liked.

'David Bowie mostly.'

Brenda wrinkled her nose. 'I don't get him. His lyrics are bonkers.'

'What are you into?'

Marc Bolan she told him.

Andy delivered a line from 'Get It On' in Bolan's pouting, preening style. 'And you say Bowie's lyrics are bonkers?'

'Yeah well, each to their own.'

They chatted some more before Brenda broached the obvious.

'How long are you here for?'

'You make it sound like I'm on holiday.' Andy took a mouthful of beer and set his glass down. He looked at her for a moment before answering her question. 'It's another extended tour. I've a bit to go yet.'

'You've been before? And you've come back for more?'

'No choice,' he said.

'I'm only jestin'. I know it's no holiday.'

Andy looked pensive. 'Sometimes I wonder why we're here. What good are we doing?'

'I must admit it would be nice to see the back of you.'

He turned down the corners of his mouth.

'I don't mean *you*. I mean soldiers in general. Then I'd know things were normal again. It's gone on so long I've forgotten what normal feels like.'

The hardest part of the job, he told her, was dealing with the aftermath of a blast. 'That bomb at the Abercorn – that was one of the worst.'

'You were there? Me too. I saw the whole place go up.' Brenda shuddered at the memory. 'It was awful.'

'It was mad that day,' he said. 'People were doing what they could to help and yet...' Andy hesitated.

'Go on,' she said.

'It was someone from their own country who planted it. That's the bit I'll never get. I can't imagine anyone from *my* home town wanting to go out and blow their neighbours to pieces.'

'When you put it like that...'

She'd never given much thought to how Belfast looked to

an outsider like Andy. He seemed bewildered by it all. She didn't know what to say to him.

'Sorry, I didn't mean to bring the mood down.'

'The thing is you're right.'

'Time to change the subject.' His face brightened. 'I'd rather talk about you.'

'What do you want to know?'

'Everything!'

She opened up about her peace work and why it was important to her. He didn't once jump in with an opinion or a criticism. In fact, he praised her.

'I wish there were more like you,' he said.

'Thanks.'

There was a glint in his eye as he added, 'Then we *could* bugger off and you would actually see the back of us.'

Brenda groaned. 'I wish I'd never said that now. You're goin' to hold it against me, aren't you?'

Andy gave her a wink. 'Always.' He reached across for her hand. 'Do you want to dance?'

Brenda gawped at him. She had never once been able to coax Peter on to the dance floor.

'Dance,' he repeated. 'You know – that thing where you jiggle about in time to music?'

'Yeah, sure.'

They danced to one song after another. Conversation was snatched over the loud music. Her voice was hoarse with the effort of making herself heard. When the slow numbers started Brenda rested her head against his chest, happy to let him take the lead. She was hot and clammy; she hoped she didn't look sweaty to him.

They were playing the final song of the evening when

Hazel appeared at their side.

'Sorry to interrupt. I've checked the car park, Brenda. Dad's already there.'

Andy pulled a face. 'You're not leaving already, are you?'

Brenda was tempted to stay. She glanced at Hazel. No, it wouldn't be right, especially as it was Hazel's dad who'd come to collect them.'

'Where's Paul? asked Andy.

'He's over there.'

Andy looked to where Hazel was pointing. His mate was locked in a tight clinch with a blonde. It looked as if he was holding her up. Both were oblivious to the fact that the disco was over and the lights were being turned back up.

Andy rolled his eyes. 'I can take him nowhere.'

Hazel handed Brenda her coat. Brenda took her time putting it on.

'Seriously, Brenda, we need to go. Dad doesn't like to be kept waitin'.'

'Hang on,' said Andy. 'I was going to ask if you fancy meeting up again?' He looked over to Paul and his last-minute conquest. 'I promise to leave him behind.' He suggested somewhere in town, maybe take in a film. 'I've heard *Dirty Harry* is good.'

Brenda rolled her eyes. 'No! Anything but that.' She'd been to see it with Hazel and a bunch of university friends. Clint Eastwood was easy on the eye but there was too much mindless shooting for her liking.

'You've seen it?' he asked.

'Yes.' Brenda saw his disappointment. 'But I'm happy to watch it again.'

Hazel was tapping her foot and making eyes at Brenda to

speed things up.

'Alright I'm comin' now.'

'Don't worry,' said Andy. 'I'll think of something else for us to do.'

He asked how he could get hold of her.

Brenda scribbled down two numbers on a bar mat. 'This one's my student house,' she said. She thought of the shared phone in the hallway, the random chance of anyone answering or passing a message on. 'You're better with this one.' She pointed to Mrs Henderson's number. 'I work there every Saturday.'

Andy stuffed the bar mat into his shirt pocket, patted it with his hand and promised to keep it safe. He cupped her face in his hands and leant in to kiss her goodnight. Brenda said her goodbyes and followed Hazel outside.

'He's over there,' said Hazel. 'It took me ages to find him.'

'A good night?' asked Mr Irwin, once the girls were inside the car.

Brenda gave Hazel a broad grin. 'Very.'

———

Back at base Andy got one of the lads to run a check on the number she'd given him. It matched the listing of university accommodation. He rang the house and asked for Brenda. The girl on the line said he'd just missed her. Did he want to leave a message?

'No,' he said. 'I'll try again later.'

Of course, there'd been other girls. They all did it and Andy was no exception. Maybe not as rampant as some of his men – they'd shag anything with a pulse – but there had been temptation; times when it had practically been served up on a plate.

It didn't feel like cheating; it was purely sex, a release. Ask any of the lads and they'd say the same. It didn't change the way they felt about their wives or girlfriends, but nevertheless they wouldn't want them finding out. Maybe the wives and girlfriends did know and accepted it went with the job. Occasionally word got back about fights with the locals – a drunken soldier making a pass at some girl in front of her boyfriend and it would all kick off.

When he'd left the disco with Brenda's telephone number he wasn't sure if he'd follow up with her. Paul told him he'd be mad not to. The girl was a real stunner. He hadn't been so lucky. At first, he thought he'd been in with a real chance with Brenda's friend but, by the end of the night, realised he was getting nowhere. As the slow music came on and the disco began to wind down he'd made his way to the dance floor in a last-minute attempt to find a girl. At that stage any girl would have done, who looked up for it.

'I was horny.'

A quick snog on the dance floor had been followed by a drunken grope in the car park. It was all he'd managed before the girl had staggered off saying, 'I'm going to puke.' He told Andy he left her spewing up over the hub cap of some poor sod's car.

But it wasn't just Brenda's looks that drew Andy to her. She was interesting, different and fun to be with. For a while he'd been able to forget the crap that went with his job and the problems in his marriage. There was none of the frostiness he got from Jenny. With her he felt wanted.

Every time she thought of him, her stomach did a little flip. Andy was gorgeous! Going to lectures this week had been pointless: she'd taken bugger all in – not even Professor Kennedy's exam hints. Apparently he'd been scattering them about like confetti.

She'd spent the week trying to reimagine every little detail about him. What she most remembered was his deep, velvety Labrador eyes. Her mum, if she ever got to see him, would like them too.

He was a good kisser. Brenda remembered that too. How could she not? Soft, butterfly kisses. No latching on to her mouth like a sink plunger or sticking his tongue halfway down her throat like some of the fellas she'd been out with.

What if he lost the beer mat he'd promised to keep safe? Or it had been reduced to pulp in the wash? She wished he'd call. All this waiting around was doing her head in.

It was late in the afternoon when Mrs Henderson handed the phone to her.

'There's someone called Andy askin' for you.'

A flicker of a smile played on Brenda's lips. Mrs Henderson gave her a curious glance then headed into the back to make a cup of tea.

'Hello,' said Brenda in a quiet voice.

'I'm sorry I haven't phoned before now.'

He sounded polite and apologetic. She said it didn't matter.

'I've been thinking about you all week,' he said. 'I'd love to see you again.' He suggested a place they could meet, said he had somewhere in mind to take her.

Brenda liked that. Peter had always left it to her to decide where they should go. It didn't feel as if he was trying to please her; it was more like he couldn't be bothered to think for himself.

'That's great,' she said. 'See you then, Andy.'

Brenda had no sooner set the phone down than Mrs Henderson appeared with a mug in one hand and a ginger biscuit in the other.

It was one of her tutors, Brenda told her, knowing full well the rosy colour in her cheeks gave her away. 'He's English, teaching over here for a couple of years.'

'Yes, but why would he phone you here?'

'I've been trying to book some time in with him to talk about my assignment. I couldn't get hold of him all week. I hope you don't mind me leavin' him the number of the shop?'

'Not at all, dear. Glad you got it sorted in the end.'

All that stuff about him being her tutor – she was sure Mrs Henderson could see it for the shite it was. Brenda hadn't intended to lie about Andy, or so she told herself. But from the moment she'd agreed to meet him again she'd decided not to tell anyone about him, at least until she knew how they felt about one another. People – Mrs Henderson, her friends, neighbours and yes, even her own family – would disapprove. More than disapprove. Her mum would be horrified if she knew one of her daughters was going out with a soldier. Why do something that would only invite trouble? Her dad, she hoped, might be more forgiving. Clare would despise her.

FOURTEEN

Brenda waited under the oak tree next to Methodist College. A heavy shower had left a glossy sheen on the tree's leaves. Every now and then a large drip landed with a splat on her head. When Andy had suggested going for a drink she'd been so glad to hear from him she'd forgotten to ask where. She knew he could only go to certain areas. What if he didn't fancy her when he saw her again? Her heart began to beat faster as she caught sight of him. She was about to find out.

He walked towards her with his shoulders back and head up, arms held stiff, not quite touching his sides. Like a gunslinger without a holster. Or in his case, a soldier minus his webbing. The closer he got, the broader her grin became. She couldn't help herself. It was a reflex action, like one of those Pavlovian experiments on dogs she'd been reading about. Brenda's chest tightened into a delicious squeeze when he crossed the road.

He kissed her lightly on the cheek. 'Have you been waiting long?'

'Bloody ages.'

'Sorry, I thought we said...' When he realised she was teasing, he broke into a smile.

'Where are we off to?' she asked.

'I thought we could go to the Wellington Hotel.'

It was literally up the road from where they stood.

'Fine with me,' said Brenda.

She didn't mean it. She'd only been in the hotel bar once or twice before. It was a bit stuffy.

'Am I alright dressed like this?'

He looked her up and down. 'More than alright.'

Brenda blushed. 'I mean, I'm not sure if I'll get in wearin' these jeans.'

'Don't worry, you'll be fine.'

He sounded confident. He'd obviously been there before. She wondered who with.

Andy put his arm around her shoulder as they turned into the Malone Road. It was already busy with drinkers making their way to the Eglantine Inn and Botanic Inn. The 'Eg' and the 'Bot' were popular Friday-night destinations. The pubs sat directly opposite each other and revellers flitted from one to the other during the course of the evening. They walked past them and on to the Wellington – or 'Welly Boot' as it was more affectionately called.

The Wellington was as Brenda remembered it. She sensed the men giving her the once-over. Some of them were close to her dad's age, for Christ's sake, but Andy soon made her feel at ease. He'd joined the Army when he was 18 years and still green behind the ears he told her. He was a sergeant now.

'So, you get to boss people around.'

'It comes with the job,' he said.

She waved a finger at him. 'Don't be tryin' it with me.'

'I wouldn't dare.'

She looked at him. 'Still, it's a big responsibility.'

He thought for a moment. 'I try my best to look out for them.'

They left the bar just after midnight. She'd loved it all – the waitress service, plush seating, soft lighting. She felt pampered. Brenda slipped her hand into his as they headed back to her room. They had only gone a couple of hundred yards when he stopped. He leant in to kiss her. It was all so effortless. No clumsy fumbling, no awkward positioning. It felt good.

As they walked along, he treated her to one impression after another. His Ian Paisley made her cry with laughter. He'd got the big man's thundering Ulster dialect spot on.

She teased him about his appearance. 'I can spot a soldier from a mile off.'

He ran his hand over his head. 'A bit of a giveaway, I suppose.'

She shook her head. 'Not the hair. I can tell by the sleeves.'

Andy looked puzzled.

'The jacket sleeves are always too short.'

Belfast men walked around in leather jackets that swamped them. The sleeves covered most of their hands, leaving only their fingertips exposed. English soldiers looked as if they should have bought their jacket a size bigger. Or at least that's how it seemed to Brenda. She made Andy stand with his arms by his sides. The cuffs rested a full inch above his wrist bone.

'See what I mean.'

It wasn't just the sleeve length. He appeared to take an interest in his clothes and she couldn't say that of any of the local fellas. He'd thought about what to wear tonight, not just thrown on the first thing that had fallen out of the wardrobe. But it wasn't quite right. The zip-up leather jacket was a light orangey tan. No doubt it looked fine back in England, but not here. All in all, he was too well groomed and too brash for Belfast. She'd tell him about it another time.

———

Brenda draped her clothes over a chair. She was already under the covers when he pushed the door shut.

'Do you want me to lock it?'

'Yes, ok.'

There was a gentle click. She was alone with a man she barely knew. She ought to be worried.

Andy stood at the end of the bed with his back turned to her. She watched him undress. The moonlight fell in shafts through the skylight window. Brenda studied the outline of his taut body taking in the muscular shoulders. A man's body, not a boy's. Her heart began to pound.

Most of the students had left on Friday afternoon to spend the weekend with their families. The house was quiet. The heating was off. Andy shivered then quickly pulled the covers back and got in beside her.

'Whoa!'

'Sorry,' said Brenda. Her feet were slabs of ice. He let her place them on top of his to warm them. When he kissed her his fine stubble lightly grazed her skin. He smelt of soap and ... sandalwood? No, it was musk. She loved that smell. She used to burn musk-scented joss sticks in her bedroom at home.

Brenda had never done anything like this before – taken someone home, invited them into her bed on the second night of meeting them. Was she mad? Probably. And yet she felt safe with Andy. He wasn't rushing anything. That made her want him more. She found herself making all the moves.

'I haven't brought any protection,' he said, gently pushing her away.

For a crazy moment Brenda considered taking a chance. 'Glad one of us is being careful,' she sighed.

'I thought that was the job of every good Catholic girl.'

'Who said I was good?'

They lay together in silence, her arm draped across his chest. She listened as his breathing settled into a rhythmic pattern of sleep. Brenda was left alone with her thoughts.

———

She woke up with a dead arm. Andy lay on his back; her arm was trapped underneath. She didn't know if she should nudge him to get him to turn over. It seemed rude somehow, too familiar. She stayed still and watched him. His breathing was hardly perceptible; he looked peaceful.

There was a slight flicker at the corner of his mouth then a smile. 'Morning.'

Her stomach fluttered at the sound of his voice.

He opened his eyes and turned his head towards her. He noticed her trapped arm. 'You should have given me a dig in the ribs.'

'I didn't want to wake you.'

He shifted his weight so she could pull herself free. Brenda's arm tingled.

'What were you looking at?'

'Your battle scars.'

A puzzled look spread across his face.

'This,' she said, pointing to a long, thin line on the underside of his chin. 'How did you get it?'

He laughed. 'That's a bit embarrassing.'

'Tell me.'

'I lost control of my go-kart. We were racing at the time.'

She tried to picture him, careering down a hill, as a young boy. 'And the one on your cheek?'

'How long were you watching me?'

Brenda coloured.

'I was drunk and heading back to the mess. I tripped and landed against a brick wall.'

'They're all self-inflicted then?'

'I'm afraid so. Have I spoilt the illusion?'

Brenda turned down the corners of her mouth in mock disappointment. 'And here's me thinkin' I'd landed my very own Action Man.'

He twisted on to his side and propped his head up with his arm. His closeness and the intensity of his gaze unsettled her. She wondered what she looked like. A wreck, no doubt.

She jumped up. From the corner of her eye she caught him staring at her, taking in the contours of her body in the soft morning light.

'I'll make us some breakfast. What do you fancy?'

'You.'

Brenda laughed. She grabbed her dressing gown from the hook on the door and wrapped it tight around her. 'I'll make us some tea and toast while you think up a less cheesy line.'

'Deal,' he said.

Brenda pulled on her moccasin slippers and padded down the stairs. Her first stop was the bathroom. She checked herself in the mirror. Jesus! Just as she thought. Panda eyes. She wet her finger and ran it under her eyelashes. She patted down the cow's lick in her fringe then headed to the kitchen. She was looking for a tray when the house warden walked in. She looked at the two mugs of tea.

Brenda ignored her as she buttered four slices of toast and piled them on a plate. 'Don't worry, Jennifer. I'll make sure to bring the tray back.' With that, she disappeared back up the stairs to her room. She pushed the door open with her foot.

Andy was sitting up, taking in the spartan possessions dotted around her room. She set the tray down on the floor and handed him his mug of tea.

'It's very basic, isn't it?'

He shook his head. 'I've lived in a lot worse, believe me.'

'What's it like where you are now?'

He shrugged. 'Pretty grim.'

Brenda imagined him bunking down with a bunch of other guys and the smells that went with it. Once on a visit to her cousin Josie's house she'd opened a door thinking it was the bathroom only to find herself in a bedroom shared by two of Josie's brothers. The stink had been overpowering – like stagnant water in the bottom of a vase where the flowers had been left to wither and die, only ten times worse.

She made him shuffle over then sat beside him. 'Yes, but seriously. What is it like?' Do you…?'

'It's just barracks life. There's nothing much to tell.'

'Don't you ever get fed up with being on the move all the time, having no real roots? I would.'

Andy nodded towards a small bookcase in the corner of the room, crammed with textbooks. 'Are you going to psychoanalyse me then?'

Brenda rolled her eyes. 'That's what everyone says.'

'Nice to know I'm so predictable.'

'People don't understand that psychiatry and psychology are two different things.'

'So, tell me then, what exactly is psychology?'

Brenda thought for a moment. 'The study of the human mind.'

Andy rubbed an imaginary beard. 'Mmm. Very interesting.'

Brenda slapped him lightly on the side of his head. He spluttered on his tea.

'Now you're just takin' the piss,' she said.

Andy looked at his watch and swore. He had to go. He kissed her and told her he'd had a great time. Brenda walked him down the stairs. He kissed her again and said he'd call her.

Then he was gone.

FIFTEEN

Brenda arrived home with two plastic bags and a holdall stuffed full of dirty clothes.

'Did you lug all that back on the bus?' asked Clare.

'Are you goin' to let me in or what?'

Clare stepped away from the front door to let her past.

'Where's Mum?' asked Brenda as she made her way into the kitchen.

'Up the stairs changin' your sheets.'

Brenda emptied the bag's contents on to the floor and began to separate the whites from the colours. She lifted up a woollen polo-neck and checked the label for washing instructions. Hand-wash. Brenda deliberated for a moment then decided to throw it in with her jeans and hope for the best.

'Don't they have a launderette at that university of yours?'

'Yes, they do. Why?'

'Just wondered.'

'It is you. I thought I heard your voice,' said Mrs

MacRae. She looked at the tumbled heap of jeans, sweaters and underwear. 'Leave that and I'll do it for you.'

'It's alright, Mum. Don't be goin' to any trouble.'

'Don't be silly. I was about to put a wash on anyway.'

'Thanks.' Brenda gave her mum a hug.

Clare rolled her eyes.

'What?' said Brenda. 'Mum offered.'

'You knew she would. She'll end up ironin' it all too, if you let her.'

'Indeed I will not. You two need to learn to look after yourselves,' said Mrs MacRae as she proceeded to load the washing machine.

They all knew she wouldn't be able to help herself. She'd have every piece of Brenda's laundry washed, ironed, folded and stacked ready for her to slip into her holdall on Sunday night.

There was a slamming of the front door followed by the clink of keys thrown into the ceramic bowl next to the telephone. The bowl was chipped round the edges. It had been sitting in the same spot for years and had suffered many near misses. A slight pause as Mr MacRae checked for mail then a thick mop of salt-and-pepper hair appeared round the kitchen door.

'Hubble, bubble, toil and trouble,' he rumbled, eyeing the three of them with suspicion. 'What are my favourite witches brewing tonight?' He set his lunch box on the table and threw his hands up in mock fear.

'Oi, you. Less of the witches,' said Brenda's mum. She flicked a damp tea towel at his leg.

'Ouch!'

Mrs MacRae took aim again. This time Mr MacRae

grabbed hold of the tea towel mid-flick and pulled his wife towards him.

He lifted her off her feet and puckered his lips. 'How's about a kiss, witchy poo?'

'You're a head case, Jimmy, do you know that?'

Mr MacRae grimaced. He set his wife down and rubbed his back in an exaggerated display of pain. 'What's for tea?' he asked. 'Eye of newt? Bat wings?'

'Very funny,' said Clare. 'You know damned rightly it's fish and chips.'

'Magic!' He said it as if it was a revelation. 'So, whose turn is it tonight?'

'I'll go,' said Clare. She stretched out an upturned hand.

Mr MacRae dug into his pocket and pulled out a fiver. 'Make sure it's...'

'Haddock. I know.'

Mrs MacRae put the dinner plates in the oven to warm.

Every Friday night followed a set routine. Either Brenda or Clare would nip out to the chip shop and bring back four fish suppers. Brenda had made the mistake of once bringing back cod. She thought her dad couldn't tell the difference. He knew with the first bite. 'Never try to trick an islander when it comes to fish.'

The moment Clare arrived with the food the hot plates were whipped out of the oven. They set their fish suppers on them and ate straight from the wrapping.

'What's the craic, Brenda?' asked her dad.

'There's not much to tell. You know ... just the usual stuff.'

For the last couple of weeks Andy had been on high alert and they'd seen little of one another. Last night, however, they'd managed to grab some time together. They'd spent most of it at her student house, the two of them alone in her room, in her bed. Brenda's cheeks coloured at the memory.

Mr MacRae stopped mid-chew to study his daughter for a moment. 'You must have been doing somethin'.'

'Lots of reading and–'

Clare snorted. 'Sounds like you're becomin' more like a nun every day.'

'I had a couple of nights out with the girls.'

'Where did you go?' asked Clare.

'The bar in the Student's Union. Nowhere special.'

Clare reached for the vinegar bottle. 'What about the talent? There must be loads of blokes to choose from.'

Brenda wrinkled her nose. 'None that I'd go for.'

'You haven't been on one single date?'

Brenda hesitated. At some point she'd have to let them know about Andy, but not tonight. 'No,' she said.

'Mmm.' Clare's curious gaze rested on her sister. 'I find that hard to believe.'

'Too fussy,' said her mum. 'That's always been your problem.'

'There's no problem in setting your sights high,' said Mr MacRae. He turned to his wife. 'Like your mum did with me.'

Mrs MacRae rolled her eyes.

'Do you still do stuff with that peace group of yours?' asked Clare.

'Why do you want to know?'

Clare gave a little shrug of her shoulders.

'Yes, what about that?' said her mum.

'I'm still involved.'

'More rallies and marches?'

'Maybe, if it helps to get our message across. There's a lot of other things we do that nobody hears about.'

'Oh?' said her mum. 'Like what?'

Brenda wasn't fooled by the innocent enquiry. Her mum knew full well there was more to Brenda's peace work than rallies and marches.

'Like that house visit we did to the lady who'd lost her husband.'

'I don't remember you sayin' anything about that.'

'It was ages ago, shortly after I joined. I didn't want to worry you. I knew you'd get all funny about it.'

'Who was she?' asked Clare.

'Some woman whose husband was in the RUC. His car was blown up.'

'A peeler?' Clare screwed up her face in distaste.

'That time it just happened to be a policeman, but we visit every woman who loses their partner to violence: police, IRA, UDA.'

'UDA?' Mrs MacRae put her hand to her throat. The very mention of the Ulster Defence Association, under her roof, was enough to set her off.

'You see? This is exactly why I didn't want to tell you.'

'I don't like you takin' yourself off to the likes of the Shankill Road on some mercy mission.'

'Too right,' said Clare. 'Why would anyone want to have anything to do with those murderin' bastards?'

Mrs MacRae turned to her husband. 'Tell her it's not safe, Jimmy and tell this one,' – she pointed to Clare – 'that she's not to curse at the dinner table.'

'You heard your mum,' admonished Mr MacRae. 'And

Brenda ...' The stern look on his face turned to concern. 'I hope you don't go to these places on your own.'

'No. You're always paired with someone.'

'Well. that's somethin' at least.'

'I'm still not happy about it,' said her mum. 'I know you believe you're doin' a good thing, treatin' everyone the same, but not everyone sees it that way.'

'I don't care what people think.'

Her parents exchanged anxious glances.

'You know, Brenda,' said her dad, 'it's a fine line between people seein' you as a bit soft, wanting to put the world to right, and a backdoor supporter of the English Government.'

'I can't believe you said that.' Brenda jerked her head towards Clare. 'You're beginnin' to sound like her.'

'I don't believe it for one moment,' he said, 'but perceptions are a funny thing.'

'I thought you'd have binned all that by now,' Clare looked archly at Brenda, 'seeing as you have so much studyin' to do.'

'We're goin' to do some animal experiments this week,' said Brenda, shifting the conversation to a safer topic.

'Yuck,' said Clare. 'Slicing up mice.'

'Worse. I think it's rats. It's disgustin'. I didn't realise we'd have to do stuff like that.'

'Not a course for the squeamish then,' said Mr MacRae lifting a forkful of battered fish to his mouth.

Brenda looked down at her plate. 'We studied fighting fish this week. Did you know that if they see their reflection in a mirror, they attack their own image?'

'What's that supposed to teach you?' asked Mrs MacRae.

'It's all to do with learnt behaviours and conditioned

responses. If the fish thinks it's being attacked, it automatically fights back.'

'Fascinating,' said Clare.

'Actually, we did cover something really interesting this week.'

'I'm glad to hear it,' said Mrs MacRae. 'I was beginnin' to wonder what the point of it all was.'

'Trauma.'

Brenda's mum looked confused.

'Like say someone's had a car accident and been badly hurt, they'll have nightmares about it afterwards. They go over it in their head and try to change what happened. That's the mind's way of dealing with something traumatic.'

'I had a terrible dream the other night,' said Mrs MacRae. 'I was being chased down an alley by Pat Docherty.'

Mr MacRae laughed. 'Jesus, Bridie, I don't know why you were scared. He's such a fat knacker, he'd never have caught you.'

'Why do I bother to tell you lot anything?' said Brenda.

It was more what she wasn't telling them. Every weekend she came home, Brenda feared she'd say something that would incriminate her. Her stomach was a constant knot – the thought of anyone in her street discovering she was going out with a soldier made her sick with fear. So why was she doing it? Because Andy made her happy ... and she fancied him like mad. That in itself was enough to keep her taking a risk.

SIXTEEN

Bangor

A s they approached the bottom of Main Street the small harbour and the sea beyond came into view. Directly in front stood a clock tower surrounded by a patch of greenery. Andy raised an eyebrow.

'Bangor's Little Ben,' quipped Brenda.

People sat on the benches that lined the sea wall, eating ice creams and soaking up the first proper dose of summer heat. Women pushed prams along the promenade; children scampered to peer over the wall at the sunbathers on the small sandy beach below. Black guillemots had made their nests in the gaps between the stones of the sea wall. They watched one fly into its hole almost under the feet of a young woman.

'That's the Queen's Court.' Brenda pointed to a rather grand, white, stuccoed hotel. 'A lot of show bands play there. I've never been myself, but Hazel has. She saw Chips there a while back.'

'Who?'

'You wouldn't know them. They're from here.'

Music was the one thing that did bring people together in Northern Ireland. Bands were a mix of Catholic and Protestant and travelled from one side of the border to the other. They were welcomed equally in both.

'Look!' Brenda pointed to the line of rowing boats waiting to be hired.

Andy grimaced.

'Come on,' she said. 'It'll be a good laugh.' Brenda had already eased herself into one. She motioned for Andy to do the same. 'You can be Captain,' she said, once he'd settled himself on the narrow seat opposite her. Andy plunged both oars into the salty water. 'Oi!' she shouted.

It was a day to treasure. The sky was cloudless, the sea a sparkling blue. A metallic smell of seaweed mixed with salt permeated the air. Brenda patted the top of her head. The midday sun already had a ferocious heat in it; her hair was hot under her hand. Everyone wore a bright smile. Bangor was glorious on days like this. It rarely lasted long, mind you. Tomorrow it could be chucking it down. The boats would be left to bob on the water, empty of rowers, the benches along the sea front devoid of people. Holidaymakers would search for an amusement arcade in order to distract their damp and despondent children for an hour or so. 'I think the sun's going to break through soon,' they'd lie, to themselves and their children.

After a while they swapped places but Brenda was no rower. Her left arm refused to work in time with her right. The boat turned in circles at first then drifted slowly and inexorably towards another, before hitting it with a thud.

105

Sorry she mouthed to the teenage boy who was jolted from his wooden seat into the lap of his girlfriend. Every boat available for hire was now taken. They couldn't row any real distance without bumping into a keel.

'I think I've had enough,' said Brenda.

They bought two large 99s, from a man in Caproni's ice-cream parlour. Andy asked for a raspberry topping. The syrup was squirted, with a swift circular movement, from a plastic bottle. Brenda had the same along with an extra topping. She watched hungrily as the man lightly rolled her whipped ice cream in a Tupperware container full of chopped nuts, coating it on all sides. A chocolate flake was added to each cone.

They walked along the seafront in the direction of Seacliff Road, past rows of large Victorian houses. The houses, painted in various shades of pastel, were several stories high. Some had B&B signs in the bay windows.

'Very grand, aren't they?'

'Yes but would, you want to live in anything that big?' said Andy. 'You'd be rattling around inside.'

'I think I could get used to it.'

'I can see it'll take more than a soldier's pay to keep you happy.'

Brenda gave a mock sigh. 'Maybe one of us will come into a fortune someday.'

'Do you know any rich relations about to kick the bucket?'

'No.'

'Nor do I.'

They dropped down on to a long stretch of sand and kept walking until they reached a small, secluded cove. Brenda pulled two rolled-up towels from her beach bag. They lay side by side listening to the harsh, disjointed cries of the seagulls and the sound of the breaking waves. It had grown hotter. A sheen of sweat appeared on the top of her lip. Brenda wiped it away.

She'd put her bikini on underneath her dress in the hope that she'd get the chance to sunbathe, maybe even take a dip in the sea. Now she was suddenly shy about taking her dress off in the open like this, in full daylight. It was ridiculous considering she'd been naked in bed with him the first night they'd met.

'I'm roastin',' she said, aware of a trickle of perspiration that had appeared between her breasts.

'Me too,' said Andy. He rolled lazily towards her and reached under her skirt.

Brenda gave a little shudder as he ran his hand up the inside of her thigh.

'Stop it, Andy,' she giggled. 'Someone might see us.'

'There's no-one around, apart from that kid who's staring at you.'

Brenda pushed his hand away and sat up. 'What kid? Where?'

'Relax. I'm joking.' He stripped down to his trunks and ran towards the water. Brenda removed her dress and followed him in.

———

She'd forgotten her hairbrush of all things. On the train back she had to pull her matted, salty hair into a ponytail.

'This will be a nightmare to untangle when I get home.'

'That was fun today,' he said. 'Amazing what a bit of sunshine can do, isn't it?'

'Puts everyone in good form.' Brenda sighed. 'I wish it was always like this.' She rested her head against Andy's chest.

Andy put his arm around her shoulder, ignoring the spreading patch her wet hair left on his shirt. She lay against him, listening to the sound of the train on the tracks.

'Brenda?'

Brenda glanced up, alerted by the uncustomary hesitancy in his voice. She watched, with a sick feeling in the pit of her stomach, as his mouth tried to form words but no sound came out. 'What is it?'

'Forget it,' he said. He looked down at her anxious face. 'It's nothing.'

'You had me going for a moment there when you went all serious on me. I thought you were about to break up with me.'

He smiled but his smile seemed strained. 'Don't be daft. Why would I want to do that?'

Brenda lay her head against his chest again. 'Right enough. Why would you?'

She was half-asleep when she felt Andy's arm stiffen.

'Blew his legs clean off.' The voice came from a man sitting further down the carriage.

'Shame they didn't get the other one too,' said his friend. 'We could have had ourselves a set of goalposts.'

The men's voices carried. So too did their laughter.

'You realise that's the lad from the Lancashires they're talking about?'

The soldier had been in the back of a Saracen. As it had

travelled along a country road near the border the IRA had detonated a land mine, which ripped through the bottom of the armoured troop carrier maiming the soldier for life. 'Say nothing,' mouthed Brenda.

'To hell with that.' Andy craned his neck trying to get a better look at them. 'I'm not listening to that shit.'

The men fell silent.

Brenda could hear the thumping of her heart. She was sure the men could too. 'Sit back, Andy. Don't let them see you.'

Andy continued to crane his neck.

'There's two of them,' she whispered. 'Maybe more.'

Andy was half out of his seat now, straining against her as she tried to pull him back.

'Please, Andy, just leave it.'

He looked at her imploring face, hesitated a moment, then eased himself back into his seat. Brenda gave his hand a squeeze and prayed he'd stay put for the rest of the journey. Each time the train pulled in at a station Brenda looked for passengers getting off. A group of girls, a young couple but no men. The closer the train got to Belfast, the more uneasy she became.

Open countryside and rural stations gave way to the sprawl of the city outskirts. Bangor had been a pleasant inter-lude, a taste of what it must feel like on a sunny foreign holi-day. The graffiti as they pulled into Belfast Central soon reminded her where she was.

Andy stood up to leave.

'Stay where you are,' said Brenda. 'Let the carriage empty out first.'

The words were no sooner out of her mouth than a fist

banged on their carriage window. A man leered in at them. His friend was on the platform behind him making an exaggerated show of pointing to his leg. They both laughed. Brenda looked at Andy.

'Fuckers,' he said.

He remained in his seat with his jaw set tight until the men moved on. They waited for a few minutes to be sure the platform was clear. Then they made their way out. Andy took Brenda's hand when she offered it up to his but she could feel the anger still pulsing through his body.

'Don't let them spoil the day.'

When he didn't reply she knew they already had.

SEVENTEEN

July 1972

They were beating the living daylights out of the 'big drums'. Dusk had now turned to blackness. Brenda knew there was no chance this tribal thunder would let up any time soon. It was set to continue well into the night. The narrow street she stood on served only to amplify the sound.

She breathed in the acrid smell of burning tyres. Rival groups of young lads had gathered at opposite ends. Tension spliced the air. So far they were just taunting each other with insults and name-calling. Each side took it in turn to edge closer then move back, like a courting ritual.

'They're just kids.'

'That's how it always starts,' said Ann Muldoon, 'with the young ones first. The older lads pile in later. Then the men with the guns.'

It was the start of the Protestant marching season and with it came growing friction. Riots had erupted throughout the city all week, starting with stone-throwing, escalating to petrol-bombing. Like the rest of her family, Brenda had been constantly on edge. It only took one misaimed petrol bomb to take hold to burn them out of house and home. It had come close last year. They'd held their breath as one skittered across their rooftop before landing with a crash of shattered glass in the alley behind the house.

This year was worse. Nail bombs were a bigger threat. The small houses shook in their wake. There was nothing they could do about it other than sit it out, wait for daybreak and pray for calm. Well, her mum did the praying. Brenda fumed inwardly and remembered how things used to be when she was growing up.

The first time she'd heard the big drums was the summer she'd stayed on her uncle's farm. The farm was in a remote part of the country, close to the border. Clare had been invited too.

'You must be jokin', she'd said. 'I can't imagine anything worse than being buried in the middle of nowhere with a bunch of *culchies.*'

Her sister had a point. Her uncle's brood were country people, born and bred. Brenda decided to go anyway.

Her mum was still talking to her brother back then. The massive fallout over their dad's will – nothing worth squabbling over as it turned out, once the debts were paid – had yet to come. Uncle Sean was as wide as Brenda's dad was tall. His armpits were always sweat-stained, his cheeks red with broken veins.

Brenda had spent the days exploring the surrounding fields with her cousins, Declan and Brian. They made a den in a copse of trees and landed themselves in trouble for trampling a path through a neighbouring farmer's crop to reach it.

The boys caught spricks from a nearby stream. Brenda had refused to handle the tiny, slithery fish they placed in jam jars. She'd no idea what they did with them once they got them home.

She slept in the guest bedroom where she had a double bed all to herself. At night, through the open window, she could hear the Lambeg drummers as they practised on the lead up to 12 July. It was like a rallying cry the way the drums answered each other, breaking the stillness of the night air and echoing across the fields, each with their own distinctive beat.

Her uncle told her it took two men to hoist the huge drum up and strap it to the drummer's chest. The drummer would beat it, he said, until his knuckles bled. Brenda was repulsed by the thought of shredded skin, yet enthralled by the noise. She'd listen to the hypnotic sound until her eyelids grew heavy and she drifted off to sleep. Now every time she heard the drums, she dreaded what would come after – the Twelfth was a thing to hate ... and fear.

Brenda made her way into the no-man's land in the middle of the road with the other women. They were greeted with catcalls and jeers from both sides.

'Fuck off home before youse get hurt.'

'I am home,' replied Ann Muldoon, 'and there'll be no fightin' here tonight. Not if I've anything to do with it.'

A stone arced towards Brenda and landed at her feet. 'What do we do now?' she asked.

'Stand our ground, that's what.'

One by one the women linked arms. Brenda's knees trembled as she stared down the mob in front of her. She could feel the venom of the crowd behind her. She glanced over her shoulder. Was it her imagination or was the crowd closer? The women remained in the middle of the road, a human chain separating the two opposing sides. Brenda flinched as another stone was lobbed in their direction and fell a little short of them.

'It's a game they play,' said Ann Muldoon. 'They're testin' us.'

How long would this test last? Brenda wasn't sure her nerves would hold. She'd heard about another such standoff that had gone on for hours. In the end the rain had determined that particular outcome as much as the women's stubborn refusal to back off. Stone-throwing had lost its allure once the boys were soaked through. Tonight was different. It was warm and dry. Perfect weather for a riot.

Something had changed. Some of the boys had split into smaller groups and detached from the main crowd. The crowd in front of Brenda no longer lobbed missiles at them. This unsettled her more than the 'just miss the target' stone-throwing game. From the corner of her eye Brenda caught a couple of moving shadows in an alleyway beside her. Whispers, a sharp smell, a clink of glass.

A boy held a milk bottle in his hands. Another struck a match; he was about to light the rag they'd stuffed in its neck. Brenda recognised him straight away. Marie Keenan's younger brother.

'Don't be stupid, Liam,' she yelled. 'Put that away.'

The boy holding the bottle jumped at the mention of his friend's name. The bottle tipped its contents over him. Liam dropped the match. There was a flash, then a scream. Ann Muldoon ran over. She covered him with her coat and made him roll on the ground. She was joined by a couple of the youths. Together they smothered the fire that engulfed the boy's body.

The boy screeched in pain. There was a smell of charred skin. Ribbons of flesh had peeled away from his arms. His face was red raw down one side. Liam was rooted to the spot, his eyes wide open in terror.

A couple of armoured personnel carriers were already on the scene. The soldiers had stayed back from the crowd at the request of Women Together. They'd been watching for any escalating hostilities, ready to intervene if things got out of hand. Ann Muldoon was now urgently asking them to get an ambulance. Brenda was crying.

'What have I done?'

'It's not your fault, love,' said Mrs Muldoon.

A furious voice cut through the woman's comforting words.

'Yes, it is. Liam lunged at Brenda. 'Fucking stupid bitch!'

'Liam ... I...'

He punched her hard in the stomach. Brenda doubled over. She vomited up a bit of sick. It tasted sour and acidic as she spat it on to the pavement. Air refused to fill her lungs.

The ambulance crew arrived carrying a stretcher. The injured boy was lifted on to it.

'Is this one causing you bother?' asked a soldier. He made ready to grab hold of Liam.

'I want to go with my friend.'

All the aggression had gone out of him. He looked and sounded like the Liam that Brenda had grown up with – a kind-hearted and caring lad, the least likely person to get in a fight.

'No,' said Brenda to the soldier. 'Leave him be.'

Liam climbed into the ambulance. As it sped off Brenda sank to her knees.

'Are you alright?' asked Ann Muldoon.

'Not really.'

Ann crouched down to reassure her. 'Don't be blamin' yourself, Brenda.' She gave her a gentle shake. 'Do you hear me?' It's the men who persuade young boys to riot in the first place who should carry the blame.'

Some boys needed little persuasion. They saw it as a mark of honour. Others, like Liam, were coerced. If he didn't join them, he'd be declared a coward and a traitor.

More soldiers appeared. They ordered the women off the street. As Brenda was helped away, the rival groups surged forward. Bottles, bricks and stones rained down on their heads. The soldiers did their best to deflect their missiles with their riot shields as they escorted the women to safety.

By the time Brenda had reached the army cordon a full-scale battle had broken out. She thought of Andy, on duty somewhere else in the city, and wondered if he too was facing down a hostile, stone-throwing crowd.

EIGHTEEN

September 1972

Brenda's mum looked at the electricity bill and shook her head.

'Your dad swore he'd paid this.' She slipped the cheque he'd written into an envelope then turned to her daughters. 'I don't suppose either of you have got any stamps?'

'Hang on, I think I've got some.'

Brenda opened her purse and pulled out a wodge of receipts. As she sifted through them, looking for stamps, a narrow strip of photographs fell to the floor. She hurriedly bent down to pick them up, but Clare was quicker, covering them with her foot and dragging them across the lino floor towards her chair.

'Here you go, Mum,' said Brenda. 'Take these.'

Clare scooped the photographs up from the floor and studied them for a moment. Her eyes widened.

Brenda had been carrying the photographs around with her all summer. The corners were now dog-eared and the images creased from being folded in her purse. Clare turned them over. Brenda blanched. She had written their names on the back, in green ink, along with the date. Clare mouthed the words.

Brenda lunged for the photographs. 'Give me those.'

Her sister transferred them deftly to her other hand.

The pictures had been taken at Woolworth's. They'd both jammed into the photo booth with Brenda balancing on Andy's knee. It had taken them ages to swivel the seat up to the right height. Then, as the camera began to click, the seat had started to sink. In the last photograph Andy was grinning straight at the camera but Brenda had slipped almost entirely from view. Only her eyes and the top of her head could still be seen.

She'd been feeling down that day, still carrying the guilt of what had happened to Liam's friend.

'Come on,' Andy said. 'Let's have a bit of that fighting spirit of yours.'

She'd made fists with her hands and let them drop. 'Right now I wish I could run away from it all.'

'Me too, but the Army doesn't take kindly to deserters.'

'I can dream.'

They'd have to stick it out for now he told her. He could if she could. The summer had come and gone and they were still sticking it out with no peace in sight.

Mrs MacRae made a mewling face as she licked the envelope flap. 'Do you see, if they cut us off,' she muttered, 'I'll swing for your father.'

'I mean it,' hissed Brenda, leaning towards her sister. 'Give me those back.'

Clare pointed to Andy.

'Who's this?'

'Nobody.'

Clare frowned. 'It doesn't look like nobody to me.'

'What doesn't?' asked their mum.

'The bloke in these pictures.' Clare waved the strip of photographs in the air.

Brenda reached across the table and grabbed them from her.

'No need to snatch,' said Clare. 'Somethin' to hide, have we?'

Brenda's mother glanced up then went back to sorting her pile of unpaid bills.

'It's just someone I hang around with in university.'

'What's he studyin'?'

'History.'

'Really?'

'That man! Would you believe it? There's another final demand here.' Mrs MacRae made her way into the hallway. She set the offending paperwork on top of the telephone table. Her husband couldn't fail to see it the moment he got in the door. 'I'll be havin' words with him later.'

Brenda tucked the photographs back into her purse and followed her mum into the hallway.

'Give me the ones you want payin'. I'll nip out and post them now.'

'Would you? That'd be great, love.'

Brenda was out the door in a flash.

———

Later that evening she heard the clattering of plates in the kitchen and the opening and closing of doors. Her dad was snoring loudly as she padded past her parents' bedroom and made her way downstairs. 'What's all the racket?' She took one look at Clare. 'I might have guessed it'd be you. Some people are tryin' to sleep you know.'

'Some people are tryin' to sleep,' Clare repeated back, mimicking her sister's voice.

'Good night out I take it?'

'Yes.' Clare took a slurp of the tea she'd just made herself. 'I don't suppose you know where Mum's put the biscuits?'

Brenda pointed to a half-open cupboard. 'In there. Top shelf.'

Her mum had taken to hiding all the biscuits in the house from her dad. It was for his own good, she said. Had he not noticed he'd been piling on the pounds lately? Clare reached up and pulled out a packet of Jammy Dodgers. She offered one to her sister.

'Wise up. I was asleep until you started all your bangin' and thumpin'.' Brenda headed back upstairs.

'Hang on a minute,' called Clare. 'I want a word with you.'

'It's late, Clare. Whatever it is can wait until the morning.'

Shortly afterwards came the sound of running water, noisy gurgling and spitting in the sink. Clare wrenched the chain once, then again. A few moments later Brenda heard her back on the landing. She opened the door to Brenda's room and tottered in.

'Go away,' mumbled Brenda from under the bedclothes. 'You're pissed.'

'I need to talk to you.' Clare plonked herself on the edge of the bed.

Brenda could smell the drink despite the peppermint toothpaste and the elaborate mouth-rinsing ritual. 'I mean it, Clare. Would you just clear off.' She tugged at the blankets and kicked with her feet. Clare wobbled for a split second then tumbled off the end of the bed. Brenda pulled the blankets back up around her and buried her head in her pillow.

Clare sat up on the floor, hugging her knees close to her chest. 'So, tell me about this friend of yours,' she said, in a loud whisper.

Brenda lifted her head from the pillow. 'There's nothin' to tell.'

'You're hardly likely to be carryin' a friend's picture around with you. He's more than that, isn't he?'

'I don't know what you're talkin' about.'

'Oh, come on, Brenda. Do you take me for some sort of idiot?'

Brenda looked her up and down. 'It wouldn't be hard.'

Her sister appeared not to hear the insult. 'He's a soldier, isn't he?'

'Why do you say that?'

'The haircut. It's a dead giveaway.'

'Short hair doesn't automatically mean he's a soldier.'

'A policeman then?'

'No.'

'UDR?'

'Look, it's none of your business what Andy does.'

Clare screwed up her face. 'He *is* a squaddie. I can tell by the way you're gettin' on.'

Brenda was kicking herself. Why had she let it get to this point? Hazel had warned her that the longer she left it, the harder it would be to ever find the right time to tell her family about Andy. She had been right about that. She was also right about the truth coming out eventually whether Brenda wanted it to or not.

'All that rubbish you fed Mum and Dad,' said Clare. 'Tellin' them you weren't seeing anyone.' Her voice had grown louder. 'I knew all along you were hiding something.'

'Sshh. You'll wake them.'

Clare scrabbled to her feet and headed towards the door.

'Maybe I *should* wake them.'

Brenda leapt out of bed. 'Don't.' She pulled Clare back from the door. 'There's nothin' to tell. Andy's a nice bloke but that's as far as it goes.'

'You're lying.'

Brenda swallowed. 'I'm not.'

Clare looked far from convinced. 'You'd better not be. People are already talkin' about you.'

Brenda's stomach lurched. 'What people?'

Clare tapped the side of her nose.

'Certain people.'

Brenda exhaled in exasperation. 'You're talkin' a load of old shite.'

'Am I now?' said Clare, squaring up to her, her voice once again growing loud.

Brenda motioned with her hands for her to keep it down. 'Why did you come here if you were only set on a fight?' she asked, in hushed tones.

'I wasn't. I came here to give you a message.'

'What message? Who from?'

'You know what? It doesn't matter. Sort your own mess out.'

Afterwards Brenda lay awake rerunning in her head everything Clare had told her. People were talking about her. Did they know about Andy? Her own sister hadn't until she'd seen the pictures. What was it she'd said that had caused Brenda such anxiety? 'Certain people.' What did she mean by that? Just thinking about the answer made Brenda's chest tighten.

NINETEEN

Brenda spent the rest of the weekend waiting for Clare to make her move. Her sister's way of landing Brenda in trouble, ever since they were kids, was to drip-feed a few hints in the lead up to the big reveal. Anything to prolong the agony. Yet there had been none of that. They'd all sat down to Sunday lunch and it was as if Clare's drunken conversation had never happened.

Back in her student digs Brenda thought on what she should do. Andy had to be told. It was his safety at stake too. She was still deliberating the best way forward when she heard the familiar three raps on the door followed by his voice.

'Are you decent?' Andy popped his head round. 'Oh, you are.' He grinned. 'Pity.'

'Come on in, you eejit.'

Andy planted a kiss on the top of her head. 'You smell nice.'

'Must be my shampoo.'

He sniffed her hair. 'Beer?'

'It's my special pub scent.' The best way to get shiny hair, she'd read, was either to break an egg over your head during the final rinse or to wash your hair in Lincoln beer shampoo. The shampoo sounded preferable.

'At least you left the stale fags out,' said Andy. 'I get enough of that as it is sharing a room with a bunch of smokers. Not to mention the whiff of their sweaty socks.'

Brenda gagged at the thought of it. 'Sounds revolting. How do you stick it?'

'No choice, have I?'

His temporary barracks had long since become permanent. He and his men were still crammed together in the same cockroach-infested building. Brenda's student room, as basic as it was, felt like a palace in comparison.

Andy pushed her down on to the bed and gave her a long, tender kiss.

'Slow down, soldier. You've only just arrived.' Brenda ran her finger over his lips.

He gave it a playful nip. 'I've missed you.' He kissed her again.

They lay on her single bed, Brenda cradled tight against him. She could feel the rise and fall of his chest with each breath he took.

'I need to talk to you about something,' she said.

'In a minute. Let me enjoy this first.'

Brenda snuggled closer. It wasn't long before his eyes began to close. When he opened them again Brenda was at her desk reading through some notes. She glanced over when she heard him stir.

'Must have dozed off for a minute or two.'

'Longer than that.'

Andy rubbed his eyes. 'Sorry.'

'Don't be. You look knackered. Tough week?'

'No worse than usual. It's lack of sleep more than anything.'

'I'd never have guessed from your snores.'

'I was snoring?'

'A little bit, yes.'

He pulled a face. 'Attractive.'

He'd been on early patrols, he said, followed by late patrols. No settled pattern. It was difficult to come down from an adrenalin high after a patrol. On top of that there was always someone coming or going in the barracks.

Andy stifled a yawn. 'What time is it?'

Brenda checked the clock on the bedside table. 'Almost ten o'clock. Are we still goin' out for that drink?'

'Do we have to?'

'Not if you don't want to. We can stay here.' Brenda hesitated. 'But I do need to talk to you about something.'

Andy sat up. 'Go on then,' he said, plumping up a pillow. He crossed his arms. 'I'm all ears.'

'Remember when we took those pictures in Woolies?'

'That was a while ago, but yes.'

'Clare found them.'

'Is that it?'

'She guessed you were a soldier.'

Andy laughed. 'Well, she's right about that.'

'It's not funny. Clare hates you.'

'She's never met me.'

'It doesn't matter. She hates all soldiers.'

Brenda had often spoken about Clare's political views but

she'd kept the true extent of her sister's bitterness from him. Maybe that had been a mistake.

'At first I told her you were a friend from university.'

Andy stared at her in mock disbelief. 'You told her I was a student?'

'Don't look at me like that. I had to. Not that she believed me.'

He gave a roguish smile. 'I'm not surprised. I mean I know I've kept my boyish good looks but...'

'Don't take the piss, Andy.' Nervousness had made her terse. 'It was the best I could come up with on the spur of the moment. Now she's threatened to tell my mum and dad.'

'Do you think she will?'

'Yes, and I'm dreadin' it. The tension in the house between me and Clare over my peace work is bad enough without adding to it.'

'Why didn't you talk to me about this before?'

'I don't know. I suppose I thought you had enough hostility to deal with without me heaping all this on you.'

He placed his hands on her shoulders and kept his eyes fixed on hers as he spoke gently to her. 'Don't worry about me. I've developed a thick skin since I've been here.'

He probably had by now, but it still didn't make it right. All that abuse he took out on the streets? It must take its toll. And Clare was adding to it.

'I need to tell my parents now, before she does. I'm not lettin' her get the satisfaction of–'

'Hang on a minute,' he said. 'Let's think about this. What has Clare got to go on? A set of photographs only she's seen? I take it she hasn't kept them?'

Brenda shook her head. 'I have them here in my room.'

'Have your parents seen them?'

'No but...'

'Has anyone else said anything to you? A neighbour, friends of your parents?'

'No.'

'Well then, you've got nothing to worry about.'

Brenda looked doubtful.

'Seriously, Brenda. There's no need to let Clare force your hand.'

'But I'm sick of all this secrecy.' Brenda's eyes filled with tears. 'I want to tell them. I should have done it ages ago.'

'I think it would be better to say nothing for now.'

'What?'

'Hear me out,' he said. 'I mean just for the time being. It'll give us a chance to work out where we go from here.' He kissed her forehead.

Brenda's panic began to subside. Maybe he was right. Clare had no real proof. 'Where *do* you see us goin'?' she asked in a quiet voice.

Andy appeared to give her question serious consideration. Then he pulled the bedclothes back. 'Here?'

———

She was more settled when he left her this morning. Andy wished he could say the same of himself. Now that he was back in barracks his heart had begun to race. Things had shifted in a direction he wasn't prepared for.

It was no secret among the lads that Andy was seeing a lot of Brenda, but his wife knew nothing about it. Andy wanted to keep it that way. Paul had cautioned him about getting too serious with Brenda. Was she worth risking his marriage for? he'd asked. Andy told him that was rich coming from someone who'd screw any old slag who bent over for him.

His friend had shrugged off the insult. 'My missus prefers not to know. Yours is different. It's only a matter of time before someone spills the beans.'

He was right. It made no odds that he and Jenny knew it was over between them. If she found out he'd been unfaithful to her, she'd still flip.

This tour would be over soon. He'd return to England on leave again. The plan was to sit his wife down and tell her face to face. They hadn't discussed a formal separation yet or what that would mean for Stevie. Andy was grappling with the idea of shared custody of the boy and how that would work, given the long stints he was away. What was the drill for something like that? He had no idea.

He'd had no choice but to slow Brenda down. Thinking time, that's what he needed.

TWENTY

Clare cursed herself for not setting out earlier. It was closing time now and the city-centre bars had just spewed out their customers. The streets were full of leering drunks.

'A good-lookin' girl like you shouldn't be walkin' home alone.'

She glanced over at the pock-faced lad staggering alongside her. How come it was always the least attractive men who fancied their chances after a few too many beers?

'You don't look as if you could walk the length of yourself,' she said, hoping she sounded braver than she felt.

His friend roared with laughter. 'That's put you in your place, Kenny boy.'

Clare watched Kenny boy's face darken. She dropped her eyes and scurried past him.

It had been a brilliant evening up until then. She'd spent it in Lavery's Bar with a group of friends from her typing course. Everyone was in full party mood, intent on making a night of it. Peter had hoped to join them, if he could, but there'd been no sign of him. When her friends suggested moving on to a later bar in another part of the city Clare had decided not to join them. It wouldn't be the same without Peter.

There was a phone kiosk up ahead. She should give her dad a call and ask him to pick her up. Inside the kiosk smelt of urine and stale vomit. Clare gagged as she searched her purse for coins. Trust this to be the night she had no loose change. She dialled the operator and asked to make a reverse-charges call. When she heard her mum's voice on the other end of the line she sighed with relief.

'Clare, is that you? Where are you?'

Clare was about to tell her mother she'd only gone as far as Donegal Pass when the line went dead. She tried the operator again, but all she got was intermittent bleeping. She slammed the phone down. Now she'd have to walk the whole way home.

As she left the city centre behind, the crowds grew thinner and the chaotic bellowing and hollering faded. Clare relaxed a little. It had begun to drizzle. Fine drops of rain misted her face; they settled on the tendrils of her hair and on the tips of her eyelashes. Clare brushed her eyelashes with her fingertip. Her wet mascara left an inky smudge; she tried to wipe her finger clean. She didn't spot the two soldiers crouched at the side of the pavement, guns loosely cradled across their forearms, until she practically stumbled on them. One mumbled something, most probably a comment on her appearance, but she ignored him. She pulled up the hood of her raincoat and quickened her pace.

'Stop!' came a voice from behind her.

She heard the unmistakable sound of a gun being cocked. Clare froze. A soldier stood in front of her.

'Didn't you hear me telling you to stop?' he yelled.

She realised her mistake. 'No. I thought...' How could she tell him she thought he was making a pass at her? And that she'd chosen to ignore the bastard.

'I told you to stop. *Twice.*'

'Well, *I* didn't hear you.'

The soldier bristled at her tone. 'You realise I could have shot you?'

Clare's eyes flitted to the soldier's blackened face and back to the finger on the trigger. She couldn't think above the slow rising tide of fear; she couldn't speak.

He called out to another soldier who was standing by the rear doors of a Saracen. 'Any female personnel around to help?'

Clare heard the crackle of a radio and a muffled exchange of voices.

The other soldier shook his head.

'Looks like I'll have to search you myself.'

She took a step back. 'Keep away from me.'

He grabbed her wrist and pulled her towards him.

'I haven't done anything wrong.' Clare's voice was shrill.

'Is there a problem?'

The second soldier had crossed the road to join them.

'No, mate. This one's just a bit hard of hearing.' He sneered. 'Isn't that right, love?' He wrenched Clare's handbag from her shoulder and tossed it to his colleague. 'Here – check this out.'

His colleague unzipped the bag and tipped the contents on the street. A make-up bag, purse and hairbrush tumbled out and landed in a puddle. He kicked them around with the toe of his boot. Tears welled in Clare's eyes.

'Nothing,' he said. 'Oh, hang on.' He picked up a small packet. 'What do we have here?' The soldier walked across to her.

Clare's face reddened. 'You know what they are,' she mumbled.

The first soldier smirked as he pulled out a condom. 'What's your name?' he asked, waving it in front of her face.

'Clare MacRae.'

'Where are you coming from?'

'The city centre.'

A fusillade of questions followed. Whereabouts in the city centre? What was she doing there? Who was with her? Where was she going now? Clare tried to form the answers in her head but they stuttered out.

'Speak up, I didn't catch any of that.'

Clare's voice cracked as she repeated it all again. She wished she'd stayed with her friends. They'd be elbowing their way to the bar right now, keen to place their last orders.

She was instructed to face the wall, raise her arms and spread her feet apart. The first soldier slung his rifle over his shoulder and began his search.

'You shouldn't be doin' this,' she said.

Her started at her ankles and slowly worked his way up rough-patting her body the whole time. His hands lingered as he reached her breasts. Clare stiffened. Her necklace snagged; coloured beads rolled to the ground.

'Find anything on her?'

'No. She's clear.'

'Are you sure? Maybe you didn't search well enough.'

The low, controlled tone of his voice unnerved Clare even more. 'Please, can I go now?' she asked.

'Not yet.'

He gripped her neck with one hand and pinned her head against the wall. Clare felt the sharp brick on her cheek; her neck was twisted to one side. An earring caught in her scarf; she thought it was going to tear through her earlobe. He pressed his body into her back. Her hands, still splayed against the wall, trembled as she tried to hold his weight. He reached under her skirt with his free hand and ran it up the inside of her leg.

'What are you doin'?'

He said nothing.

'Get off me, you bastard,' screamed Clare.

He reached the crotch of her tights and gave a quick tug. She felt a rip. He tugged again. Clare gasped as his cold hand touched her skin. She clenched her thighs. His rasping breath filled her ears. What was he doing? Dirty fucker!

She couldn't believe this was happening to her, in a street near her home. Surely someone would see what was going on; someone decent would come over and put a stop to it. But who? The street was deserted apart from the soldiers and the squat green bulk of the armoured vehicle.

'Don't, please don't,' she kept repeating.

It all happened very quickly.

He pulled her pants to one side and slipped his hand inside. His fingers jabbed and probed. 'Hiding anything in here?'

A flash of pain. Clare retched.

Clare lowered her arms and remained facing the wall. She didn't want to look at him but he ordered her to turn round. He tilted her chin up and forced her eyes to meet his. Clare shuddered.

'You can go now,' he said.

She ran over and scooped up the contents of her handbag from the wet ground. She straightened her clothes. As she walked away, she felt the nudge of a rifle butt in the middle of her back.

'Off you go then,' they said in unison.

Every muscle in Clare's body yelled at her to run but she didn't. She wasn't going to give them the pleasure of seeing her flee. The street seemed to go on forever. Were they still watching her? She was too scared to look back. She thought she heard them laughing. A bin lid clattered to the ground in a darkened side alley. Clare jumped. She hurried on. The rain was heavier now. The wet pavement glistened yellow with the reflected lights from the street lamps.

She hadn't heard him. A simple mistake, and yet they'd treated her like scum. Would they have done that if she'd stopped as they'd told her to? Or were they waiting for a girl, any girl stupid enough to be out on her own? She should have elbowed him in his ugly pig face. She should have grabbed his gun and shot him. Instead, she'd done nothing. *Nothing.* She'd let those disgusting fingers violate her. She felt dirty. She hated herself. She hated him.

As Clare neared her own street, she sprinted for home. By the time she reached her front door she was gasping for breath. Her hands were shaking; it took her ages to get the key in the lock. She threw the door open and rushed inside.

'Is that you, Clare?' Her mum glanced into the hallway to

check for herself. 'Oh good, it is you. You're just in time for a wee bite of supper.'

Clare heard the click of the kettle and the clatter of cups and saucers. Her mum was humming one of her indecipherable tunes.

'Did you have a nice time?'

Clare didn't respond.

'As long as you enjoyed yourself, that's the main thing.'

'I'm knackered. Think I'll go straight to bed.'

'Why on earth did you walk home in that rain?' called her mum from the kitchen. 'Your dad would have been happy to pick you up.'

'S'alright, Mum.' She had just reached the top of the stairs when Brenda appeared on the landing.

'Oh, you're back. Mum's been waitin' up for–' Her voice trailed off at the sight of Clare's bloody cheek and dishevelled clothes. 'What happened to you?'

'Nothing.' Clare pushed past her and into the bathroom.

Brenda followed and knocked the door. 'Is everything ok?'

'Yes.'

'What happened to your face?'

'I fell.' Clare filled the sink with water and a little antiseptic. She soaked a face cloth in the liquid then dabbed her cheek.

'How much have you had to drink?'

'Fuck off, Brenda.' Clare unbuttoned her raincoat. She pulled off her tights, rolled them up and stuffed them into her pocket.

'That's lovely, that is. I was only checkin' if you were alright.'

'Well you've checked. Now go away.'

As Clare made her way to her bedroom she could hear Brenda reporting back to her mum.

'I'd say she's had a skinful. I doubt she'll be wanting any supper.'

Clare sat on the edge of the bed and fought back hot, angry tears. Let her think what she wanted. As usual her sister had got it all wrong about her.

TWENTY-ONE

A week had passed and Clare had told no-one. Not even Peter. She blamed him in part. If he'd turned up as he'd promised, she'd never have found herself walking home on her own.

As she stood in the chip shop, waiting her turn, memories of the checkpoint flashed into her mind. She could still see the soldiers' mocking faces. The images combined with the smell of the frying fat made her stomach churn. It still hadn't settled when she placed her order for four fish suppers with Liz.

The girl had just started her shift but already there was a sheen to her face. They were out of haddock. Did she want to wait while they fried another batch or would she take cod?

Clare groaned. She just wanted out. 'Cod will do, if that's all you have.'

'Salt?' Liz's hand hovered, ready to pour.

Clare nodded. 'And plenty of vinegar.'

'I suppose you've heard about Peter?' Liz liberally

doused each fish supper with vinegar before wrapping them in paper.

'What about him?'

'He's been arrested.'

Clare felt her chest tighten at the news.

'Pulled over at a checkpoint.' Liz handed Clare her change.

Clare took her fish suppers and stepped to one side. It was Friday night and there was a hungry, impatient queue of people behind her.

'Found explosives in the boot of the car he was drivin'.'

That couldn't be right. Peter moved guns around, not explosives. Clare would have known if he'd had a hand in that.

'Unlucky,' Liz glanced over the counter at Clare while keeping a watchful eye on the battered sausages sizzling in the deep fat fryer, 'or just a bit thick.'

———

'What kept you so long?' said Mrs MacRae. 'I was about to send out a search party.'

Clare dumped the parcels on the kitchen table. In breathless tones she recounted what she'd been told.

'Explosives?' Her mum looked horrified. 'I didn't think he'd get himself in that deep.' She turned to her husband for reassurance.

'It wouldn't surprise me, Bridie,' he said, unwrapping his fish supper. He motioned for them to take their seats at the table. 'Come on, girls. Let's eat this food before it gets cold.'

Clare turned to her mum. 'The soldiers probably made it up. It happens all the time.'

'Oh, come off it,' said Brenda. 'You don't seriously believe that's what happened?'

Clare could feel the anger bubble up inside her. 'I wouldn't put it past them.'

Mr MacRae set down his fork down and looked at his youngest daughter. 'Tell me this, Clare – why are *you* so keen to stick up for him?'

'Because...' Clare felt flustered under his watchful gaze.

'You think it's ok to plant bombs?'

'I didn't say that.' Clare hesitated. 'But sometimes you have to fight back whatever way you can.'

She might as well have punched him in the guts the way he reeled from her words.

'I can't believe I'm hearin' this from a daughter of mine.' Her dad ran a despairing hand through his hair. 'So let me get this straight,' he said. 'That bomb that went off in the Abercorn, for example...'

Clare squirmed. She could see where he was going with this one.

'...the one that almost killed your mother and sister. Is that the sort of fightin' back you mean?'

'That was *different*.'

'Really? In what way?'

Of course she wouldn't want to see her family get hurt. Her dad knew that, but he was intent on making a point.

'Peter says...'

'I'm not interested in what that fella has to say. I was askin' *you*.'

Clare was no match for her dad's clever logic. Whatever she said would be wrong.

'And as for Peter,' her dad added. 'He's a piss-poor choice of a boyfriend.' He shot a look at Brenda. 'At least you had the sense to realise it.'

'Yeah. Brenda's the sensible one, isn't she? So, what do you think of her latest choice?'

'Clare, don't.'

Clare caught the flicker of fear in her sister's eye. Her dad had noticed it too.

'Are you seein' someone else, Brenda?' asked Mrs MacRae.

Her question hung in the air for a while, unanswered.

'Go on,' said Clare, savouring her sister's discomfort. 'Tell them about the soldier you've been screwin'.'

'You're what?' Her mum reacted as if she'd been electro-cuted. 'Is this true?'

'Yes but–'

'What the hell are you thinking?' She turned to her husband. 'Jimmy, talk some...' She stopped when she took in his expression. 'You knew, didn't you?'

'No, I didn't and I'm tryin' to understand what's happening here.'

'Mum, let me explain,' said Brenda.

Her mum's face was beetroot, her chest was puffed up so much Clare thought it would burst. She knew what she was like when the red mist took hold of her; there was no point trying to talk her down. She didn't want to anyway. Her sister deserved their mother's wrath.

'I want it to stop, do you hear me?'

'You don't know him,' said Brenda. 'He's a decent bloke.'

'I've no intention of gettin' to know him. Keep him well away from this house, do you hear me?'

'A decent bloke wouldn't be over here killin' our people.' Clare looked to her mum for support. 'Tell her, Mum.'

'I don't want to see any of our boys gettin' killed, but I don't want to see soldiers getting killed either. A lot of them are just youngsters, in over their heads.'

Clare stared at her. 'So, you're excusin' them?

'I'm just sayin' they don't know what they're gettin' into. You, on the other hand,' she pointed a finger at Brenda, 'you knew exactly what you were gettin' into and the trouble it would cause.'

Mr MacRae placed a steadying hand on his wife's shoulder. 'I think everyone needs to calm down. I–'

She swiped it away. 'Don't try to make light of things the way you always do. We have a problem here and you know it.'

'People will call her a traitor,' said Clare. 'They'll say we're all in on it.'

Suddenly all the puff went out of Mrs MacRae. She looked anxiously at her husband. 'That's what happened to that woman I was tellin' you about the other day, Jimmy. What is it you call her?'

Her husband shook his head. 'No idea who you're talkin' about, Bridie.'

'The one that helped the injured soldier.'

'Mrs Leith?'

'Mrs Leith, yes. She found a young soldier lyin' on the path outside her house. He'd been shot in the leg. All she did was put a pillow under his head. Any mother would do the same. When the Provos found out they told her to pack up and go. And her with a house full of young ones. Said she was a traitor.'

'I know her,' said Clare. 'She's an informer.'

'She's no more an informer than I am,' snapped her mum. 'Not that it matters. Once they take it into their heads...' She looked at Brenda. 'How long have you been seein' this soldier of yours?'

'Since the summer,' Brenda said quietly.

For a moment Clare thought her mum was about to reach out and strike Brenda.

'Is that what you've been gettin' up to in that student's house of yours?'

Brenda lowered her head.

'I thought as much.'

Mrs MacRae looked at their untouched food. 'Dinner's cold now.' She snatched up her plate and threw the contents in the bin. Half of it missed and landed on the floor. 'Are you done with this?' Her husband's plate was whisked away before he had time to answer. There was a sound of breaking crockery as the plate and its contents were thrown into the bin too.

'Happy now, Clare?' said her dad.

'That's right. Twist it on to me. That's what you always do.'

It was so unfair and yet typical of her dad. Brenda was the one who had crossed the boundary but it was Clare being made to feel bad.

Mr MacRae went to his wife.

'What sort of daughters have I raised?' she asked him.

'One sneakin' behind our backs like a common tramp, the other traipsin' after a criminal.'

'Peter's not a criminal,' blurted Clare.

'You just told me he's been arrested.'

'He's a freedom fighter.'

'Freedom my arse,' said her dad.

Brenda took a step towards their mum. 'Mum, please...'

'No. Whatever it is, I don't want to hear it.'

'But...'

'I mean it!'

Brenda's eyes filled with tears. 'You're one fuckin' bitch, Clare.'

Mr MacRae took hold of his wife's hands. 'Just leave me with your mum for a while, Brenda,' he said. 'And you too, Clare. The pair of you, get out of my sight.'

As Clare followed her sister to the door he cautioned her: 'This needs to stay with us. Not a word outside this house.'

TWENTY-TWO

Brenda bumped into one table, spilling a pint. She offered to replace it but, following a few choice words from the drinker, was waved away.

'How's about ye, Brenda?' came a voice from the shadows. She peered at a group of men sitting next to the bar. 'Oh, Mr McManus. I'm grand, thanks.'

Shit! What was he doing here? His usual haunt was the club at the end of the street.

'I don't see much of you these days,' he said.

Brenda set her handbag on the sticky counter. 'I'm up to my eyes in coursework.'

Mr McManus nodded like he understood the demands of her timetable. 'What is it you're studyin' again?'

'Psychology.'

'That's it – psychology. Aye well, you'll find plenty of head cases around here.'

The men at the table started pointing to one another.

'You've got that right,' said Brenda, casting her eye over the group.'

'Pay no heed to them. They're only jestin'.'

Brenda forced a smile. She turned back to the bar and began to rummage in her handbag for her purse.

'Here, let me get this one.'

Mr McManus had appeared beside her.

'No honestly, you're alright.'

'I insist. Now what will it be?'

Brenda stopped fumbling in her bag. 'A Bacardi and coke, please.'

'And what about that lovely sister of yours?' Mr McManus smiled in Clare's direction.

Clare smiled back and lit up a cigarette.

It had been Clare's idea to come here tonight. Their dad had encouraged it. He said he was glad to see the two of them spending some time together instead of being at each other's throat. But that was just it: they weren't. For the last two weeks, the atmosphere in the house had been calm. Clare had curbed her tongue and Brenda, in return, hadn't spoken of Andy, at least not to her family.

'I feel as if I'm denying his existence,' she told Hazel. 'How can that be right?'

Mr McManus coughed. He was waiting to know what drink to get Clare.

'Sorry ... she'll have the same as me.'

He ordered the Bacardis and a Guinness for himself. He watched as the young barmaid tilted the glass and slowly topped up the black liquid. The stout clouded and she put the glass to one side to let the pint settle. 'Actually, I'm glad I bumped into you, Brenda.'

'Oh?'

'Another couple of minutes,' said the barmaid, tapping the glass.

Mr McManus winked. 'Take your time, love. There are some things in life you shouldn't rush and a good pint is one of them.'

He drummed the counter with his fingers. His oppressive closeness made Brenda uneasy.

The young barmaid returned and thumped the beer glass down on the counter.

'Oops,' said Brenda as the creamy top spilled over and trickled onto the counter.

Mr McManus scowled. 'You never let the black stuff spill like that.' He wiped the glass clean with his thumb.

'It's only a bit of beer,' said Brenda. She gave the barmaid a sympathetic smile.

Mr McManus took a long, slow sip of Guinness. He smacked his lips in appreciation then turned to Brenda. 'I hear you've got yourself a new boyfriend.'

Brenda's stomach lurched. Was he one of the *certain people* Clare had spoken of? She didn't want to hang around to find out.

'An Englishman,' he added.

Brenda hastily thanked him for the drink. 'I need to be gettin' back to Clare.' She glanced over at her sister.

Clare looked away and took another drag of her cigarette. A second man from Mr McManus's table had come to the bar. Brenda found her path blocked. The barmaid approached to take his order but was waved away. She picked up a cloth and busied herself with polishing glasses.

'A soldier.'

Brenda swallowed. 'I don't know where you got that from.'

Mr McManus fixed her with a cold stare. 'The thing is, Brenda, we have a problem with that.'

The significance of the word 'we' didn't escape her. Brenda was suddenly hyper alert.

McManus leant closer. 'Sometimes our girls get led astray.' He grabbed her arm and squeezed it tight. Brenda gasped with the pain. 'They get attracted by the glamour of it all, dating someone different to what they know. I can understand that.'

'You're hurtin' me.'

'Brenda?' Clare had stood up to get a better view of what was happening. She looked as if she was about to come over but one of the men blocking Brenda's path motioned for her to sit down.

'They can't see that they are being used,' continued Mr McManus in a low growl. 'Corrupted. Sometimes we have to save them from themselves.' He released her arm.

'I don't know what you're talkin' about.'

He stared coldly at her. 'A smart girl like you? Surely I don't need to spell it out.' He turned away from her and went back to his pint.

Realising he was done with her, for now, Brenda left the Bacardi and cokes on the counter and hurried back to her table. 'Drink up,' she said. 'We're goin'.'

Clare stubbed out her cigarette and grabbed her coat.

'What's goin' on?'

'I'll tell you when we're outside.'

Out on the street Brenda gulped in the cool night air.

'Are you alright, Brenda?' Clare's face was full of concern. 'What was all that about?'

Brenda turned to face her. 'Guess.'

'Oh shit!'

'Did you tell him?'

'What?' Clare shook her head. 'No!'

Brenda searched her sister's face, seeking the truth, wanting to believe her.

'I swear I didn't tell him anything.'

'Then how does he know?'

Clare looked at her as if she was crazy to even ask. 'It's what I've been tryin' to tell you. He has people all over the place. He knows *everything*.'

Brenda felt sick. Of course, he did. What if he'd been watching her, tracking her movements? She'd never forgive herself if something awful happened to Andy because of her.

On the way home neither girl spoke. After a while Clare began to lag behind. Brenda stopped to wait for her up and, as her sister walked towards her, she thought she detected a smile on her face. It had vanished by the time she caught up with her.

TWENTY-THREE

Peter sat hunched over a table. When he lifted his head to greet her, Clare gasped.

'What happened to you?'

'I fell on one of their fists.'

His right eye was half-closed with bruising.

She reached forward and touched it with her finger. 'Soldiers did this to you?'

Peter flinched. 'And more.'

'Tell me.'

He shook his head. 'It doesn't matter. It's done now.'

'Tell me, Peter. I want to know.'

He said they'd made him stand spread-eagled and lean against the wall with only his fingers keeping him up. 'It went on forever. Fingertips position while they fired questions at me, over and over. When I got too tired to stay like that and fell down, they hit me.'

Memories of her own treatment at the hands of soldiers came flooding back. That too had started with being told to stand spread-eagled against a wall. 'Bastards.'

Others had spoken about the torture methods Peter described and worse. Men who had been rounded up by the Army on dawn swoops and later released. They told of being ordered to stand as Peter had, for hours on end, forced to run over broken glass, deprived of sleep. It didn't matter if they were guilty or innocent; they'd all been treated the same way.

'Have they charged you yet?'

Peter nodded. 'They did me for possession of explosives.'

'Explosives?' Her stomach twisted into a knot as her mind raced through the consequences. 'Peter, this is serious. You could be inside for a long time.'

'I'll know soon enough. I'm in court in a couple of days' time and I can guess how that's goin' to pan out.' He gave an expansive sweep of his arm. 'Welcome to my new home.'

'That's not funny, Peter.'

'Who's laughin'?'

Clare looked around her. The old Victorian jail was as grim inside as it was outside. Up until she was a child, people had been hung inside this building. The place gave her the creeps. All those ghosts of previous inmates. Peter must feel it too.

'Just my luck to get caught, huh?'

'Keep your voice down, Peter.' Clare glanced over at the prison guard who stood close by.

Peter gave him a nod. 'Alright there, mate?'

The prison guard scowled.

'It makes no difference what he hears,' said Peter. 'It won't change anything.' He held his hands up. 'Guilty as charged.'

Clare took hold of his hands and pulled them down to rest on the table. 'Even British justice still has to prove it, Peter.'

'They found the stuff on me. There's no arguing my way out of that.'

Clare had hoped the girl in the chip shop had got it wrong. She'd clung to the possibility that Peter had been framed. Now as she sat here, looking at Peter's battered face, she realised it no longer mattered to her if he was innocent or guilty. It didn't change how she felt about him.

'The laugh of it is I wasn't supposed to be drivin' that car in the first place.'

'What do you mean, Peter?'

'There was a group of them lined up for the job. They'd been plannin' it for ages. One of the men bottled at the last minute and I was asked to step in.'

'You could have said no.'

Peter sat tall in his chair and drew his shoulders back. 'I was proud to be asked.'

'Sorry. I don't know why I said that.'

He shrugged. 'It was just my bad luck they sent me on that route.'

'And these explosives – they were in the boot?'

'Incendiaries, all primed and ready. I was told to deliver them to the lads who were goin' to plant them. They were to leave them in the doorway of the Kings Arms.'

Clare had heard of the place. It was well known for being a loyalist drinking den. 'So, what happened?'

'I was pulled over before I got there.'

Clare imagined the scene: Peter handing over the car keys; soldiers opening the boot to take a look inside; guns turned on him as they dragged him from the car; a crack on the side of the head with a rifle butt; questions barked at him

– Who were they for? Where was he taking them? Peter slammed against the wall.

'They wanted names but I didn't give them any.'

'What about the others? Are they in here too?'

'No. Just me.' Peter sat back in his seat. He looked at her for a moment. 'Of course, what the bastards really wanted to know was who gave the orders.'

'You didn't...'

'I'd rather take a few more kickings in here that than offer up that information.'

'Oh, Peter, don't say that.'

'What pisses me off is that I haven't heard from him the whole time I've been in here. As long as I keep my mouth shut, that's all that matters. The only time he'll take an interest in me again is if I start talkin'. And that meeting would be short and painful.'

The wardens began to signal that visiting time was almost up.

'Piss off,' muttered Clare.

The room reverberated with the sound of disgruntled murmurs as relatives and friends said their goodbyes.

'How long do you think they'll give you, Peter?'

'I don't know.' A touch of panic crept into his voice. 'I don't want to think about it.'

The room began emptying of visitors. Clare got ready to leave.

'Hang on, before you go...'

She knew what he was about to ask, wondered why it had taken him so long.

'Did you do what I asked you to?'

'If you're referring to Brenda – yes.'

'The boys caught up with her then?'

'Let's just say, if they were hopin' to scare her, it worked a treat. I don't think she'll be seein' *him* again any time soon.'

Peter's plan had been carried through and yet it didn't seem to please him. 'In a way it's a shame.'

For a moment Clare thought she had misread his mood.

'But it had to be done.'

'Yes.'

'You'd better go,' he said, 'before they lock you in too.'

'I'll come and see you once you're...'

'Settled?' Peter gave a bitter laugh.

Clare leant across and kissed him. 'Take care of yourself.'

'I'll do my best.'

Once outside she took a closer look at the hateful building that kept him from her. She cursed its dark grandeur, its solid stonework, the gate topped with barbed wire. Everything about it filled her with anger. It was so unfair. Why should Peter take all the beatings and be locked in this hellhole when others stayed free? She couldn't give up on him, no matter what her dad thought of him. Peter needed her now more than ever.

TWENTY-FOUR

England

J enny had walked out taking their son with her. Andy flew back only to find she'd stripped the house bare of all traces of them, apart from one family photograph and a couple of wedding gifts – a crystal carriage clock and a china tea service. She'd never liked them. She'd taken her albums and tapes from the shelf that housed their music collection, the cushions and rugs she'd bought to cheer the place up, the bedlinen, even the lampshades. Stevie's toys too.

On the kitchen table was her letter. It was over between them. She'd gone to stay with her mother. He wasn't to follow her. In three short sentences she'd ended their life together.

Andy called his mother-in-law's house and demanded to speak to his wife.

His exchange with Jenny was stiff and formal. She'd enrolled Stevie in a new school. It was just around the corner from her mum's place; he would start next week. She and her mum had sorted out a bedroom for him. They'd painted it in the same colour as his old one so that things would feel less strange for him.

'Mum's happy for us to stay here as long as we want. She's been rattling around in the place anyway, since Dad died.'

'Good old Mum, eh? She's got you all sorted.'

Jenny gave a long sigh. 'She's only trying to help.'

'Yeah, right.' What about Andy? Did they expect him to drive all that way every time he wanted to see his son? Her mum's house was miles away from the Army base. 'Jenny, how are we going to manage this?'

'I don't know.' Jenny hesitated. 'We need to work something out ... whatever's best for Stevie.'

'Yes, but when? How?' He suggested letting Stevie stay with him, for a weekend, maybe longer, the next time he was back on leave.

She refused. 'It would be too confusing for him. Maybe once things are settled between us then I'll think about it.'

'That's big of you.'

'I've contacted a solicitor,' she told him. 'I want a divorce.'

'Could we not have talked about it first, like two sensible adults, instead of you running off to your mum's then dumping this news on me?'

'Don't make me out to be the unreasonable one,' she said. 'You're the one who had the affair.'

'Call it an affair if it makes you feel better.'

She gave a derisory laugh. 'Believe me, it doesn't make me feel any better to know you've been screwing behind my back. You humiliated me, Andy. Hearing about it from the other wives – you made me look a fool.'

It was Paul who had spilt the beans in the end. He told his missus. Once Paul's wife knew it hadn't been long before everyone did, including Jenny. No mention of love from her, he noted, just wounded pride. 'You and I both know our marriage was over long before I started seeing Brenda.'

'Brenda.' She said the name like it was a bad smell. 'So, who is she? Some little tart you met on a night out with the lads?'

'It wasn't like that.'

'Has she no shame, chasing after married men?'

A silence fell between them.

'Oh my god. You haven't told her, have you?'

'I was trying to find the right moment.'

'You're pathetic.'

'Don't talk to me like that, Jenny.'

'I won't. From now on my solicitor will do the talking for me. He'll be in touch soon.'

———

He parked across the street from the school gates and waited. His son had always been a dawdler. He waited until the stream of children became a trickle. And there he was – neat and tidy in his shirt, tie and blazer, surprisingly presentable for the end of a school day. Andy had hated wearing a school uniform when he was a boy. Every school photograph showed him with his top button undone, his tie askew and his shirt tails hanging out. It was ironic that he'd ended up in the Army and now wore a uniform every day.

Stevie's limbs were as skinny as before but the boy himself was taller. He looked as if he'd been stretched.

Andy rolled down the window. 'Stevie!'

'Dad?'

Andy got out of the car and went to meet him. 'Thought I'd surprise you.'

Stevie gave him a wary look. 'Does Mum know you're here?'

'Yes, of course.'

The boy relaxed his shoulders and ventured a timid smile.

'I thought we could go for a bit to eat,' said Andy. 'How does burger and chips sound?'

'Can we go to Wimpy?'

'Yes, but you'll have to show me the way.'

Stevie threw his bag into the back of the car then took a seat in the front beside his dad.

———

They ordered cheeseburger and chips, a coffee for Andy and a double-thick strawberry milkshake for Stevie.

'So, how are you finding your new school?'

'It's alright. Most of the teachers are alright too, except for Mr Wilson. He's the Maths teacher and no-one likes him.'

'Are you making new friends?'

Stevie shrugged. 'S'pose so,' he said, sucking his milkshake loudly through his straw.

'Good. I'm glad to see you've settled in. It was all a bit sudden ... the move and everything.'

'Yeah.' Stevie flicked a glance at his dad.

'I'm talking to your mum about how we can get to see each other.'

'You, me and Mum? But I thought...'

'I meant just you and me.'

'Oh.' Stevie kept his eyes on his glass.

'Look, I don't know what your mum's told you...'

'She said we wouldn't be living in the same house anymore.'

Andy frowned. 'That's right but you and I can still spend time together. You can come and stay with me whenever you like.'

'Where I used to live?'

'Maybe there or I might get posted somewhere else. We'll see.'

Stevie pushed his milkshake to one side. 'I've finished. Can we go now?'

Back in the car he kept his gaze on the road in front of him. He appeared to have nothing left to tell his dad.

Andy filled the gaps in their conversation. He offered to take him to a football match the next time he saw him. 'You like football, don't you?'

'Yeah.'

'But you've never been to a match before?'

'No.'

'Well, that'll be my treat to you,' said Andy as he pulled into his mother-in-law's driveway.

His son retrieved his schoolbag from the back seat of the car and ran to the door. Jenny had thrown it open before he had a chance to ring the doorbell. She reached to hug him.

'Where have you *been*?'

He looked at her in bewilderment. 'Dad told me you knew.'

'No, I didn't.' Jenny fixed Andy with an icy stare. 'What do you think you're playing at? You do realise we were about to call the police?'

'We weren't gone that long.'

'More than two hours, Andy.'

Jenny's mother appeared on the doorstep. 'You're such a selfish man. My daughter was worried sick.'

'Keep out of it, Gill. We don't need you sticking your oar in.'

'Don't you speak to my mother like that.'

Stevie looked from one warring parent to the other. 'Stop it,' he shouted.

'Mum, take Stevie inside.'

'Remember what we talked about,' said Andy as Stevie was led inside.

'How dare you take my son without permission.'

'I've as much right to see him as you. He's my son too.'

'My solicitor will be hearing about this.'

'Don't threaten me with that solicitor bullshit.'

Jenny's mother had reappeared. She beckoned for her daughter to come in.

As Jenny turned to go Andy caught hold of her arm. 'Wait!'

Jenny lost her footing and fell to the ground.

'Right, that's it,' said her mum. She helped her daughter up then turned her fury on Andy. 'If you don't go now, I *will* ring the police.'

Andy looked at his wife's grazed hands. Tiny pieces of

gravel were embedded in the shredded skin. 'I'm sorry,' he said.

The sight of his son's tear-stained face at the window told him he'd blown it. He'd managed to scramble a few days leave but tonight he'd have to return to Belfast. He'd be stuck there for months. The solicitors would take over and any chance of building bridges would be lost. 'It doesn't have to be like this, Jenny. We can sort something out,' he pleaded. His words were lost as Jenny and her mum disappeared inside.

TWENTY-FIVE

Belfast

Brenda switched the television off.

'Hey, I was watchin' that.'

She motioned to Clare to keep quiet and listened again. No, she hadn't imagined it; the noise was definitely coming from the street.

'Can you hear people shoutin'?'

'It's probably some eejits havin' a fight.'

Brenda shook her head. She had an uneasy feeling about this. There were too many voices for it to be a street fight. The noise grew louder. Clare ran over to the window and peered through the curtains. She looked puzzled.

'What is it?'

'There's a whole crowd of people at the head of our street. I can't make out who they are. Oh, hang on, I can see now. They're headin' this way. Oh Jesus!' She turned and stared at Brenda. 'They've stopped at our house.'

Brenda's stomach lurched. They both knew why they had come.

Fists pounded the front door. Brenda's dad was changing out of his work clothes when he heard the commotion. He rushed down the stairs and wedged himself against the door.

'What in the name of fortune is goin' on?' Her mum's voice came from the hallway.

'Open up. We need to speak to Brenda,' roared a male voice.

Clare was rooted to the spot. She shot her sister a terrified glance.

'Brenda's not home,' yelled their dad.

'Open the door, Jimmy. We know she's in there.'

Brenda's body stiffened. She could scarcely breathe.

'I'm tellin' you she's not here.'

There was a moment's silence. Then the order was given.

'Kick it in!'

Brenda heard the splintering of wood and her mum's screams followed by a loud crash as the door gave way.

'Don't you dare lay a finger on her,' shouted her dad as he made one last frantic attempt to hold them back.

Brenda's legs could barely support her. She put a hand on the wall to steady herself, took a deep breath and stumbled out to face them. 'Get away from him. Leave him alone.'

Two men in balaclavas tightened their grip on her dad's arms as he writhed and kicked.

'What are you doing?' yelled Clare. 'Stop it!'

Blood streamed from his nose and there was an angry red welt on the side of his face.

Brenda saw the club swing but it was the sound when it hit his head that shocked her into action. 'Dad!' She rushed over to him and flung her arms around his neck. He was a dead weight. Two more masked men wrenched her from him and frogmarched her outside. The crowd clapped and cheered. Someone shouted, 'Turncoat'. A young girl ran up and spat at her then darted back into the crowd.

'Where are you takin' me?' The men ignored her. 'What are you going to do to me?' She was terrified they would shoot her.

They dragged her along the street, past the rows of terraced houses and parked cars until they stopped at the lamp post in front of the chip shop. A woman stood by the side of the road holding a length of rope. Marie Keenan. At the sight of the familiar figure Brenda's reserve crumbled and she began to cry. 'Please, don't do this,' she pleaded.

The taller of the two men clamped her head between his hands. She could smell the nicotine on his fingers as he held her steady while his accomplice taped over her mouth. They made an efficient team.

Fingers clawed at her blouse, ripping it open and pulling it down over her shoulders. Brenda's eyes darted around the braying crowd. Her heart thumped wildly. This couldn't be happening – not to her. This sort of thing only happened to girls in other parts of the city and in other streets, not her street. She'd grown up among these people. How could they suddenly hate her?

Marie stepped forward with the rope. She looked at Brenda with dead eyes. 'You were warned,' she hissed, 'but you wouldn't stop.'

They wound the rope around Brenda's chest and tied her to the lamp post. The rope dug into her exposed skin. She tugged at it, trying to free herself. A club slammed into her hand. She whimpered as pain shot through her fingers and up her arm. Another slam of the club and she stopped struggling.

She caught the flash of blades in the street light. Marie grabbed a fistful of hair and began to hack it off. One by one, large tufts of long, auburn hair grazed the pavement. The scissors bit into her scalp, slicing her skin. The pile of shorn hair grew higher until it covered Brenda's feet. Marie turned to the crowd and nodded. Another woman took her cue and stepped forward. She carried a large can of black paint, which she emptied over Brenda. Marie handed the woman a sack of feathers. The woman shook them over Brenda's head. The crowd murmured in satisfaction as the feathers tumbled down and settled in the sticky fluid. Brenda's eyes were squeezed shut but the paint still managed to seep in. Her eyes were on fire.

The crowd grew quieter as, one by one, the women drifted away. They'd got other things to be getting on with – they needed to make the dinner, put their kids to bed. Only the masked men remained, keeping vigil. She felt their shadowy presence as they paced up and down behind her. Every now and then they stamped their feet and blew on their hands to keep warm. It was getting dark. The street light had just come on.

'Here you go, lads.' She recognised the voice. It was McManus. 'I thought you could do with a bite to eat.'

There was a rustle of paper. The smell of vinegar saturated the air. Brenda felt sick. The men ate their chips and discussed their work.

'I don't like doin' the women,' said one man. 'All this hangin' around afterwards is borin'.'

The other laughed. 'Wait til you get your first kneecapping. You'll not be bored then. They squeal like butchered pigs.'

The shutters of the chippie were being pulled down and the door bolted. It must be ten o'clock. How much longer were they going to keep her here? Brenda shivered uncontrollably. The cold made her want to pee.

All through the evening they flagged down passing cars and spoke to the drivers. The drivers shone their car lights on her face: they'd been told to take a good look and spread the word that this is what happened to a 'soldier doll'. Some wound their windows down and shouted abuse. One driver got out of his car and walked up to her. He leant close and snarled obscenities in her ear. He told her in graphic detail what they should really do to her, said he'd pay her a visit himself once they'd finished with her. Brenda wet herself.

Eventually they all tired of their sport. Even the hooded men went home. Brenda was alone. She thought of her dad, beaten and bloodied, and hated herself for bringing that on him. For all she knew they could have killed him. What about her mum? Clare? They could have turned on them too. How could she have been so selfish? She hadn't stopped to think how she might be putting her family in danger. If she had, she'd never have gone out with Andy. But that wasn't true, was it? Brenda had been led by her heart and chosen not to think of the consequences. Until now.

She wished he could come and get her. She wanted to be with him, somewhere, anywhere, as long as it wasn't here. But it was her dad who cut her loose and wrapped her near-unconscious body in his coat. He peeled the masking tape off her mouth and tried to wipe the paint from her face. It was rock hard and wouldn't budge. He plucked at a feather that had stuck to her eyelashes. Brenda winced and pushed his hand away. He scooped her up in his arms and carried her down the street.

A milk float drove past them. Women, in their dressing gowns, gathered up milk bottles from the doorstep then hurried back inside and shut the door. Nobody looked at them. Nobody spoke to them.

'I'm sorry, Dad,' she whispered. 'I never meant to–'

'I know you didn't. Hush now. I've got you, you're safe.'

But they both knew she wasn't safe and that she couldn't go back to her old life. Everything had changed.

TWENTY-SIX

A young nurse, not much older than Brenda, whisked her off to a side cubicle and pulled the curtains shut. She struggled to mask her shock at the sight of black paint and feathers welded to Brenda's skin but tried to sound reassuring.

'The doctor's on his way to you right now.'

After a few minutes the curtains parted and the doctor appeared beside them. 'What have we got here then? Oh...' His voice tailed off as he took in the scene. He turned to Brenda's dad.

'She didn't want to come.'

'No, of course. I understand,' said the doctor. 'Ok, let's take a look.' He asked Brenda's dad to leave.

'I'll be right outside if you need me, love.'

The nurse tilted Brenda's head back and held it steady. Brenda could hear the echo of her dad's footsteps as he paced up and down the corridor.

The doctor rubbed cream on to her eyelashes; he tried to tease the top and bottom lashes apart. Brenda gasped. Her dad's footsteps stopped suddenly.

'What's goin' on?'

Brenda took a deep breath. 'It's ok, Dad.'

'You're doing really well,' said the nurse. 'We're nearly there. I just need you to put your head back one more time.'

Brenda squeezed the arms of the bed and bit her lip. The doctor pulled her eyelids back and rinsed her eyes with a saline liquid. The liquid was cold and made her want to blink furiously. She tried to remain still and keep her eyes open as he washed them out for a second and then a third time. Once he'd finished, the nurse called Mr MacRae back.

She'd been lucky, said the doctor. There was no lasting damage but her eyes would continue to smart for a while. She should try not to rub them, if she could. Her vision would be a bit blurry too. He said he'd like to keep her in overnight.

Brenda leapt up. 'No!' She wasn't going to let him put her in a ward. 'I won't have everyone gawpin' at me.'

'Take it easy.' Her dad placed a hand on her shoulder. 'No-one's forcin' you to stay.'

'Get me out of here, *please*.'

'Look I really appreciate what you've done,' said Mr MacRae, 'but I can take care of things from here.'

The doctor nodded. 'Alright but what about yourself? Maybe we should take a quick look at...'

'I'm fine. Just sort my daughter out.'

The nurse cleaned Brenda's face and hands and tidied her up as best she could. Her pristine blue uniform was covered in black streaks.

Brenda's dad led her back out into the full glare and clamorous din of the accident and emergency department.

They made their way across the crowded waiting room, attracting curious glances and hostile stares in equal measure.

A man dripping in blood from a slashed arm stood in front of them. He looked Brenda up and down. 'Been screwin' squaddies, have you?'

Brenda's dad shoved him to one side and the man stumbled backwards into a trolley scattering bottles of pills, swabs and bandages over the grey linoleum floor. They left him floundering on his back, trying to hoist himself upright with his one good arm as they hurried towards the exit. They half-walked and half-ran across the car park.

As soon as they were both in the car, Mr MacRae locked all the doors from the inside then drove off as fast as he could. 'Shit!' He slammed his foot on the brakes and the car jolted to a halt.

The Army had set up a checkpoint outside the hospital gates. Two soldiers, holding rifles, stood in the middle of the road. One of the soldiers walked round to the driver's side of the car. Mr MacRae rolled down the window.

'Where are you off to in such a–?' His voice tailed off when he saw the state of the driver's face.

'I'm takin' my daughter home from hospital.'

The soldier peered into the back of the car. His eyebrows creased as he took in the dishevelled figure wrapped in the car rug. 'Driver's licence, please.'

'Are you serious? Can't you see what's goin' on here?'

'Licence now, sir.'

His driver's licence was inside his wallet, which he'd left on the hall table. The soldier walked round to the front of the car. He radioed in the registration number and waited for the response. Brenda's dad drummed his fingers on the steering wheel.

The soldier took another furtive glance at Brenda. He shuffled his feet in embarrassment at the delay. 'Away you go,' he said when the All Clear finally came through.

Mr MacRae rolled the window back up in disgust and drove off.

They made their way through the city and down the Falls Road. To Brenda it seemed like the longest journey of her life. Every time the car stopped at traffic lights she pulled the rug up to shield her face and slid further down the seat. They passed rows of plain, two-up two-down brick houses. Huge paintings of men dressed in paramilitary uniform, brandishing guns, filled the tall corrugated iron 'peace' wall that kept the two warring communities apart. Their eyes, staring out through the slits in their balaclavas, seemed to follow her. Burnt-out and boarded-up buildings were daubed with 'Brits out' slogans and Irish flags. At last they turned into their own street. The traces of feathers and paint were still visible on the pavement outside the chippie.

It was after lunch when they arrived home. Her mum rushed out the moment she spotted them, oblivious to the sniggers of the kids playing in the street as she helped Brenda out of the car. She cupped her daughter's face and kissed her forehead.

'I'm alright, Mum.'

'Thank god for that but look at you. How could they let you out in such a state?' She ushered Brenda inside the house and led her straight through to the kitchen. 'Come on, let's get you properly cleaned up.' She placed Brenda on a chair in the middle of the kitchen floor and cut away the remainder of her torn blouse. A large block of butter sat on the table. 'Don't stand there with both arms the same length, Clare. Come and give me a hand.'

Mrs MacRae took a lump of butter. She smeared it over a section of Brenda's skin and began to massage it in. Clare did the same. The paint was dry to the touch and little cracks had formed in the folds of Brenda's skin. The more they rubbed the butter in, the looser the paint became. They each grabbed a towel and wiped the paint off before starting on another section.

'What about my hair?'

'We'll have a go at that in a minute. Let's sort this out first.'

'Be honest, Mum. How bad does it look?'

Brenda had caught a glimpse of her reflection in the hospital window. She knew she looked a fright but she was hoping they'd tell her something different. They said nothing. Clare concentrated on rubbing the butter, one small circle at a time. She couldn't meet her sister's gaze.

'That bad then,' said Brenda. She began to sob.

Clare let go of Brenda's arm. 'You should never have got involved with a squaddie in the first place.'

'What?'

'Now you're payin' the price.'

'Stop it, Clare,' said Mrs MacRae. 'She doesn't need to hear that from you of all people.'

They lathered Brenda's matted hair with soap and rinsed it over the kitchen sink. Some of the paint refused to budge despite their repeated attempts to wash it out. In the end they agreed there was nothing for it other than to crop her hair even shorter. When they were through Brenda rubbed her hands over her head. It felt like the soft bristles of a baby's hairbrush. She went upstairs and ran a bath. She pulled off her soiled clothes and stuffed them in a bin bag.

In the bath Brenda scrubbed furiously at her skin. Grease from the butter and flakes of paint residue floated to the top of the water and formed a scum. Her body ached all over; her right hand was red and swollen. She dried herself, wiped the steam off the full-length mirror on the inside of the door and took a proper look at herself. One glance in the bathroom mirror crushed all hope. She went to her bedroom, locked the door and curled up on the bed. Her racking sobs could be heard throughout the house.

TWENTY-SEVEN

Her sister had been locked away in her bedroom like this for the last couple of days. Clare knocked on the door.

'Yes?'

'Did you not hear Mum callin' you? Dinner's on the table.'

Brenda opened the door. 'Tell her I'll be down in a minute.'

Their mum was doing what she always did in a crisis: trying to keep a lid on her feelings and carry on as normal. She'd made Irish stew – comfort food. There was enough in the large pot to feed the street. Their dad, on the other hand, could barely contain his rage. He was so unlike himself, it scared Clare.

They ate in silence.

Brenda picked at her food. 'I take it there's still been no word from him?'

'If you mean lover boy, then no,' said Clare. 'Looks like he's done a runner.'

Brenda put down her spoon.

'Andy's not like that.'

'They all are.'

Mr MacRae slammed his fist on the table. Brenda's spoon bounced; the salt pot ended up on the floor.

'I'm sorry but it's obvious.'

'That's enough, Clare.'

'I'm only sayin' what everyone's thinking.'

'I said that's enough!'

Clare swallowed her frustration and forced herself to hold her tongue.

'I can't eat any more,' said Brenda, pulling out her chair. As she made her way into the living room, her dad went after her.

Clare gathered up the half-empty bowls and took them to the sink. She washed; her mum dried. Through the window she could see next-door's ginger tomcat on its evening prowl. It tiptoed along the fence, arched its back and leapt on to the coal bunker that took up most of the space in their back yard. It sat on the bunker and stared back at her. As if it knew.

Clare plunged her hands into the washing-up bowl. How had things got so out of control? They weren't supposed to hurt Brenda. Peter had said the boys would have a word in Brenda's ear. Enough to scare her off, nothing more than that. Clare had trusted him to keep his word.

'Mum,' Clare handed her another plate to dry, 'you don't think she'll try to see him again, do you? I mean that would be crazy.'

'She'd better not.'

'What if she does?' Clare wouldn't put it past her. Her sister was too stubborn for her own good. 'You'd better have words with her,' she said. 'It's obvious Dad isn't goin' to say anything. Someone needs to get her to see sense.'

The phone in the hallway rang. They both stopped what they were doing and looked at each other.

Brenda had rushed to answer it. Clare could tell from the flat tone in her voice it wasn't who she hoped it would be. She tried to piece together the conversation, work out who the caller was, but Brenda was saying very little. Suddenly her sister's voice grew loud and agitated. 'Don't you tell me who I can and can't see!'

Mrs MacRae threw down her tea towel and stormed into the hallway. 'What is it now?'

Mr MacRae grabbed the phone from Brenda. 'Who is this?' He began to shout at the caller, told him he was a faceless coward, scum of the earth. His words made no impact. The caller had already hung up.

Brenda was shaking.

'I swear to god when I catch up with them I'll...'

Mrs MacRae put her hands on her hips. 'You'll what, Jimmy? Go on, tell me. What exactly are you goin' to do apart from make things worse than they are?'

'I'll find them and put a stop to it. That's what.'

Mrs MacRae snorted. 'You don't even know where to look.'

Clare had ventured out of the kitchen and now stood at her mum's side. 'Please, Dad, promise me you won't do anything silly.' The resolute look on his face made her stomach knot with fear. 'I mean it. You've no idea what you're gettin' into.' She rounded on her sister. 'Do you see what you've started?'

'What *I've* started?'

'Yes ... you!'

'What about them? They're the ones makin' the threats.'

'You're not the only one who feels threatened. We all do, thanks to you.'

'That's not fair. You can't blame me for what they did.'

'I'll tell you what's not fair,' screamed Clare. 'The way you dragged us all into your mess.'

'Enough!' bellowed Mr MacRae.

All three women fell silent.

He looked at his warring daughters. 'Havin' you at each other's throats won't solve anything.' He turned to his wife. 'And if you think I'm goin' to sit back and watch my family be terrorised in their own home, you're wrong. I know exactly where to find the lowlife involved in this. I've lived here long enough to know which stones to look under.'

———

The following morning Clare and Brenda did their best to ignore one another. As the chilly atmosphere slowly thawed they progressed to monosyllabic grunts. After a few hours they were able to manage short, civil exchanges, mostly about routine domestic arrangements, all under the watchful eye of their mum. Did anyone fancy a cup of tea? Had the paper arrived? What else needed to go on the shopping list? Their dad stuck to his Saturday routine. He polished off a hearty Irish breakfast of bacon, sausages, potato farls, black pudding and a fried egg. At midday he headed to the pub for a couple of pints.

It was only when he'd left the house that Brenda remembered her Saturday job. In all the commotion no-one had thought to let Mrs Henderson know she wouldn't be in today. Clare offered to stop by the shop and speak with her. She needed to pop out anyway and get some groceries in. Brenda looked unsure.

'You can't go in the state you're in, Brenda.' Clare stuffed the shopping list into her pocket and stepped out into the watery sunshine. She was glad to escape the oppressive atmosphere in the house.

Through the glass panel in the shop door she could see Mrs Henderson tidying up inside. She was folding babygrows and putting them back in their cellophane bags. Clare rapped the glass with her knuckles and Mrs Henderson spun round. She opened the door and cast her eyes up and down the street. Then she motioned for Clare to step inside. 'Come in dear. It's Clare, isn't it?'

'I won't keep you, Mrs Henderson. I don't know if you heard what happened to Brenda but...'

She could immediately tell from her face that Mrs Henderson had heard everything.

'Terrible business altogether ... just terrible! I do hope she's alright.'

'It's shaken her up. It'll be a while before she's back.'

'Actually, I've been meaning to have a word with Brenda,' said Mrs Henderson. 'The thing is, it's a bit quiet in the shop at the moment.'

'That's funny. Brenda said she was run off her feet last Saturday.'

Mrs Henderson didn't dispute that last week had indeed been one of their busiest, but generally, things were quiet and she didn't need the extra help any more. If business picked up, she'd be sure to let Brenda know.

'You've no intention of takin' her back, have you?'

'I can't risk my business.'

'She's goin' to be really upset. She loves this job.'

Mrs Henderson turned away from her and went back to folding babygrows. 'Tell Brenda I was asking after her.'

Clare slammed the door behind her. So much for loyalty. Brenda had worked hard for Mrs Henderson. What if Clare hadn't gone to see her? How would Brenda have known she was no longer wanted? She could guarantee Mrs Henderson wouldn't have popped round to their house to tell Brenda herself. The worst of it was that Mrs Henderson was right. If she was seen to side with a traitor both she and her shop would be targeted.

On the way home Clare stopped off at the grocer's. As she emerged, laden down with two full carrier bags, she caught sight of Mrs Doyle from across the street. She hollered hello but her neighbour looked right through her. Clare felt herself go hot under the collar. She continued making her way down the street. Girls she'd gone to school with nudged and pointed at her when they spotted her coming towards them. She'd hung out with these girls during school breaks, but now they crossed the street to avoid her. Why were they turning on her? Clare was no lover of soldiers. Her friends knew that. Yet the way they were getting on you'd think Clare was the one who'd been screwing Andy.

Clare quickened her pace. How long would they keep this up? Would her mum get the same cold-shoulder treatment?

'We'll have to tough it out,' said her mum as they unpacked the groceries. 'Things will settle down.'

'Maybe you're right. People do forget after a while, don't they?' Clare tried to convince herself as much as her mum. She thought about the chain of events she'd put in place. Only now did she realise Brenda's punishment was merely the start of her family's torment.

TWENTY-EIGHT

Andy sat on the end of his bunk polishing his boots. It had started. His split from Jenny was actually happening and with it came all the decisions he'd been putting off – custody; maintenance money; where Andy would call home. On top of all that there was Brenda to consider too. His jaw tightened at the sound of his Paul's voice.

'Listen mate, I'm sorry Jenny found out about...'

Andy spat on a toecap and rubbed it with his cuff.

'Me and the missus were having a chat. It just, sort of, slipped out.'

Andy sprung to his feet.

'Take it easy.' Paul took a step back.

Andy grabbed him by the collar and pushed him against the wall. 'You fucking idiot!'

Paul pushed back harder. 'Screw you.'

Andy fell on to his bunk.

Paul straightened his shirt collar. A button had worked loose. 'Fuck's sake. You almost tore my head off.'

Andy looked at the solid, square face sat on top of a bull neck. 'I don't think I could even if I tried,' he said. 'Sorry. It's been a shit couple of days.'

'S'alright.'

Andy sat for a few moments staring at the floor. 'You were right.'

'I was?' Paul looked confused.

'I should have told Jenny about me and Brenda ages ago.'

'I don't remember telling you that. I was worried you'd get found out, that's all.' Paul gave a tentative smile. 'And thanks to me, you did.'

'In a way you did me a favour. Things couldn't go on the way they were.'

Paul gave a small bow. 'Glad to be of service.'

'Don't push it, you arsehole. This wasn't how I wanted it to happen. Jenny went off on one. I lost my temper. Her mum threatened to call the police.'

Paul whistled through his teeth.

'Stupid, I know.' Andy glanced up. 'It gets worse. Brenda doesn't know I have a family. It's all a mess.'

Paul reached down, grabbed Andy's arm and pulled him to his feet. 'What are you going to do?'

'Some of it's already been taken out of my hands now that Jenny's moved in with her mum, but I don't know what to say to Brenda.' He cast his mind back to when they met. 'Do you remember that first night when I went back to Brenda's room?'

'I thought you were a lucky sod. Still do, if I'm honest.'

Andy smiled. Paul was undoubtedly an arsehole but he was an honest one, like he said.

That first night Andy hadn't expected anything more than

a quick shag. Brenda had seemed up for it, inviting him into her bed the way she did. And yet they didn't have sex. He had been content to simply lie next to her. Not that he'd have admitted that to any of the lads, least of all Paul. 'I think even then I knew she was special.'

'Steady on, mate. You're sounding like a right sop.' Paul gave an uncomfortable cough.

'I know. I don't know why I'm telling you all this,' said Andy.

'It's not that.' Paul hesitated. 'It's Brenda.'

'What about her? Has something happened?'

'The bastards tarred and feathered her.'

'They *what*? When?'

'A few nights back when you were away.'

'Are you sure it was her?'

'A couple of lads stopped a car outside the hospital. They did a number-plate check and her surname came up. MacRae. Kendal Avenue.'

'That's her,' said Andy.

'They saw a girl on the back seat. It was obvious what had happened to her.'

Andy remembered how anxious she'd been the last time he'd seen her. She'd been convinced her sister knew about them. If her sister knew, she'd told him, others would too. He'd played down her fears, told her she was overreacting. All because he wanted to buy time with his wife. 'Do we know who did it?'

Paul shrugged. 'It could be any one of those fuckers.'

'Where is she now?'

'At home, I think.'

'I need to go to her.'

Paul placed a restraining hand on Andy's arm. 'Where do you think you're off to?'

'Her house. If she's there, I want to see her.'

'Don't be ridiculous.'

The thought of Brenda's attackers going unpunished filled Andy with fury. 'I'm going to find out who did it.'

'And just how are you going to do that?' Paul asked. It was a civil matter he told him, nothing to do with the Army. It was up to Brenda to decide what to do, if she wanted to report it. In most cases the girls didn't. What was the point? It would only make things worse for them and their families.

'I can't sit around and do nothing.'

'Mate, you need to get a grip. If you turn up there, do you really think it will calm the neighbours?'

———

His CO told him to stop acting like a love-struck idiot.

'Get your anger under control. You're an officer with responsibilities. Tensions on the streets are running high enough without you wading in like a total dick.' He gave him a long reminder of current hostilities – the bombings and shootings, the recent killing of one of their own. The young soldier had been separated from his patrol and mistakenly left behind. Provo gunmen had shot him dead. Lessons needed to be learnt from that. 'You're not to go anywhere near her. Have I made myself clear?'

He had. Perfectly clear. He was to do what he was told and follow the rules.

Screw the rules.

Andy went straight to the pay phones the lads used to

make their calls to their loved ones back in England. As he dialled Brenda's number his mind drifted to the first time Brenda had told him she loved him. Lying next to him, her head nestled in his arm, she made it sound like the most natural thing in the world. They had been going out for a month. Andy laughed. 'We hardly know each other.'

'I mean it,' she said, without any embarrassment.

At the time he didn't feel the same way. Brenda was a beautiful girl and he enjoyed being with her, but there was nothing more to it. Andy would return to England on leave and that would be the last he would see of her. At least that was the plan. He'd told her he'd get in touch when his leave was over. She believed him even if he didn't believe it himself. Then he found himself in Belfast, back on tour, seeking her out. She'd been so openly happy to see him, it was infectious.

'I missed you,' she said, planting a kiss squarely on his lips.

'Me too,' he told her, taken aback by how much he meant it. Before long he couldn't imagine his life without her.

The phone rang for a long time before a girl answered it. 'Is Brenda there?' he asked.

'She's in her room.'

'Could I speak to her? Tell her it's Andy.'

'You've got a nerve phonin' here,' she said. There was no offer to go and get Brenda.

Andy had primed himself to deal with the mum and dad. From the way Brenda spoke of them, her parents sounded like reasonable people. The sort he could at least have a sensible conversation with. This had to be the younger sister,

Clare, the soldier-hater and she, on the other hand, was being obstructive.

'Have you any idea what we've been goin' through?'

'I know about the tar and feathering, yes.'

'And the rest!'

'What do you mean?' he asked. 'Has something else happened?'

'Stay away from her. You'll only make things worse.'

'I need to talk to her,' he said, struggling to keep his temper in check. 'I've asked you once already. Now would you please just go and get your sister.' He immediately regretted the insistence in his voice.

'Who do you think you are, givin' *me* orders? I don't have to take your shit, you know.'

Andy tried to back-track. He told her he was sorry for being short with her.

'Save your breath,' she said. 'She wants nothin' to do with you.'

'Did she say that?'

'Do you want to get her killed the next time? Leave her alone. You're the last thing she needs in her life. And you see if you phone here again, I'll report you for harassment.'

'Tell her–'

She set the phone down.

TWENTY-NINE

Brenda could still hear the sickening thud of fists slamming into her dad's body. He wouldn't give in, her mum said, kept pulling himself back on to his feet. So they hit him harder. In the end, they clubbed him until he lost consciousness.

'Is he ... alright?' asked Hazel.

'Yes, but they gave him a right hidin'.' Brenda took a sip of tea. 'Fuck. I forgot. Her bottom lip stung like hell.

Hazel winced. 'What about you?'

'I'm ok now.'

'Really?'

Brenda squirmed under the concerned gaze of her friend. 'No,' she said in a quiet voice. She ran a hand over her shorn head. 'Looks terrible, doesn't it?'

'You know,' said Hazel, checking the back and sides of Brenda's hair, 'it's not as bad as you think.'

Brenda rolled her eyes.

'Just a wee bit of length on it,' Hazel held her index

finger and thumb to indicate an inch of growth, 'will make all the difference. It'll grow in no time.'

Brenda snorted.

'Honestly, it will.'

'Wise up, Hazel. I look like one of those mental cases they lock away in Purdysburn.' Brenda pulled a face. 'Mind you, if I have to spend any more time in this house, I'll go mad myself.'

The problem was that they were all cooped up in the house together. Her dad was off work and trying not to get under her mum's feet. Her mum was cleaning obsessively. 'Lift,' she'd bark as she shoved the hoover under her husband's legs. 'Put a coaster under that, Jimmy,' she'd scold if he dared set his cup down on the freshly polished table. 'You'll leave a ring on it.'

Clare was doing her best to freeze Brenda out. She'd leave the room the moment Brenda walked into it. If she brushed against her in the hallway, she'd stiffen as if the slightest touch would contaminate her.

Brenda smiled at her friend. 'You shouldn't have come here, but I'm glad you did.'

'I was shittin' bricks in case I missed my stop.'

Brenda had told her which bus to take from the city centre. She was to watch out for the primary school, get off there and she'd be almost at her house.

'Everyone was eyein' me up and down,' said Hazel.

'You're imaginin' it.'

'No, I'm not. I felt like the only vampire in daylight. I didn't know what to think when the woman in front of me made the sign of the cross. Then everybody on the bus did the same thing.'

'You must have passed a chapel.'

'I know now. Thanks for the warning, by the way. I ended up copying them, but I might have got it the wrong way round.'

Brenda laughed. 'You do realise you could have burst into flames?'

'It's alright for you to laugh. You weren't the one sitting with a carrier bag from the butcher's on the Ormeau Road.'

Brenda glanced down at the carrier bag by Hazel's feet.

'I wanted to bring something to cheer you up.'

'Meat?'

'No! Magazines and chocolates. I was in a hurry to get out of the house. I lifted the first bag I could find.' Hazel reached into the bag and pulled out a box of Milk Tray. 'Fancy one?'

'I'm alright, thanks.'

'Mind if I...?'

'Go ahead.'

Hazel helped herself to a caramel square. 'What will you do about university?'

'I've spoken to the course tutor. I told him I needed a few weeks off for personal reasons.'

'What did he say?'

'That it was ok, but he still wants to see me to have a chat.'

'That's good.'

'No, it's not. How can I show my face lookin' like this?'

'Maybe if you explained what happened...'

'No! I'm not tellin' him my business.'

Hazel raised her hands. 'Ok, ok.'

Brenda went to the sideboard and picked up a letter.

'Here.' She stuffed it into Hazel's hands, 'This came the other night.' Special delivery.'

'What is it?'

'Read it.'

It had been pitch-black outside when a plain brown envelope was pushed through the letterbox. Brenda heard the shuffling of footsteps as she went to the door to pick it up. Inside were two typewritten sheets of paper. The letter itemised the reasons for carrying out her punishment.

'A warning?'

'Yeah.'

'It says here you're not to *fraternise with the enemy.* Fraternise?'

'I know,' said Brenda. 'They make it sound like I'm doin' it with my brother.'

Hazel looked over at Brenda. 'If you had one, that is.'

The letter read like a final demand from the electricity company. But its cold formality didn't cancel out Brenda's feelings for Andy. She couldn't control her love for him like an on/off switch.

'*More severely dealt with*?'

'Yeah, if I ignore the warning.'

'Who knew those wee shites paid enough attention in English classes to produce something so correct?' Hazel handed the letter back. 'Seriously though, Brenda, what are you goin' to do?'

Brenda gave a long sigh. 'I don't know.'

'What does Andy say?'

'I haven't heard from him.'

'Nothing? But it's been over a week.'

'I *know*,' snapped Brenda. She could deal with the threats.

She could handle the tensions in the house – just about. What she couldn't handle was Andy's silence.

Hazel was all for confronting him on Brenda's behalf.

'How are you goin' to do that?' Brenda asked her.

'You know where he's based, don't you?'

'Yes, sort of.'

'Well, I'm goin' down there,' fumed Hazel, 'to give him a piece of my mind.'

Brenda was sure she would, if Brenda wanted her to. 'I don't think so. You're meant to be a peacemaker, remember?'

'Bollocks to that.' Hazel narrowed her eyes. 'Men can be right shites at times and they need to be told so.'

It was Brenda's dad who suggested she should go away for a while. Just until things settled down, he said. At first, Brenda wouldn't hear of it. She wasn't about to slink off with her tail between her legs. Yet the longer the threats continued the more she'd come round to the idea. If this was to be the way of things, it would be better if she wasn't there.

In the days following the tar and feathering, her dad been a raging storm. Brenda had dreaded what he might do, but he'd battened down his fury – he still had to work and live among these people. Her mum had been outraged when Brenda had been singled out for punishment. How dare they make a spectacle of her daughter! She was full of fighting spirit when the first hate mail arrived. 'When I find out who it is, I'll tell them to their face what I think of them.' But her mum's bluster waned as the intimidation intensified. When she found herself spurned by the people she'd previously considered friends, she began to spend more time in the house. She stopped seeking out company. More and more she relied on Clare to run errands for her, much to Clare's annoyance.

Clare being Clare, had made her feelings known. Yesterday she'd arrived home in a thunderous mood, laden with grocery bags. She'd scarcely uttered a word to Brenda as she unpacked the food.

'Do you want a hand?' Brenda offered.

She got no response. Clare opened and slammed shut the fridge door. A bag of potatoes was hurled on to the larder floor. Jars clinked ominously as they were jammed into cupboards.

'Oh, for pity's sake,' said Mrs MacRae, 'there's no need for all that bangin' and clatterin'.'

Clare upended the contents of a bag. A bottle of brown sauce rolled across the work top and smashed on the kitchen floor. She turned to Brenda. 'There you go. It's all yours.'

'What the–? Come back here, you,' yelled Mrs MacRae but Clare was already out the door.

If Brenda wasn't around maybe her mum's life might return to normal too.

Hazel helped herself to another chocolate.

'I might go to Harris,' said Brenda.

'*What?*' Hazel dropped her chocolate on the floor.

'My dad says I could stay with my nan.'

'Oh, Brenda, no. Don't hide yourself away. That would be givin' into them. And don't throw in your studies.'

'That's easy for you to say, Hazel. It's not your family's lives bein' made a misery.'

'At least go to the meeting with your tutor,' pleaded Hazel.

'That old git? Only if you come with me.'

'Deal.'

Together they phoned the administration building to book an appointment. What did Brenda wish to discuss with Professor Kerr, asked the enquiring voice on the other end of the line. None of her business whispered Hazel. Brenda gave Hazel a dig in the arm. 'It's personal,' she replied. Professor Kerr was a busy man, explained the administrator. The soonest he could see her was next Wednesday. A half-hour slot in the afternoon. Would that do? Brenda looked to Hazel. She nodded. 'Yes, that's great. Thanks.'

'Good,' said Hazel as Brenda set the phone down. 'At least that's sorted.'

They chatted for a while longer until Hazel said she needed to go. She wanted to make her trip back while it was still light.

Brenda hugged her. 'Thanks for comin'.'

'No bother. Take care of yourself and I'll see you next week.'

'Yeah.'

Hazel gave Brenda a reassuring smile. 'Things will sort themselves out in a few weeks.'

Brenda wished she could share her optimism.

————

In the end her tutor was really nice about it all. He said she could hand in the coursework when she could. She'd be fine as long as she kept on top of her reading list. He continued to look concerned, but hadn't quizzed her any further. Brenda had seen a side of him she never knew existed.

'You see,' said Hazel. 'Aren't you glad you went to see him?'

'Yes,' she told her but that was before she bumped into a couple of lads on the steps of the Student's Union. Brenda didn't recognise them as students but they seemed to know her.

'What are you doin' back here?' asked the one in the green anorak.

'What's it to do with you?' said Hazel.

'I'd shut that gob of yours if I were you.' He held a clenched fist close to Hazel's face. 'Or I'll shut it for you.'

'Leave her alone,' said Brenda.

The lad in the anorak lowered his fist. 'You wanna pick your friends a bit more carefully, Hazel.'

'How do you know my name?'

'Come on,' said Brenda, tugging at her friend's sleeve. She was shaking as she made the call to her dad. 'Can you please come and pick me up?'

———

They arrived back to an empty house. Her mum had been coaxed into an afternoon's shopping in the city centre with Clare.

'It'll do her good,' said her dad, 'to get away from this house and this street for a while.'

'This country more like.'

He gave Brenda a searching look. 'What happened today?'

'It doesn't matter. It was a mistake to think I could go back to university.'

'I thought you said...'

'Forget it, Dad. I don't want to go back now.'

He didn't press her.

They were drinking the tea he'd made them when he raised the subject of Andy and his apparent indifference to her. 'If it was my girlfriend who'd been attacked, nothin' would keep me from her.'

Brenda smiled. 'I don't doubt that for a second.'

Her dad shook his head. 'I just don't get it.'

'Maybe Clare's right. He's done a runner. As simple as that.'

'Never mind what Clare says. Is that what *you* think?'

'No,' said Brenda. Her shoulders sagged. 'I don't know any more.'

'Can't you call him? At least you'd know, once and for all, where you stand.'

'I don't have his number. Andy always phoned me. That was the arrangement.'

He didn't need to comment. Even to her own ears Brenda's words sounded ridiculous. Yet it was true. Brenda had always been the one waiting for the call. At the time she hadn't given it much thought. She'd been so caught up in the excitement of going out with him. Was it his way of keeping her at arm's length? 'You know, when I think about it, Dad, I'm not sure I really know him.'

'I wouldn't get too hung up on it. Look at all the years I've been with your mother and still the woman manages to confound me.'

'That's called keepin' you on your toes.'

'Aye well, it works.'

'What I mean is, when you first start goin' out with someone...'

Her dad began to laugh. 'Now you're testin' my memory.' His laughter faded as he took in the serious expression on Brenda's face.

'You want to know about their family, their home, things like that, not because you're nosy but because you're interested in them.' Brenda paused. 'Andy never wanted to discuss personal things. I had to prise it out of him.'

'People don't always want to talk about their past. Your mum never did.'

'She's good at that, the not talkin' thing.'

Brenda was finding it impossible to communicate with her mum these days. A shutter had been pulled down and any mention of Andy's name was met with a stony face.

'All this has been very hard on your mum.'

'Not just her.'

'You know, your mum's childhood wasn't a happy one.'

'What's that got to do with anything?'

'Her father had a drink problem. Turned nasty when he'd had a few too many.'

This was news to Brenda. The only mention her mum made of her dad was to say he hadn't coped very well after her mother's death.

'She was only little when her mum died. Things got worse at home,' he said. 'She was taken in by relatives living near here. It was only when she came to Belfast she felt safe.'

Brenda laughed at the irony.

'I know,' said her dad. 'Hard to believe. But she said her life began when she moved to Belfast.'

Her mum had always followed the same routine week in,

week out. Meeting the same group of friends she'd known for years. To Brenda she'd seemed stuck in her ways. Now she understood why. She felt bad for destroying the bonds it had taken her mum a lifetime to build. And for what? A man Brenda loved who didn't appear to love her back?

She turned to her dad. 'You think I've been taken for a fool, don't you?'

'It's not for me to say.'

'You do, don't you?'

Her dad let out a deep sigh. 'If you want my honest opinion – yes.'

Brenda gave a thin smile.

'Then again,' he said. 'What do I know?'

'The thing is I really believed he was interested. More than that. I thought...'

Brenda's dad put his arm around her shoulder. 'I know, love, but could it ever have worked?'

Maybe. She'd wanted it to. Still did. But what chance was there of that now?'

THIRTY

The large suitcase had only ever travelled to the Antrim coast and back. This would be its first trip overseas. Brenda sneezed as she wiped the powdery film of dust off with her sleeve. Too big for one person but it would have to do.

The same frayed blue canvas suitcase had served all their family holidays over the years. Her mother would pack it neatly with clothes for four. Then her dad would load it on to the roof rack, cover it with tarpaulin and secure it with ropes.

Brenda recalled one family trip in particular to Portrush. It was the first time she was to stay in a caravan and she couldn't wait to get there. They'd only gone a few streets when the rope holding the tarpaulin cover worked loose. The suitcase landed with a thud in the road. A Ford Cortina swerved and narrowly missed it. Amid the blaring of horns, mumbled curses from her dad and much rolling of eyes from her mum, it was eventually restored to its place on the roof of the car.

It rained every day. Most of the holiday snaps were of her

and Clare with the hoods of their anoraks up – sitting on the beach, at the amusement arcade or eating ice cream on the harbour wall. Long afternoons had been spent inside the caravan, playing cards, as they waited for the sun to break through the clouds. At night Brenda lay on her bunk bed and listened to the torrential rain as it beat, loud as pebbles, on the metal roof.

On one of the few sunny days, she'd seen eels, dozens of them, swimming along the sluices of the harbour walls. Horrible grey snake-like fish that slithered through the dark water. At first, she hadn't spotted them. Then she caught a rippling movement. It was only when she peered closer that she realised the water was thick with them. Her dad grabbed her ankle and she almost fell into the harbour waters with the fright of it. He said they'd buy some and try them for tea.

That night, when her mum served up potted herring and mashed potatoes, Brenda had eyed the grey-white fish, soaked in vinegar and rolled into a parcel, with suspicion. She'd touched none of it.

'Now see what you've done. You've turned the child's stomach with all that talk of frying eels.'

Brenda had nightmares about eels for the rest of the holiday. She imagined them slithering out of the sluices, wriggling their way across the caravan site and into her bunk, coiling about her waist and chest and squeezing until she could no longer take a breath.

She stared at the case lying open on her bed and wondered what to put in it. She'd asked her mum what the weather was like in Harris at this time of year.

'Fierce altogether,' was how she'd described it. 'Make

sure you take a proper coat with you, not that flimsy thing you wear at the moment.'

'Windy,' was all her dad said.

Brenda searched her wardrobe for anything that might accommodate fierce and windy – her warmest jumpers, woollen tights, thick cords. What about shoes? She tossed her only pair of flats into the suitcase. They'd do.

She pulled a stack of books from under her dressing table and selected three from the pile. They were placed in the suit-case, along with a thick lever-arch file full of lecture notes. She picked the case up. Too heavy. She took them out again. There was no point in taking them anyway. This year was written off.

When her dad had suggested Brenda could go to Harris, her mum had been quick to agree. Too quick, considering she'd only ever had bad things to say about the place. Now it was different. It wasn't a lonely spot, it was a *quiet* one. It wasn't bleak, it was *rugged*. It wasn't backward, it was *quaint*. Her mum's change of heart was unconvincing. It was her dad's enduring love of the island that persuaded Brenda.

'The people there are decent,' he said. 'They look out for one another.'

Decent. She liked the sound of that.

———

She said her goodbyes to her mum and Clare in the house. Between the two of them they made her feel as if they couldn't wait to get her out the door. Not because of what they said. It was the lack of words that spoke volumes. A desultory 'Ok, bye,' from Clare as she stood by and watched

Brenda gather her things together. A brief hug from her mum: 'Have you got everything you need?' Nothing about letting her know when she arrived. 'Say hello to your nan for me,' as an afterthought. Brenda imagined she heard the small, terraced house sigh with relief the moment she was in the car.

Her dad drove her to the Belfast–Liverpool boat. For the whole journey he chattered non-stop. He passed comments on other drivers – 'Did you see the way he cut me up there?' – and on drinkers making their way home after an evening pint – 'Would you look at the state of that? These young lads, staggerin' about. Making fools of themselves. Can't hold their drink to save their lives.' Her dad was still commenting on everyone and everything when they pulled up at the docks. When the car stopped, so did her dad's chatter. A strong pine smell filled the car. It came from the green air freshener, shaped like a frog, that dangled from the side of the driver's mirror.

His hands gripped the steering wheel; he stared straight ahead. 'I'll miss you,' he said softly. Brenda glanced across to the driver's seat. His left eye was still puffy from the beating. The bruising had turned from blue-purple to a jaundiced yellow. The little muscle in her dad's jaw twitched, betraying emotion. He lifted her suitcase out of the boot, offered to carry it for her, but she wouldn't let him come with her to the terminal. She couldn't.

'See you soon, Dad,' was all she said.

As she walked away from him, she'd never felt more alone.

THIRTY-ONE

Isle of Harris

The murmur of voices grew louder. Brenda opened her eyes. The book she'd been reading had fallen to the floor and people now stretched across her, craning their necks for a better view of the land that slipped by her window. She was shocked at how close the craggy outline was to the boat.

Brenda had been travelling non-stop for two days, her world one of buses, trains and boats. This was the last leg of her journey aboard the Calmac ferry that would take her to her father's island. She gathered up her things and made her way on to the deck to take a closer look.

The ferry glided past one rocky outcrop after another, some softly rounded and capped with grass, others devoid of all vegetation. The tiny islands were a mottled camouflage of colours like the pattern of a soldier's combat jacket, every possible hue of sage and brown. Late-afternoon sun lit up hillsides and cast shadows on dips and hollows. Every now and again the boat sailed past harsh and jagged grey rocks that looked as if they had been planted vertically in the ocean by some giant hand, with the sole intention of gashing the side of any vessel that dared to venture too close.

Brenda's dad had spoken of ships sunk by such rocks, lives lost within sight of their loved ones waiting on the shoreline as vessels were pounded and torn apart by raging seas. She could see for herself how that might happen, but today the sea was calm. A soft breeze stroked her face. Grey-and-white seagulls wheeled overhead, occasionally hitching a lift on the gentle current.

The chain of tiny rocky islands, dotted either side of the boat, gradually linked together to form two long outstretched arms. As the boat steered a narrow course between them the land closed in on her. Brenda felt it could bring its arms together at any moment and give the boat a squeeze. She could see whitewashed houses now, dotting the mountain-side. A large, sombre grey building – a church – appeared to have been carved into the very rock it stood on.

Fáilte gu Tairbeart (Welcome to Tarbert) said the sign as Brenda stepped off the boat. She headed straight to the Tourist Office at the end of the street to ask about buses. A short, white-haired lady in horn-rimmed glasses was tidying up the various piles of photocopied pamphlets. Brenda asked for a timetable.

The old lady rested her glasses on top of her head. 'There aren't any,' she said. 'No need to waste more paper. Where are you headed, dear?'

Brenda pulled out the piece of paper with her grandmother's address and passed it to her.

The woman slipped her glasses back on to read it. 'North-ton? Oh yes, that's a lovely spot. You'll be needing the Leverburgh bus.' She turned to a well-worn map of the island stuck to the wall with yellowing Sellotape and showed Brenda the route the bus would take. 'Northton's here, just before you reach Leverburgh,' she said, pointing to the bottom left-hand corner of the map.

'What time does the next bus leave?' asked Brenda.

The woman looked at her watch. 'In five minutes. You'd best catch it. The next isn't due for hours.'

Brenda grabbed her suitcase and hurried to the exit.

'Just tell the driver where you're headed and he'll drop you off at the door,' the woman shouted after her.

The carnival-red-and-cream colours of the bus made it easy to find. It was almost full by the time Brenda clambered on board, hauling her suitcase after her and panting for breath. She pulled a fiver from her pocket and gave it to the driver.

'I'm afraid I can't take this,' he said.

'Why not?' Brenda looked at the note he'd just handed back.

'It's Irish money.'

Brenda pointed to the stamp. 'See here, where it says issued at Belfast. That means it's sterling.' She knew she was wasting her time; she'd encountered the same problem on the mainland. In the end she'd taken her dad's cash to the bank and changed it all for Scottish notes. This one had slipped through. Brenda dug into her handbag and pulled out her purse. By now she'd attracted the attention of everyone on board. Her cheeks smarted as she made her way to the only spare seats right at the back.

The bus wound its way up a steep hillside leading out of the port. Brenda looked down at the little boats moored in the harbour. Colourful buoys bobbed in the water far below. She bounced up and down on the back seat as the bus began to pick up speed on the narrow, bumpy road. All signs of life were soon left behind as the bus and the people on it were swallowed up by a stark mountain range.

There were no houses here. Not one. Weirder still, there were no trees either. Only rocks, blackened heather and even blacker pools of water that lay among the rocks. It looked like a torched planet. And yet there were sheep everywhere, on the slopes of the mountains and by the roadside. Some lay in the middle of the road, playing chicken with the bus as it hurtled round a blind bend. Spring lambs with black faces and hooves suckled on their mothers. She wondered how the sheep had got here and who looked after them. It wasn't at all how she remembered it. Her early childhood memories were of beaches and sand dunes.

On and on the bus jolted, passing mile after mile of barren, rocky landscape. Swirling clouds played peek-a-boo with the mountain tops, exposing then hiding their peaks. An enormous bird sat on a post by the roadside. As the bus passed, it ruffled its glossy ink-black feathers and extended its wings. Brenda shivered. She had never seen a bird as big or as menacing.

The bus continued through miles of the same terrain. Just as she was beginning to think the oppressiveness of the dark mountains would never end, the light began to change; it became brighter yet softer. Through the gap in the mountains she spotted the beach and the ocean beyond. Brenda felt a childlike urge to *ooh* and *aah*. As the bus rattled its way down to the shoreline the harsh mountains gave way to gently rolling green fields leading to miles of dazzling white sand and a turquoise sea. It was like one of those exotic places she'd seen advertised in the travel agent's window. Brenda's spirits lifted. She gave a little smile.

The bus finally emerged into the vast openness of the coastline. It stopped at Seilebost to let some passengers off. To her right was a derelict stone house; only the gables remained standing. Abandoned farm machinery lay rusting in the front garden. Other newer, rendered houses had been built close by, leaving the old one to crumble. At least there was some sign of life.

'There's nothing grand here,' her nan had warned, 'but yer welcome to stay as long as ye like.'

Her journey ended outside a cottage overlooking a small cove. It was the same cottage Brenda had seen in the sepia-coloured, dog-eared photographs at home. A welcoming curl of smoke drifted up from the chimney. Her grandmother stood by the front door. She was older than in the photographs but still wore a pinny. She watched as Brenda stepped down from the bus and made her way up the slippery stone path. Then she opened her arms in a welcoming embrace.

Brenda was led through to the living room where a crackling fire gave off a wonderful peat-reek aroma. Her grandmother took a seat on the sofa and beckoned for her to join her. Her hair was white now, not pewter. She was still slim and, when she sat, it was with a ramrod back.

'How was yer trip?'

'Alright thanks, but I don't want to see another ferry for a while.'

'No, I'm sure, but yer here now, that's the main thing. How's everyone at home? I trust they're keeping well?'

'They're fine.'

'And what about yerself?' Brenda's grandmother gave her an appraising look. 'I understand you've had a rough time of things lately.'

Brenda sighed. Here, in the quiet setting of her grand-mother's house, riot-torn Belfast seemed a million miles away. 'Do you mind if we don't talk about that right now?'

'That's alright, dear.' Her nan stood up. 'You can tell me later. You'll be wanting yer room first, I expect.'

Brenda took that as her cue to follow her.

The bedroom was sparsely decorated with a small wardrobe and a chest of drawers that also doubled as a bedside table. A plain wooden cross hung on the wall above the single bed. A quilt, with its kaleidoscope of heathery hues of pinks and purples, provided the only splash of colour. Everywhere smelled of polished wood.

'I've cleared some space in the wardrobe. Let me know if you need any more hangers.' The wooden floorboards creaked as her nan crossed the room. 'I'll leave you to unpack.'

The wardrobe's metal key was stiff in the lock. Brenda needed both hands to twist it. Her nan had pushed a couple of tweed skirt suits and a crisp cotton blouse to one side. The blouse was so heavily starched Brenda was sure it would support its own form if she stood it on the floor. At the bottom of the wardrobe sat a pair of brown brogues. Beside them were a couple of woollen shawls, still in their cello-phane packaging. Brenda spotted an Anderson and McAuley label on one. A Christmas present from her parents? There were three empty wire hangers in total and one plastic skirt holder. They soon sagged under the collective weight of Brenda's jeans, cords, shirts, cardigans and coat.

The chest of drawers was full of freshly pressed bed linen. Only the top drawer was empty, apart from a little, midnight-blue, leather-bound bible. The book was pristine, its parchment-thin pages edged in gold leaf. Brenda took it out and turned the cover. James MacRae, 1938, read the inscription. It was funny to see her dad's name written down like this.

All the first-born males in his family were christened James. Her dad had always been proud of the name and that it had been handed on like a baton, from generation to generation. Yet to everyone back in Belfast he was known as 'Jimmy'.

He'd given up trying to correct people years ago. Only his parents still called him James. And Brenda's mum. But that was usually in the middle of an argument when she wanted to emphasise a point. It was weird how she'd suddenly become all formal and correct when she was riled.

Brenda wondered if the book always stayed in this drawer or if her nan had deliberately put it there. Maybe she thought she would appreciate having something that once belonged to her dad. Or (Brenda had a moment of panic) that she might actually read it. There was as much chance of that happening as Ian Paisley inviting the Pope round for tea. She caressed the cover of the bible before placing it back in the drawer. In a strange way, it did bring her some comfort. She liked that it connected her to her dad's past.

From the window she looked out at her nan's neat flowerbeds, the vegetable patch and whitewashed fence. By contrast, next-door's front garden was full of what Brenda could only describe as 'toot' – useless bits of rusting machinery, an old washing machine, a jerry can, empty plant pots and battered plastic containers. In front of her lay a golden beach and open water.

Delicious smells had begun to waft up from the kitchen. Brenda's growling stomach reminded her she hadn't eaten. She slid her empty suitcase under the bed made her way downstairs.

'Sit yerself down,' said her nan.

Brenda took a chair next to her grandfather as her nan dished up generous ladles of lamb stew into bowls. The dark meat broke apart with the lightest touch of Brenda's spoon.

'Good?'

'Mmm ... lovely. Even nicer than Mum's.'

Her nan gave a little smile. 'Harris lamb is hard to beat.'

For a while they concentrated on the food. Her nan was the first to speak again.

'It's good to have some young company. I get tired lookin' at that auld face all the time.' She nodded in the direction of Brenda's grandfather.

He turned round to check if there was anyone standing behind him. 'I take it it's me yer referring to?' he said, breaking into a crooked smile.

His wife tutted. 'Ye were just a bairn the last time we saw ye. Look at ye now. You've turned into a fine young woman.'

'Aye, she has that,' said her grandfather. 'A little peaky, mind. We'll have to put some colour back in those cheeks.' He suggested a few long walks, helping out in the garden.

Gardening? Brenda didn't know one end of a spade from another. 'I understand things are pretty bad over there.'

'Well...' What could she tell him? That people relied on a form of social Russian roulette when deciding where to go or what to do – What are my chances of getting caught up in any trouble today? That they clung to their everyday routine like a life raft? 'Yes, it's bad.'

'We heard about yer own bit of bother.'

Brenda glanced at her nan.

'Yer father told us all about it.'

Brenda's face grew warm. How much did they know?

'I'm surprised he didn't come with ye,' said her nan. 'It's not like him to leave his daughter to make a trip like that by herself.'

'He didn't want to leave Mum on her own.'

'Yes, I can well believe that.'

Brenda detected a note of censure in her nan's voice. 'And Clare too,' she added. 'The Provos sent letters; they phoned the house threatenin' all sorts of things. He had to stay. He was worried for both of them.' Her dad had said not to mention anything about his injuries, not to worry them unduly, but it felt wrong to keep it from them. 'It wasn't just that,' she said. 'They ... beat him up.'

Her nan's hand flew to her mouth. 'They hurt him?'

Her grandparents' anxious faces stared back at her. 'Nothin' broken,' she said, 'but his ... his face still looks a mess. He didn't want you to see him like that.'

'I'll call him first thing tomorrow,' said her nan. 'I knew he was holding something back.' She got up to wash the dishes; her husband was told to take himself into the living room. Brenda remained at the table, unsure if she should join him or stay where she was. Why had she come here? It was all a big mistake.

Halfway through rinsing out a pot her nan stopped. 'Well,' she said, holding a tea towel in her hand, 'are ye going to dry these or not?' She handed her a plate. 'Tell me, Brenda, this soldier ye were seeing…'

'Andy.'

'What does yer father think about ye going out with him?'

'Dad? He, he ... understands. He says it's up to me who I choose to see. He just wishes I'd told him.'

'Why didn't you?'

'I don't know. I was scared. You can't imagine what it's like in Belfast at the moment. Dad might have been ok with it, but there are plenty who aren't. I suppose I thought, by not tellin' him, I'd protect him ... all of them ... in some way. Stupid, huh?'

'Where is Andy now?'

'He's still in Bel–' Brenda thought for a moment. 'I don't know.'

By the time the dishes were done she had told her everything. About the peace movement, Andy, her punishment, the tensions at home, what drove her to leave. Her nan had said nothing other than the odd 'I see'. It was this neutrality and her soothing presence that encouraged Brenda to reveal more and more of her story. As she'd filled her nan in on what happened to her, her situation had sounded ridiculous, the place she called home chaotic, ugly and spiteful.

Brenda was exhausted when she climbed the stairs for bed. She wasn't sure where she stood with her grandparents or if they even liked her. She had left them to take it all in. These sorts of things didn't happen in her grandparents' world.

It was so dark here and eerily quiet. It scared her. Brenda left the curtains open to let some light in but all she could make out was a sliver of moon and a black sky. It took her a while to focus her eyes and realise the sky was saturated with stars.

THIRTY-TWO

Belfast

With her sister gone, the phone calls stopped. Her mum was still jittery but she could at least watch the television without interruption. Tonight's programme seemed to take her mind off things. Clare was glad to see her so engrossed in it. She, on the other hand, was struggling to keep her eyes open. The combined heat of the fire and the drone of the narrator's voice had made her sleepy.

She jumped as the key turned in the front door. There was a careful scraping of feet on the mat then her dad appeared in the living room. Clare looked up and smiled. Her smile soon vanished as she caught sight of his face. She could tell that he knew.

Her mum tried to peer round her hulk of a husband. 'I can't see through you, you know.' She shooed him away with her hand.

Mr MacRae took his seat by the fire and kicked off his

shoes. He wiggled his toes in front of the flames and sighed. 'Is that all that's on?'

'Uh huh.' Clare's mum didn't take her eyes off the screen.

He picked up the *TV Times* from the magazine rack by the side of the chair and studied the programme listings. 'There has to be somethin' better than this.'

'Sshh, Jimmy. I'm tryin' to listen.'

Clare stared at the screen, occasionally glancing at her dad from the corner of her eye. She knew he wasn't reading anything; he was biding his time. Then again, maybe she'd misread the look on his face and her own guilt had made her assume the worst. She sneaked another look at him. No, she hadn't imagined it.

The sombre voice of the narrator was replaced by the saccharine sound of the latest advertising jingle.

'How come you're back so early?'

'Oh, I'm allowed to speak now, am I?'

Mrs MacRae squinted in the direction of her husband. 'What's that on your shirt?'

He rubbed his finger over the large stain his wife had spotted. 'Frying fat.'

'How did you get that all down you?'

He was about to answer her when the commercial break ended. Clare's mum turned back to the television.

The documentary eventually reached its shocking conclusion.

'Well, that was cheery,' said Mr MacRae, setting the magazine to one side.

Clare's mum dabbed her eyes with a tissue. 'It just goes to show – there's always someone worse off than yourself.'

'Livin' here at the moment isn't exactly a picnic.'

'I know, Jimmy, but at least we're not starvin'.'

'That's true. We might be killin' one another but, thank the Lord, it's on a full stomach.'

Clare's mum rolled her eyes. 'You can't take anything seriously, can you?'

'I wouldn't say that.' He turned his gaze on Clare. 'There are some things I take very seriously.'

Clare felt her stomach knot.

'There was a lot of talk flyin' about the pub tonight.'

'What sort of talk, Jimmy?'

'Stuff I wish I hadn't heard.'

Clare got up from the sofa. 'Anyone fancy a cup of tea? Dad? Mum?'

'Jesus, wonders will never cease. I can't remember the last time you offered. Yes, I'll have one.'

Clare turned to her dad. 'What about you?'

'I think I will, thanks.'

From the kitchen she could hear her parents' voices, low, as they talked. Clare switched the kettle off and listened. All she could make out were the bongs that signalled the headlines on the ten o'clock news. Her dad said something. Her mum laughed. That was a good sign, wasn't it? She took the supper tray into the living room and offered round some biscuits. Her mum's hand hovered over the plate until it landed on a Bourbon Cream.

Her dad waved the plate away. 'Sit down, Clare. There's somethin' I need to ask you and I want a straight answer.'

Clare's mum was alerted by the sudden change in tone. 'Sounds like you're in trouble,' she said, half-joking.

Clare froze in her tracks.

'I said sit down, Clare.' Her dad's voice was calm but there was an edge to it.

Her mum set her half-eaten biscuit on her saucer. 'Jimmy?'

Clare returned to her seat on the sofa and waited.

At first, he said nothing. Clare had expected an outburst of anger; she was ready for it. This prolonged silence was much worse.

Mrs MacRae looked from daughter to husband. 'Jimmy? Clare? What's all this about?'

'Go on, Clare. Explain to your mother.'

'It's not how you think, Dad. I didn't deliberately...'

'That's not the way McManus tells it.'

Clare's mum set her cup and saucer on the table with a thump. 'Would one of the pair of you tell me what's goin' on here?'

'She's the one who tipped the Provos off.'

'What are you talkin' about?'

'It was her all along. *She* told them Brenda was goin' out with a soldier.'

Mrs MacRae wheeled round to confront her daughter. 'Is this true?'

'I didn't think they'd go as far as they did.'

'You knew what they were plannin' to do?'

'Yes. I mean *no*! Peter said they'd just–'

Mrs MacRae's eyes shot up at the mention of Peter's name. 'When were you talkin' to him? Sure he's in prison.'

Brenda's dad switched the television off. He turned to face Clare. 'Are you goin' to tell her, or will I?'

216

There was a hush in the room.

'Tell her!'

'Alright, alright, so I've been to see him. But you have to believe me ... I didn't know he ... *they* ... were goin' to do *that* to her.'

'What exactly did you say to Peter?' asked her mum.

'There was this one night ... we were in the social club. I'd had too much to drink. He'd been askin' a lot of questions about Brenda. I told him she'd met someone else. I said it to shut him up. He kept on and on at me, wanting to know more about him. I said he was good-lookin' ... if you're into squaddies. I didn't mean to, but it was too late to take it back.'

It had been Peter's idea to get 'the boys' to have a few words in her sister's ear and Clare went along with it. He'd seemed satisfied when she told him it appeared to have done the trick. He gave no hint of any sort of punishment to follow. It was only later, on her final

prison visit with him, that he told her they had always intended to make an example of Brenda. Clare grew hot with shame as she recalled their conversation.

'Oh, come on,' he'd said. 'What did you think we were goin' to do? Give her a little wrap on the knuckles? You know how it works.'

'I didn't think–'

'Yeah, keep tellin' yourself that.'

She was still telling herself that.

Clare looked up to find her dad watching the struggle with her conscience play out on her face.

'We're a family,' he said. 'When you betray your sister, you betray us all.'

'They were only supposed to warn her off. You know ... shake her up a bit.'

He took a long, searing look at her. 'I can't stay in this room,' he said. 'I don't trust what I'll do next.'

'Dad, wait! You don't understand. She shouldn't have gone out with him, not with a soldier ... not after...'

There was no point in trying to explain. Her dad's thoughts, as always, were with Brenda. He wasn't interested in hearing what his other daughter had to say. Not that Clare would ever speak of what happened the night she had been assaulted, least of all to her dad. It was too humiliating.

'Leave him be,' said her mum.

'But–'

'He's in no mood for excuses. And frankly, neither am I.'

———

It was her mum's anxious voice that woke Clare later that night. It wasn't the first time it had happened. Her mum had been having trouble sleeping for weeks, kept thinking she could hear noises downstairs. She'd shake Clare's dad awake and tell him to listen for strange sounds – scuffling, low voices, a door being prised open. Sometimes she insisted on him getting up to check it out and she'd follow behind him. This time there was real fear in her mum's voice.

'You better get down here!'

Clare leapt out of bed.

Her parents had just reached the bottom of the stairs when there was a loud crash of breaking glass. Brenda's dad flung the living-room door open. They saw the first billow of flame engulf the curtains. The smell was unmistakable.

'It's a petrol bomb!' yelled her mum.

Her dad ripped the curtains from the rail. Between the three of them they managed to beat and stamp the flames out before the fire had a chance to rip through the house. The curtains and carpet were ruined. So was the furniture nearest the window. Black soot covered the ceiling. Her dad held Clare's trembling mother as she took in the damage.

'We're lucky we weren't burnt alive!'

'It's alright, Bridie. No-one got hurt.'

'Look at the state of this place!' Her eyes lingered on each charred item in turn, then fixed on Clare. 'See what you've done! Your father warned you not to say anything about Brenda and that soldier of hers, didn't he?' Despair was written all over her face. 'Why did you defy him?'

'I've said I'm sorry. What more do you want from me?'

'I've heard all the apologies, but nothin' that's come out of that mouth of yours tonight explained *why.*'

'I told you. I had too much to drink. It just slipped out.'

'Drink might loosen someone's tongue, but it doesn't make them say or do things they aren't already thinking. I should know. I lived with a drunk for long enough.'

'I'm not like *him*,' said Clare, horrified at the comparison to her mum's father.

'Of course, my father had a mean streak in him long before the drink took a hold of him.'

Clare swallowed. 'Do you think I have a mean streak too?' She thought of the delicious thrill she'd felt when Peter first suggested putting the frighteners on Brenda. She had known it was wrong but the prospect of doing wrong excited her. Peter had been quick to spot that in her.

She'd been gutted when he told her not to visit him

anymore. Her family had shown their disloyalty and he couldn't be linked to that. At first, she thought he'd been coerced into saying it. Then there was a slow dawning. Disloyalty had nothing to do with. 'This is about you, isn't it? Your chance to get back at Brenda.' He wouldn't have it, called her stupid, but she knew she was right. 'You couldn't accept she left you for someone else.' That's when he told her to piss off. She hadn't seen him since.

'This might be my fault, Bridie. If I hadn't lost my temper...'

It took Mrs MacRae a moment to tune into what her husband was saying. 'Dear god.' Her voice dropped to a whisper. 'What have you done?'

'I was passin' the chip shop on my way home. McManus called out to me. Said he was sorry to hear about the unfortunate business with Brenda. He was goadin' me. We both knew he was responsible. Somethin' inside me snapped. I had to wipe that false smile off his face.'

'What have you done?' repeated Clare's mum.

'I decked him but not until I got the truth out of him first. It's surprisin' what a man will tell you when you're holdin' his hand over a deep fryer.'

'Are you crazy?'

'I couldn't help myself. I saw Brenda slumped at that lamp post, my daughter beaten and humiliated. I wanted to hurt him, *really* hurt him.'

'And did you?' asked Clare.

He didn't answer her. Instead he put his arms around her and her mum and pulled them close. 'If anything had happened to either of you tonight, I'd never have forgiven myself.'

They remained in the living room all night, afraid that the people who'd done it would return.

'I won't let them drive me out,' insisted her mum. 'Do you hear me, Jimmy? I won't!'

The next morning her dad boarded up the broken window. He told them they had no choice but to leave.

THIRTY-THREE

ndy was one of four from his regiment who had been volunteered to attend the community relations meeting. The idea was to discuss ways they could 'positively engage' with local people. All over a cosy chat, a cup of tea and a sandwich.

'You'll be expected to show your face for a couple of hours,' said Major Warrington. Richard 'Dickie' Warrington was the senior officer who had drawn the short straw of civic duty that evening. 'At all times be respectful and polite.' He surveyed the men in front of him. 'And at least *try* to look interested.'

They were only a quarter of an hour into the informal get together when the young soldier in front of Andy showed signs of boredom. 'Do we seriously have to listen to this lot rabbit on?' he muttered.

'I'd pay attention if I were you,' said Andy.

The young soldier looked startled.

'These women could teach you a thing or two.'

Andy surveyed the middle-aged matrons with their

sensible cardigans and roller-set hair – the Women Together delegation he was here to meet. He could see why the young soldier had been so ready to dismiss them. It was as if they were listening to their mam dishing out advice on the best way to deal with an armed attacker.

But Andy was well aware that the women had a good grasp of both military and paramilitary goals. They understood how each side operated, their tactics, their frustrations. They also witnessed the impact all this had on the lives of ordinary people. Worth talking to. In more ways than one. Andy had spent the last few weeks in torment, unable to see Brenda. He didn't expect her to be among these women but they might have news of her.

From the far side of the room he could hear the major's clear, confident voice.

'I do understand your concerns. The recent incident was ... most regrettable but, in times of conflict, there is always a chance an innocent civilian will get hurt.'

'Innocent child.'

'Sorry?'

'The civilian you're talkin' about was a 10-year-old child.'

'Yes, yes indeed. Most regrettable.'

Andy looked over to see who was taking the major to task in such a strident fashion. The young, scowling face looked familiar. Hazel? He couldn't believe his luck. If he could just nab her now while he had the chance. This tea-and-sandwiches nonsense was a preamble. They'd be sitting down soon to more serious discussions.

'Killed by a rubber bullet as he stood by his bedroom window.'

She's really getting stuck into old Dickie. Andy made his way across the room.

Major Warrington was trying to maintain his best 'taking on board your comments' expression. 'That's why we rely on your help,' he said, 'to keep civilians off the street and away from trouble.'

'He wasn't out on the streets. He was in his own house.'

'I think what Hazel is trying to say,' said another woman, 'is that it's stirring up more anger, making ordinary people feel bitter.' She smiled at the major. 'You have a hard enough job, Richard, trying to win people over. Using rubber bullets doesn't help.'

'Hello again,' said Andy. He smiled at Hazel.

'Do you two know each other?' asked the major. He looked grateful for the interruption.

'Yes.'

'No,' said Hazel.

Major Warrington gave her a puzzled look.

'I mean yes ... sort of.'

He waited for Hazel to explain but all that followed was a strained silence.

'Richard,' said the other woman, steering him towards a different group, 'let me introduce you to Bridget. She's been doing some great work for us.'

'You look rough,' said Hazel.

'It's been a rough couple of weeks.'

'Poor you.'

Andy glanced over at the Major but, thankfully, his attention was now on his new acquaintance. 'How is she?'

'I take it you mean Brenda? Not great, if you really want to know.'

'I've been worried sick about her.'

Hazel raised an eyebrow. 'Have you? Well, you've a funny way of showin' it.'

'Come on, Hazel,' Andy gave an ingratiating smile, 'don't be like that.'

'How do you expect me to be?'

The young soldier Andy had spoken to earlier was now observing him with open curiosity.

Andy nodded towards a quieter part of the room. 'I wanted to see her,' he said, when he was sure they were out of earshot.

Hazel's face clouded. 'Don't give me that.'

'I was ordered to keep away, and I had other stuff to deal with.'

'Like what?'

'Personal stuff.'

Jenny had followed through with her threat of solicitors. She was pushing for custody of Stevie, no doubt with her mother's encouragement. And if her mother had anything to do with it, Andy wouldn't get a look in.

'I'm sure you could have done something.' Hazel's voice was sharp and accusing.

'What should I have done?' Andy snapped. 'Gone AWOL, bowled up to the house one Sunday afternoon and demanded to see her?'

'No, of course not.'

'What then? Sent her a bunch of flowers?'

'Now you're being ridiculous.'

'Sorry,' said Andy, reining in his irritation. It would get him nowhere with Hazel and, right now, he needed her on his side more than ever.

'It's Brenda you should be apologising to. She thinks you deserted her.'

Of course, he hadn't. Is that what Brenda thought – that he'd cut and run at the first real sign of trouble? Hazel obviously did.

'Do you know what they did to her?'

'Hazel, this isn't the place to–'

They had begun to attract more curious glances.

'They dragged her out of her own home. Hacked off her beautiful hair.'

'I know what happens when someone's tarred and feathered.'

'Do you know they beat her with clubs?'

'No.'

'She spent the whole night roped to a lamp post. They spat on her, called her all sorts of disgusting names, threatened her with rape. She was terrified.'

She might as well have skewered his guts. Andy had tried not to imagine any of it. It was the only way he could calm the rage inside. He didn't need Hazel conjuring up every last horrible detail. Not here. Not like this.

Hazel's voice grew quieter. 'Anyway, there's no point in you bowlin' up at the house. You'll not find her there.'

'What do you mean?'

'She's gone to Harris.'

'The place her dad comes from?'

'Uh huh.'

'But that's in the middle of nowhere. Brenda said so herself.'

Hazel began to walk away.

'Whoa, hang on a minute.' Andy stood in front of her,

pleading with his hands. 'You can't dump that news on me and go.'

Hazel stopped.

'We can't talk here,' he said. 'Meet me. He pressed a scrap of paper with his phone number into her hand. Take it, please.'

Hazel placed it in the pocket of her jeans. 'I'll think about it.'

The woman who had rescued Major Warrington had returned. 'Sorry to interrupt,' she said. 'They're about to start the meeting.' She led Hazel away.

Andy got the nod from Major Warrington that they should make their way there too.

For the duration of the meeting he followed little of what was discussed. All he could think of was Brenda. Why had she run off like that? He could have explained everything if she'd only waited. Every so often he glanced over at Hazel, trying to read her intentions. When she caught him looking, she dropped her gaze. On the few occasions their eyes did meet, hers were full of angry distrust.

Did others notice her hostility towards him? Did Major Warrington? Andy wanted to reach across and shake Hazel. That wouldn't have helped community relations but it would have made him feel better. Stupid girl – she'd got him all wrong. She had no idea what he was going through or how he felt about Brenda.

THIRTY-FOUR

Her mum said she could tell by the colour of a girl's skin: it took on a yellowish tinge. Brenda studied her face. She did look a bit sallow. Or perhaps it was the glow from the strip light above the mirror? No, she couldn't possibly be. She squeezed toothpaste on to her toothbrush. Oh god, what if she was? She attacked her teeth with the brush and spat out a mouthful of toothpaste and blood. Idiot. Idiot girl!

In Mrs Henderson's shop she'd served so many girls who'd found themselves in the same situation. Silly wee hussies, she'd called them. They couldn't see beyond the street they lived in, settling down, having kids – not always in that order. She'd sworn she wouldn't end up like them.

Brenda took another look in the mirror. Maybe she was just imagining the worst. She had none of the obvious symptoms. No throwing up in the morning, no tender breasts. But she was late. Brenda was never late. And she had a persistent feeling that something had changed. She couldn't put it into words. She just felt different somehow.

Her nan was serving up breakfast by the time she made her way downstairs. 'I hope yer ready for this.' She set a plate of bacon, eggs and pancakes in front of her.

Brenda didn't gag. Surely that was a good sign? She gave her nan a smile and tucked in.

———

The small grocery store in Leverburgh also served as a post office. It had a telephone too, something her grandparents' cottage didn't.

'I'll be with ye in a minute,' said the large woman behind the counter. She was rounding off a conversation with another customer: a ruddy-cheeked man with dirt-encrusted fingernails.

The inside of the shop was the size of her nan's front room. There was a long counter and some roughly hewn wooden shelves that held rows of canned food, sacks and cardboard boxes of various shapes and sizes. The contents of the boxes were listed on the outside with a black marker for easy identification. An antiquated fridge hummed in the corner.

The minute the woman promised stretched into several. Life on Harris, Brenda had discovered, had a pace all of its own: slow, stop, slow. She struggled to curb her impatience until, at last, the conversation reached its long drawn-out conclusion.

'Say hello to Janet and the little ones frae me.'

'Indeed I will.'

The storekeeper's full attention was now on Brenda. 'So, what can I get ye?'

Brenda rattled off her nan's list.

The woman knitted her brow. 'Sorry, dear. I didn't quite catch that.'

Yet again Brenda was talking too fast.

In conversations back home words tumbled like a fast-flowing mountain stream. Silences had to be filled. In Harris such gaps were an essential part of the conversation. They provided time to ponder.

It wasn't just the speed at which Brenda spoke that singled her out. The island accent was soft and rounded. Brenda's was as jagged as the outcrops the ferry had sailed so close to on her journey here. To Brenda's ear, the woman behind the counter trilled and Brenda cawed. She repeated her order, slower this time.

The woman eyed her up and down, making no effort to move. 'I'm thinking you must be Moira MacRae's grand-daughter?' she said after what seemed like an eternity.

'Yes.'

'I heard ye were visiting.' Still the woman didn't move from her spot behind the counter. 'How long are ye planning on staying?'

'I'm not sure.'

'No, of course not.'

It struck Brenda as a strange thing to say as if she knew the workings of Brenda's mind better than Brenda herself.

'I like the way you've done yer hair.'

'Erm, thanks.'

'Like that actress, the one in Peyton Place, married to Frank Sinatra. Now, what's her name?'

Mia Farrow?'

'That's the one.'

Was she taking the piss? This was no pixie cut she was modelling. With her hacked-off hair Brenda looked more like someone from Belsen than a Hollywood star.

The woman walked over to a large set of brass scales that sat on the far end of the counter. She lifted a bulging hessian sack from the shelf behind her. As she opened it up a puff of white flour escaped and settled in a fine ring on the counter top. She selected a couple of weights and placed them on one of the scales. Then she reached deep into the sack with a scoop and heaped its contents into the other scale. The woman closed one eye, added more flour, shook her head, took a little off. Then she tipped the flour into a brown paper bag and made her way back to Brenda.

'What made ye come to the island?' The woman stood weighing Brenda up with as much precision as she had measured out the flour.

So many questions. Brenda was beginning to wish she'd never come in. 'Visitin' my grandparents,' she said. The news was met with a nod of approval. 'And the place I was born.'

'Ah yes, indeed.' The woman counted out coins from a tin cash box. As she handed Brenda her change she added, 'I remember ye as a little girl.'

'Really?'

'Ye used to come in here with yer father to buy sweets. Dolly Mixtures were yer favourite.'

'I don't remember.'

'Aye well, it's been a long time. I'm Mrs McDonald, by the way.' She shook Brenda's hand. 'Welcome back, dear.' Mrs McDonald gave her a broad smile. 'I hope ye enjoy yer time with us.'

'Oh! Thank you.' The sudden warmth of the greeting took

Brenda by surprise. 'I like it here,' she mumbled. It feels peaceful and...' Her voice trailed away.

What was wrong with her? One friendly gesture and she'd almost gone to pieces, almost forgotten the real reason she'd come.

'One other thing, Mrs McDonald. I need to make a call home. My nan said I could use the telephone here?'

'Yes, of course. Help yerself.' She turned the phone to face Brenda. 'I'm just nipping into the back garden,' she said. 'I'll settle with ye when yer done.'

Brenda was alone in the shop. She placed her call to Hazel and hurriedly told her of her fears.

'Don't panic. I'm sure you're not.'

'Are you just sayin' that to make me feel better?'

'No, of course not. Why would I do that?'

A smile played at the corners of Brenda's mouth. 'Aye right enough.'

'I bet it's all the travellin' that's made you late. It's quite common, you know, for a woman to miss her period after a long flight.'

'That's a relief,' said Brenda. 'Except I haven't been on a flight, have I?'

'No but–'

'Where did you get that from anyway?'

'I read it in *Cosmopolitan*. Look, you know what I mean. You had a nightmare of a trip gettin' there and, what with all the stress you've been through, I'm not surprised your body clock's messed up.'

Hazel's theory sounded absurd but Brenda wanted to believe it. For a moment she almost succeeded until the panic took over. 'Oh Christ, what am I goin' to do? How will I let Andy know? What if he doesn't–?'

'Whoa! Slow down, Brenda. You're just guessin'. You don't know for sure.'

'You're right. I'm gettin' ahead of myself. Like you say, it's probably a false alarm.'

'I saw him a couple of nights ago.'

Brenda's stomach fluttered. 'Andy?'

'Yes.'

'Why didn't you tell me straight away?'

'I would have but you threw me with all this talk of being pregnant.'

Brenda listened excitedly as Hazel recounted their chance meeting – how, at first, she'd had a right go at him for leaving Brenda in the lurch, then he told her he'd been ordered to keep away.

'I knew he wouldn't have abandoned me like that, not if he could help it.'

'I dunno. I think there's more to it than that.'

She told her Andy was dead keen to meet up with her again so that he could 'explain everything' to her, whatever that meant. 'It's up to you, Brenda. If you want me to go, I will.'

'Yes, I do. And when you see Andy, tell him I–'

Mrs McDonald had reappeared with a wicker basket hooked over her arm. 'That's one beautiful mornin'. Even the chickens are in fine form.' She tilted the basket at Brenda. 'Tak a look.'

The basket was full of eggs – brown, white, speckled. The odd feather stuck to some of them.

'Can't get any fresher than that,' said Brenda.

'What?' It was Hazel on the other end of the line.

'Eggs.'

'Huh?'

'Mrs McDonald's brought in a basket of eggs. Her hens laid them fresh this mornin'.'

'Oh!' said Mrs McDonald. 'I didn't mean to interrupt yer chat.'

'You can't really talk, can you?' said Hazel.

'Uh huh, that's right.'

Hazel gave a frustrated sigh. 'I wanted to ask you how late you are. Ok, just say the number of weeks.'

'Four, maybe closer to five.'

'Oh.' When Hazel spoke again, she sounded less sure. 'Maybe you should go to the doctor just for ... you know ... peace of mind.'

'I was thinkin' the same thing,' said Brenda. There was a catch in her voice as she said her goodbyes. 'Speak to you soon.'

Mrs McDonald looked over. 'Is everything alright, dear?'

'Yes, fine.'

'Are you sure? Ye seem a bit upset.'

Brenda told her it was nothing to concern herself over. She was simply feeling a bit homesick. She left before she could question her further.

Outside was bright and sunny. Oystercatchers, with their black-and-white plumage, waded in the waters close to the shoreline. They stabbed at shells with their long orange-red bills. It was indeed a beautiful morning but it was lost on Brenda. An Atlantic seal popped its head above the waves and stared inquisitively at her. With its bright, intelligent eyes it seemed to sense her anxiety.

As she made her way back to the cottage, she thought on what Hazel had said. Brenda did need to see a doctor and soon. The problem was that Harris had only one and he was ancient. Doctor MacKay had delivered most of the children on the island, including Brenda's dad. He'd treated them for mumps and measles, patched them up after scrapes and tumbles, some more serious than others.

Her dad had told her of the time he'd been trapped under a capsized boat as a young boy. They'd hauled him from the icy waters, half frozen to death. The doctor turned him on his side and held him as he vomited up brine. When his insides had emptied, the doctor wrapped him in blankets, sat him upright and administered a generous slug of whisky from his hip flask, much to the disapproval of Brenda's nan.

'It's just a wee dram to warm his bones. It won't do him any harm.'

Her dad swore that was the point he became a whisky drinker. For all the years he lived in Belfast, he never once drank Irish whiskey; it had to be Scottish single malt.

It would be too embarrassing to go to her dad's old doctor but there was no-one else to see. Then again, Hazel could be right about Brenda's body clock being all up the shoot. Maybe she should leave it for another couple of weeks. She wouldn't want to go seeking medical advice only to find it was a false alarm. And if she was pregnant, leaving it for another couple of weeks wouldn't change anything. It wasn't as if the situation could be reversed, unless ... Brenda shook her head free of the thought. That was willing something bad to happen.

THIRTY-FIVE

He'd suggested they meet at Linda's, a coffee shop in Lisburn, a small town south of Belfast. The town was made up of predominantly loyalist Protestants. A safe choice and it wouldn't be busy at this time. At most there would be a few housewives rounding off their morning shopping trip with a hot drink, a slice of cake and gossip.

Andy stuck his head round the door but there was no sign of her. What if she didn't show? Then what would he do? A ginger-haired waitress tried to usher him to a table. He said he'd come back later.

Bollards blocked off both ends of the main street, turning it into a pedestrian-only zone. It was a safety precaution to stop cars, packed with explosives, being driven into the town centre and left outside shops. Through the large glass panes of the Woolworth's store front he could make out groups of young kids crowded around the Pick 'n' Mix section. They were stuffing selections of brightly coloured sweets into brown paper bags. Further down the street he saw the familiar green-and-white striped awning of Eason's, the newsagents. He popped in and bought a paper. The headline spoke of Vietnam. The last American troops were being pulled out after eight years of fighting. *Poor bastards*, he thought. *It must have seemed like it was never going to end.*

Andy returned to the coffee shop and found a quiet corner table. Behind the serving counter they were setting up the day's tempting hot food offer – Irish stew, vegetable soup, steak-and-mushroom pie. It was certainly a step up from Taff's cooking. He glanced towards the door and caught Hazel peering through the misted-up window. She stepped back when she realised he'd spotted her. A moment later she pushed the door open and strode in.

'Thanks for coming,' he said.

Hazel pulled out a wicker chair and sat down. 'I can't stay long.'

It was warm in the coffee shop but she kept her coat on. The ginger-haired waitress came to take their order. Andy asked Hazel if she wanted something to eat. She shook her head. The waitress hovered as they deliberated over their drinks.

'Talk about not giving you a chance to decide,' said Andy, with a bemused grin, as the waitress scurried back to the serving counter.

'You wanted to see me?'

He took in the pinched face, the stiffened body. This wasn't going to be easy. 'You really threw me the other night when you told me Brenda had gone.' Andy pulled a face. 'To Harris of all places.'

'I know. I couldn't believe it either,' she said, grimacing too. 'She's stayin' with her grandparents.'

'Whereabouts?'

'Some place called Leverburgh or close to it.' She took a piece of paper out of her pocket. 'Here,' she said. 'Brenda asked me to give you this. It's her address.'

'How long's she there for?'

'Dunno. I don't think Brenda knows either.'

'So, you've spoken to her?'

'Of course.'

The waitress placed two steaming mugs of hot chocolate on the table.

Andy cupped his drink in both hands and raised it to his mouth. 'This is good. Aren't you going to try yours?'

'She thought you'd dumped her,' said Hazel. 'That was part of her reason for leavin'.'

'Hopefully I've put you straight on that.'

Hazel reached for her drink. 'Sort of,' she said, taking a sip. 'I know you'd been told to keep away but surely...'

'It wasn't just that.'

Hazel eyed him warily. 'I thought there was more to it.'

'That's what I wanted to talk to you about.'

Hazel sat back in her chair and folded her arms. 'I'm listenin'.'

'I had to go back to England suddenly,' he said. 'Family business. My wife–'

'I fuckin' knew it!'

A woman at the opposite table glanced up from a plate of apple pie.

'There was always somethin' about you that didn't ring true.'

They were beginning to attract the attention of other tables. Maybe it hadn't been such a good idea to come here.

'I take it Brenda doesn't know you're married?'

Andy shook his head.

'I thought as much.'

'I didn't deliberately set out to keep things from her, if that's what you're implying.'

'Yeah, right. Who are you tryin' to kid?'

Andy slammed his mug down on the table. Hot chocolate sloshed everywhere. 'Now you're just being stupid.'

'Stupid, am I?' Hazel's voice had risen to a shrill. 'Because I happen to think it's wrong for a married man to screw around?'

The waitress appeared at their table with a cloth to mop up the mess. She looked pissed off. 'Do you think you two could save your lovers tiff for somewhere else?'

'Yes, of course,' said Andy. 'Sorry.'

'I'm not with *him*.' Hazel glowered at Andy.

The waitress raised her eyebrows. 'Well, that's put you in your place.' She leant closer and whispered, 'And just so you know, that accent of yours is sticking out like a sore thumb. I'd keep it down if I were you.'

Hazel and Andy continued their conversation in hushed tones.

'So, when did you plan on tellin' her?'

Andy thought of the times he'd tried to broach the subject then bottled at the last moment.

'Were you ever goin' to tell her?'

'Yes, of course I was. What do you take me for?'

'You really don't want to know.' Hazel pushed her chair back and stood up. 'Brenda's goin' to be gutted when she hears this.'

'Hang on, Hazel. Don't go.' If she was going to relay their conversation to Brenda, and he was sure she would at

239

the first opportunity, then he wanted her to have the full story to pass on. 'At least let me finish what I was trying to say before you shoot off.'

He wasn't sure if it was his pleading that convinced her to change her mind or naked curiosity on her part.

'Go on then,' she said, taking her seat.

Andy rattled out his explanation. They'd been married very young. He and his wife had grown apart over the last few years. Their marriage had been merely bumping along. His story was so clichéd even he found it laughable.

With every disclosure Hazel's face grew more thunderous. 'Your wife didn't know about Brenda. Brenda didn't know about your wife,' she said once he'd finished. 'Nice little set up you had goin' there.'

'I didn't want to hurt anyone. What was I supposed to do?'

'Tell the truth?'

'I did try but it wasn't easy.'

'Why?' Hazel studied him for a moment. 'I thought you and your wife had grown apart.'

'We have, but I had my...' Andy held back from telling her more. It didn't feel right to bring Stevie into things.

'It seems to me the only person you were thinkin' about was yourself.'

'That's not true, but I can see I'm not going to convince you of it.' It was obvious he wasn't getting anywhere. What had he hoped to achieve anyway? Hazel was clearly set against him. Andy pulled a fiver out of his wallet and tossed it on the table. 'That should cover it.'

'I don't want your money.' She pushed the note towards him.

He put his coat on. 'Suit yourself.'

By the time he reached the end of the street he was cursing himself for losing his patience. He almost turned back then thought better of it. Why should he have to justify himself to someone he hardly knew? Still, in one way, it hadn't been a totally wasted trip. Brenda was with her grand-parents, he'd discovered, and he had an address.

THIRTY-SIX

S unday on Harris was a day of serious worship. There was no washing or hanging out of clothes, no tending to crops, no fishing, no cooking. Her nan's lamb stew had been prepared the night before. Brenda lifted the lid of the pot and wrinkled her nose. A fatty skin had formed on top. At least she didn't have to eat it cold. The Lord didn't take offence to the heating up of food on the Sabbath. He did, however, object to the cutting up of vegetables, braising of meat and making of gravy on the day itself.

Brenda thought of the kids back home, turfed outside once Sunday dinner was over and told to amuse themselves. She missed the sound of their laughter as they played a game of tag or kicked a football about. The kids would stay out until bath time when their skin was scrubbed clean and their hair washed, ready for a new school week. Here the children weren't allowed to play games on Sunday. Instead, they spent the afternoon in Bible class.

Every Sunday her grandparents asked if she wanted to go to church with them. Every week she politely turned them down. Usually she liked this quiet time, away from the inquisitive stares of strangers. Today the panicked thumping of her heart filled the silence. Her dad was planning a visit and Brenda was fretting about how to tell him her news. In person was better than the dreaded phone call but, either way, she couldn't hide things much longer. Soon she'd be starting to show. Brenda pulled on her coat. Sitting here on her own, trying to imagine the conversation, was adding to her anxiety.

She could hear the singing as she neared the church. Voices rose and fell in unison. Brenda listened for a while then wandered into the small churchyard overlooking the bay. Every islander was laid to rest facing the sea, something Brenda found surprisingly moving, different from the large cemetery back home with row upon row of graves set next to a busy motorway.

She walked around studying the headstones. They were simple slabs devoid of any carvings or embellishments. No fanciful wording, just a simple beloved father, mother, son, daughter. Whole families buried in the same plot. MacLeans, Campbells, MacLeods and... MacRaes. She stopped to take a closer look.

The date told her this James MacRae was her great-grandfather. Una, his wife, was buried five years after him, aged 95. Brenda thought of her nan's robust good health and smiled. She turned to the grave next to it. More MacRaes, but this time there was only one name etched on the headstone, that of a 6-month-old child. A lump came to her throat as she took in the tiny grave. Alice was her name and – she did a quick calculation – she had died a couple of years after her dad was born. Her dad had never mentioned he had a sister and yet her name was here for all to see.

There was a murmur of voices as the first of the congregation emerged from the church. The churchgoers stood around in small groups, exchanging pleasantries. Brenda spotted the upright figure of her nan amongst them.

Her nan beckoned her over. 'This is our granddaughter,' she said, introducing Brenda to a woman with hair scraped back into a tight bun, which glinted blue-black in the sunlight.

'Were ye here for the service?' she asked.

'Brenda's not much of a churchgoer.'

'Oh.' The woman studied her for a moment.

Brenda felt horribly aware of her casual clothes.

'Well maybe we'll see ye in there some time.'

They lingered for a while saying their goodbyes before heading home.

'She makes the worst dumplings on the island,' said her nan, as soon as they were out of earshot. She gave a little choking sound by way of demonstration.

'That's a very uncharitable thing to say.' Brenda's grandfather grinned. ''Tis true, mind you.'

Her grandparents filled her in on the service (a good choice of hymns this week), who was in the congregation and who was missing. The island doctor again, and it hadn't gone unnoticed. Talk turned to Brenda's dad and how much they were looking forward to his visit.

'Mind you,' said her nan, unable to resist a dig at her only son, 'it's long overdue.'

They were nearing the cottage when Brenda stopped. She looked towards the headland. 'You go on. I'm goin' to take a walk along there for a bit.'

Brenda had only gone a short distance before her ears

throbbed from the biting cold; her jaw hurt too. At the far end of the point were the ruins of a small chapel and an ancient, circular stone building. A broch, her nan called it. Brenda had stood inside the broch the other day. It was so quiet and still, she'd struggled to make out the crashing waves. She couldn't hear anything other than the beating of her heart. Brenda wished she could stay there, encircled with stone, protected from the world outside.

Beneath her feet a myriad of green shoots pushed their way through sandy soil. Within the next few weeks the first of the machair flowers would burst into bloom. A carpet of yellows and whites to begin with; the reds and blues came later. A wonderful sight, her nan said. Brenda knelt down to take a closer look at the tiny leaves mixed with rabbit droppings. She couldn't picture it.

Below her stretched an empty beach and a white-capped sea. Brenda zigzagged her way through the dunes and down to the beach. The white sands glowed in the sunlight as if lit from beneath by hundreds of candles. She followed the solitary tracks of a bird to the water's edge, her own footprints huge beside the tiny claw-shaped indentations. The crash and roar of the Atlantic waves filled her head. In front of her, a huge rock loomed out of the sea.

'It's called Irishman's Rock,' a voice shouted over the wind.

Brenda turned to see her grandfather making his way towards her.

'Here you are. Yer grandmother thought ye could be doing with this.' He handed her a woollen hat.

Brenda gratefully tugged it down over her ears.

He stood beside her and gazed out at the vast expanse of

water. 'I know every one of those rocks, and every inch of that coastline.' He tapped the side of his head with his finger. 'I carry it all in here, like a map. I had too. Back then there was no such things as radar.'

'I always thought you were a crofter.'

'Crofting, fishing, a bit of everything. Whatever it took to earn a living.'

Brenda stared at the choppy seas. She tried to imagine her grandad, as a younger man, negotiating the treacherous coastline in a fishing boat. Those she'd seen in Tarbert harbour were so much smaller and insubstantial than the ferry.

'A dangerous business,' he said, reading her mind. 'Every time I went out in the boat yer grandmother feared I wouldn't come back.' His face clouded. 'Some didn't.'

Brenda jumped. 'What the–?'

A number of large white birds had appeared from nowhere; they began dive-bombing the water.

'Gannets,' said her grandad.

Brenda watched, fascinated, as they repeated the spectacle over and over again. Every so often one emerged triumphant from the water, gripping a fish in its beak.

'Why did he leave? Dad, I mean.'

It was almost as if he had been expecting the question. He answered without hesitation. 'Because yer mum wanted to. She'd had enough of the place, and of yer...'

Brenda shot him a sideways glance. 'They didn't get on, did they?'

'Yer mum and yer grandmother? No.'

Brenda's mum and dad were newly married when they moved in with her grandparents. From everything she'd heard, the two MacRae women had clashed from the very start.

'It got worse when you came along.'

'So, it's my fault?'

Brenda's grandfather gave a gentle shake of his head. 'No, you weren't to blame. To be honest, I can't remember the half of what they disagreed about. Only that it all came to a head over the pram.'

Brenda's grandmother believed a baby needed a good dose of fresh air every day. She'd often leave the pram, with Brenda asleep in it, in the back garden. Brenda's mum worried that her baby would catch a chill. She was furious when she came back one day to find Brenda had kicked the blankets loose.

'She said yer feet were like ice.'

She tore into Brenda's grandmother. Was she trying to kill the child? How could she trust her with you? Brenda winced as she remembered the times her mum had rounded on a neighbour. She could have a vicious tongue on her.

'Yer mum cut deep that day. Deeper than she could ever know.' He paused for a moment. 'Yer grandmother isn't one to open up with her feelings but I could tell.'

He told her about the little girl they'd lost a couple of years after her dad was born.

Brenda recalled the small grave in the churchyard. 'Alice? I saw the name on one of the gravestones.'

'Aye, that's her.'

The baby had been out of sorts all day. Brenda's grandmother had taken her to the doctor but he couldn't find anything wrong with her. The next morning, she went to lift her from her cot, but the child was cold and lifeless. Brenda's grandfather had been tending the garden. He remembered her throwing open the window and yelling his name. A fearful sound.

When he got to the bedroom he found Brenda's grandmother sat in a chair with Alice in her arms. 'She refused tae let go. Wouldn't let me tak the baby from her. When the doctor arrived she wouldn't let him tak the baby either.' In the end Brenda's grandfather fetched Mrs McDonald from the post office. She was the one who persuaded his wife to give up the body. 'I'll always be grateful to Janet for that.'

After the funeral she shut herself away from everyone for a week. 'Yer grandmother did all her grieving in that one week. She never spoke of Alice's death again.' The doctor couldn't explain what had happened. The child had seemed in good health when she'd brought her into the surgery. For Brenda's grandmother the not-knowing was the worst thing. 'We didn't have any more bairns after that.'

THIRTY-SEVEN

Her dad's injuries had healed but Brenda could see he wasn't back to his old self. His face, always so ready to break into a smile, was taut. Wound up tighter than a fiddle string was how her nan described him. It wasn't until the second day of his stay that the reason became clear.

'They petrol-bombed the house.'

'They *what*?' exclaimed Brenda.

Her nan was at the kitchen sink. She spun round to face him. 'Oh, dear Lord, James.'

'The living room was destroyed. We put the fire out before it spread but you could still smell the stench of it everywhere.'

Brenda had seen plenty of houses gutted by petrol bombs. She knew of families who had barely escaped with their lives, been forced to move on. Through her peace work she'd tried to help them. But this was her own home, her own family. It didn't seem real.

Her nan stood wide-eyed, clutching a saucepan in one

hand, dripping soapy water on to the kitchen floor. 'Ye could have been killed.'

Brenda's dad placed the pot on the draining board and took her wet hands in his. 'Nobody got hurt.'

'What sort of people would do such a thing? I don't know why ye don't pack up and leave that dreadful place once and for all.'

'Because it's our home.'

Her nan gave him a reproachful look.

'You and I both know Bridie will never leave Belfast,' he said.

She threw her hands up in despair. 'That woman would have ye all burnt in yer beds before she'd see sense.'

'It won't happen again. We're in a different house now. We're safe there.'

Brenda stared at him. 'You've moved? When did that happen?'

'A couple of weeks back. I didn't say anything because I wanted to tell you to your face.'

Brenda's thoughts flew to her mum. She'd be devastated to leave that street. She knew everyone by first name or so it seemed, if you walked the length of it with her. Her years there had been happy ones before everything changed. It was those happy memories that kept her going through the bad times. Her mum doggedly believed things would improve. She'd still been hoping that on the day Brenda left. Now they'd have to start all over, in an unfamiliar place.

'This is my fault,' said Brenda. 'If I hadn't...'

'Your sister needs to take a share of the blame.' Her dad hesitated. 'And so do I.'

'What do you mean, James?'

He gave a quick shake of his head. 'Nothin'. Forget it.'

For the next couple of days Brenda's nan kept a watchful eye on him. She fed him well and encouraged him to spend time out on the island with his daughter.

They went to her dad's favourite spot on one of their walks together. It was where Brenda had first ventured into the sea, he told her. She was a toddler at the time. They'd taken their shoes off and stood at the water's edge, letting the water lap over their feet. 'You were trembling with fear.' He remembered her little hand clutching his and Brenda pleading with him to go further in.

'Into that freezin' sea?' said Brenda. 'That's child cruelty.'

'You're the one who wanted to go in. I was doin' my best to hold you back.'

As the water ebbed, the pull had been too strong. She lost her balance and tipped forward. Her dad caught her before she hit the water and scooped her into his arms. Then he set her down to rinse the sand off her feet before slipping her feet back into her shoes. As they walked towards the dunes she kept turning round, wanting to return to the shore. She offered excuses – *I've lost a shoe. I need to wash my feet again.* He laughed at the memory.

The tide had been going out that day. Today it was coming in. Once again Brenda stood by her dad's side. They watched the waves break and churn on a nearby outcrop of rocks, sending a white spray high in the air.

'What's the new house like, Dad? You haven't said much about it.'

'It's alright but...'

'Mum hates it, doesn't she?'

'Yes.'

'And what about you?'

'Different house, different street,' he said. 'It takes a bit of gettin' used to, that's all.'

She could imagine him saying the same thing to her mum and her mum having none of it. 'The other night, when you were tellin' us about the house being petrol-bombed,' Brenda paused, 'why did you say you were partly to blame?'

'Because I was.'

'I don't understand.'

'If I hadn't lost my temper with that bastard, McManus...'

'McManus?' Brenda's stomach flipped at the mention of his name. 'What's he got to do with it?'

'Let's just say we had a bit of a set to.'

'Over me?'

Her dad turned to meet her horrified gaze. 'Yes.'

'Oh, Dad.'

'I know, I know. I shouldn't have let him get to me.'

Part of her felt bad for placing her dad in that situation. A bigger part hoped he'd kicked the crap out of McManus. 'You don't have to explain,' she said.

'The thing is, Brenda, I knew better than to go pokin' a snake.'

The waves ran up the beach towards them, covering their shoes with lacy foam. Water soaked into Brenda's socks.

'Ugh,' she squealed.

They took a few dancing steps back to avoid the next rush of water.

'Is it always this cold?'

'Pretty much,' said her dad.

'And I thought the sea at Portrush was bad.'

'Tropical compared to this, but look around you, Brenda.' The strain on her dad's face melted away. 'You'll never find anything as magnificent as this back home.'

They walked the length of the beach, each lost in their own thoughts. Every so often he pointed out a seabird, delighting in the discovery that he could still recall its name. When they ran out of golden sands, they turned round and retraced their steps.

'What else is on your mind, Dad?'

'Hmmm?'

'I know you. I can tell when you're tryin' to hide something.'

He raised his hands in fake surrender. 'Sussed.'

Brenda waited.

'It's Clare,' he said.

Brenda groaned. 'What's she done now?'

Her dad stopped and turned to face her. 'She told them everything.'

'Told who? Told them what?'

'The Provos. About you and Andy.'

'Oh, come on, Dad. It's one thing her tellin' you and Mum. She couldn't wait to drop me in it with you two, but she wouldn't–'

'I know for sure it was her,' he said.

'How?'

'From McManus himself. When I confronted your sister, she didn't deny it.'

'So that night they came for me...' Brenda felt queasy at the memory. 'Clare knew?' She'd been prepared to learn it was a neighbour – Magda or one of her crew, or someone at the university – anyone but her own sister.

'She didn't realise they'd take things that far. She thought they'd have their chat with you and that would be it.'

'And that makes it alright, does it?'

'I didn't say that but I believe her when she says she's sorry for what she's done.'

'I don't!'

Brenda's mind began to race. That night, in the pub, when she'd had her run in with McManus and his cronies ... She'd been scared out of her wits and Clare had watched it all. Her sister was the only reason Brenda had been there in the first place. All that guff about sharing a drink, saying she wanted to patch things up between them. 'That sick bitch set me up. I hate her!'

'I know you feel that way now but ... maybe when you're back home, when things have settled...'

'I'm not comin' anywhere near a house she's in. You can tell her that from me.'

'Alright. Let's leave things as they are for now,' he said. 'It's probably for the best. Your mum can't cope with more. Not on top of everythin' else she's dealin' with.' The pinched look had returned to his face as he spoke of her.

'You're worried about her, aren't you?'

'Yes, she's the innocent party in all this.' He gave a heavy sigh. 'I never thought I'd see the day the family turned on one another.' There was an uncommon note of defeat in her dad's voice when he said it. It's not right, he told her. Family were supposed to have each other's back. That's what he'd been brought up to believe. It made him sad to think he hadn't passed those values on to his own family. He felt he had failed.

'Daddy, stop! You're not to think that way.'

Her father had always tried not to take sides. Resolutely kept an open mind in all his dealings with people, regardless of their beliefs. Brenda had spoilt that for him. She'd brought the troubles right into his home. Her family was split now and her father, the great pacifier, no longer knew how to mend things.

Tears welled in Brenda's eyes. 'What a mess,' she said. 'All from one stupid decision to have a drink with a soldier. I wish I'd never set eyes on Andy.'

Her dad put his arm around her. 'It wasn't the choice you made; it was the place you made it in. You shouldn't be blamed for that.'

'I wish you didn't have to go back.'

Her dad gave a heavy sigh. 'So do I.'

They stood a while longer, watching the waves creep steadily closer. As the broad stretch of golden sands shrank to a narrow strip, Brenda thought about how he was always there for her. When she was right; when she was wrong; when she cried; even when she lied. He was always there when she needed him most. She glanced up at her dad's troubled face. This wasn't the time to burden him with any more worry.

THIRTY-EIGHT

November 1972

The tiny doctor's surgery was full. Brenda waited as the receptionist, a wiry woman with intense deep-set eyes, busied herself filing medical notes. When she was happy they were all in the right place, she turned to Brenda.

'What is it yer here for?'

'I'd ... um ... rather talk to the doctor, if you don't mind. It's personal.' Even with her back to them, Brenda could sense the growing interest of the people in the waiting room.

'I remember ye now. Brenda, isn't it? Are ye here for the results?'

Brenda's face flushed crimson. 'Yes.'

'Well, you'd best tak a seat,' said the receptionist. 'I'm afraid yer in for a wait. We're very busy this morning.'

Brenda looked around the room. Every seat was taken.

A woman lifted a toddler on to her knee and shuffled along a wooden bench. 'Sit here,' she said, patting the empty space beside her.

Brenda squeezed on to the end. She unbuttoned her coat and placed her handbag on her knees. The toddler immediately made a grab for the strap.

'Ah ah ah!' chided the woman. 'Don't be putting that in yer mouth.'

Brenda teased it out. The strap was covered in drool.

'Teething,' said the woman. 'His gums are on fire.'

Brenda discreetly wiped her hand on her jeans.

'He's here for his jab.' The woman pulled a face. 'Poor wee mite.'

The words were no sooner out of her mouth when another mother appeared with a bawling child.

'Who's a brave girl then?' she said, stooping to stroke the child's cheek.

The child spat out the sugar lump she'd been given. She looked at her mother then the red swelling on her arm and proceeded to bawl even louder.

During the commotion, Brenda picked up a magazine and began reading it in the hope no-one would strike up a conversation. It was an Easter edition from a couple of years ago. She worked her way through the knitting and crochet special, a dramatic real-life exclusive and a simple step-by-step guide to cooking the perfect chicken dinner. She was on the problem page at the back of the magazine when her name was called.

The woman with the toddler nudged the person beside her. 'MacRae,' she said, in a loud whisper. 'Isn't that...?'

'Moira's granddaughter? Aye, I reckon it is.'

A dozen pair of eyes followed her as she made her way back to the reception desk. She cleared her throat, trying to catch the receptionist's attention. 'Sorry, which way is it again?'

The receptionist's head was buried in more paperwork.

'If yer lookin' for the doctor's room,' it was the woman who had made space for her on the bench, 'go down the corridor and take the first door on the right.'

Brenda mumbled her thanks.

She stood for a while outside the room, her hand hovering over the door handle. She thought of leaving but that would mean walking past all those strangers again. In the end Doctor MacKay decided for her by opening the door.

'Come in,' he said with a welcoming sweep of his arm. He wore a brown tweed jacket and matching waistcoat over a crisp white shirt and tie. His bald head looked as if it had been buffed into a shine. 'How are ye?' he asked, sinking into a large, well-worn leather chair.

'Fine,' said Brenda, feeling anything but fine. About to throw up was closer to the mark.

'Then why are ye here?'

She began to stutter an explanation.

'I'm only joking,' he said.

Brenda was in no mood for banter.

The doctor looked out the window. 'Still raining, I see. Turning bitter with it too.' He proceeded to give a lengthy account of his drive to the surgery that morning, in a heavy downpour with only one windscreen wiper working.

Brenda's nerves were stretched taut. 'Anyway,' she said. 'Have you got my results?'

Doctor MacKay leant forward in his chair and rested his elbows on the desk. 'Aye, that I do.'

Her heart thudded.

'Well now,' a smile crept across his face, 'I believe congratulations are in order, Brenda. Yer going to be a mum.'

Brenda gawped at him.

'Maybe it's not the news ye wanted?'

'I didn't plan on gettin' pregnant, if that's what you mean.' It sounded more curt than she'd intended. 'Sorry.' Brenda pulled a tissue, already soggy from the rain, out of her pocket ready to dab away the tears that threatened to spill. Doctor MacKay mentioned something about dates, check-ups, a district nurse. His words rolled over the top of Brenda's head. 'Mum' was the only one she heard.

'Yer in luck! Jean is in today. She's giving out rubella jabs.'

'Sorry, who?'

'Jean, the district nurse. She can book in her visits straight away.' He explained that Jean would come to the cottage regularly to check everything was as it should be with Brenda and the baby.

'Oh yes, thanks.'

Brenda knew he was only making sure she got the follow-up care she needed but it irritated her. She hadn't taken in the news herself and this man was determining her future. What would her nan say? Would she even want Brenda to stay in the cottage?

'Is there anything else you want to ask me?'

She couldn't think of anything. Doctor MacKay saw her to the door. He smiled one last time and clicked it shut.

Brenda didn't stop to seek Jean out. She walked past reception, through the waiting room and out on to the street.

———

'You sound out of breath,' said Hazel. 'Where are you?'

'In the post office. Honest to god, the smell of Dettol from this receiver is enough to–'

'Never mind all that. What did the doctor say?'

'I'm pregnant.'

There was a sharp intake of breath from Hazel. 'Are you sure?'

'Yes, I've just come from the surgery.'

'I see. How do you feel about it?'

'Pissed off!' said Brenda. 'I keep thinking, how could I be so bloody stupid?'

'These things happen.'

Brenda screwed up her face. *These things happen*? Was that the best Hazel could come up with?

'Have you told your parents yet? Your nan?'

'No.'

'You'll have to tell them soon.'

'I know, I know, but not yet. I need to think first.'

Brenda had looked to Hazel for reassurance. She'd hoped she'd say everything would work out fine. Instead, she'd made her panic more. She imagined the phone calls she was yet to make. Her mum would go ballistic when she found out her first grandchild was to be born in sin. Her dad would … what? Brenda shrank at the thought of having that chat with him. Christ only knew what her nan would think. And then there was Andy. She'd ask Hazel for his number. All those conversations. Brenda dreaded each and every one of them. She wanted to curl up into a ball and hide from the world.

'You don't have to have it, you know.' Hazel's voice had become quieter, more hesitant. 'There's other options. You could...'

'Get rid of it? No, I'd never do that.'

'Sorry. I don't know why I said that.' There was a brief silence on the end of the phone. 'Listen, Brenda, there's something I need to tell you.'

Brenda gave a half-hearted laugh. 'Don't tell me you're pregnant too?'

'It's not that.'

'It was a joke,' said Brenda. 'Obviously not a very funny one.'

'I saw Andy again yesterday.'

Brenda's pulse quickened.

Hazel continued in a tight voice. 'Look I don't really know how to say this, but ... Andy's married.'

No, no. Hazel had got it wrong. 'He can't be! I'd know if he was.'

'Believe me, he is. He said so himself.' Hazel recounted the scene in the coffee shop: how Andy told her he and his wife had grown apart; that he hadn't meant to deceive Brenda; how he had never wanted to hurt her or his wife. Hazel had taken him to task on that. She'd asked him why he couldn't have been straight with Brenda from the start. 'He had no answer for that.'

Hazel was on her high horse and Brenda couldn't handle it. She knew her friend was only sticking up for her, but it wasn't Hazel's place to tackle Andy like that. Didn't she realise every time she had a go at Andy, she was having a go at Brenda too? Brenda felt stupid enough. Her friend had discovered more about him over a coffee than Brenda had in the whole time she'd been seeing him.

———

Hailstones pelted the hood of Brenda's coat as she pushed open the cottage door. The back of her hand felt like it was being punctured by dozens of miniature pitchforks. The doctor had been right about the sudden dip in temperature: both the pathway and garden were now covered in a blanket of white.

Balls of ice landed on the doormat and rolled, like marbles, into the hallway. Brenda quickly shut the door. She flung her coat on a hook, tugged off her shoes and set them next to her grandad's mud-caked wellington boots. Small, perfectly formed circles of water dotted the flagstones where each hailstone had begun to melt.

She went straight to the fire in the living room. *Fuck it!* She stabbed at it repeatedly with the poker. What was it with this place? She'd never known weather like it. She piled another block of peat on top of the flames. Was she the only one round here who tried to keep this thing alight?

Her ears filled with the cracking noise of the hailstones as they smashed against the windows of the house and bounced off the corrugated roof of the shed. She was sure something would break. Not that she cared. She was still reeling from what Hazel had told her.

How had Andy managed to keep all that from her? It must have taken considerable effort on his part to make sure he never tripped up. That's what hurt the most – the deliberate, calculating way he'd gone about keeping her in the dark.

His mate, Paul, had been in on the deceit too, giving the impression they were both single lads. When Hazel joked about them having girls back home, Paul had laughed it off.

'He's too ugly and I'm too smart,' he'd said.

When Andy had told her how much she meant to him,

was he acting then too? She'd been wrong to think they had something special. Yes, he said he was crazy about her but he'd never actually told her he loved her. She'd told him though. More fool her.

A chunk of smouldering peat landed on the rug in front of Brenda's feet. She watched it glow and singe its way through the wool. To have kept it from her for so long – she couldn't believe she hadn't sensed it. Except that wasn't entirely true.

That time they'd gone to Bangor for the day, on the train, on the way back to Belfast, he was about to tell her but changed his mind. She could see that now. She'd misread the signals, thought he was about to break up with her. There were other times too. She could have teased it out of him if she'd tried. Deep inside she'd always feared he was hiding something but she'd chosen not to probe too deeply. What sort of person did that make her?

'Brenda!' Her nan grabbed the tongs, lifted the chunk of peat and placed it back on the fire. 'Are ye trying to burn the house down?' She tutted then made her way into the kitchen. A few minutes later she stood in front of her holding two cups of tea. She offered one to Brenda. 'So, when are ye due?'

'How...?'

'I had a fair inkling before ye even went to Doctor MacKay.' She sat down beside her. Tiny orange flames licked the side of the fire as she spoke. 'Does James know?'

'I haven't told Dad yet – or Mum.'

'I see.'

'I didn't know for sure myself until this mornin'. I was hoping...'

'Do ye want me to speak to yer dad?'

'What? No. I'll do it. Please don't say anything yet.' All hell would break loose soon enough but first Brenda needed time to take it in herself.

Her nan moved on to practical matters. 'Where will ye have the baby?'

Beads of sweat formed on Brenda's brow. The doctor had assumed she'd have the baby on the island but Brenda couldn't think that far ahead. Her mind was taken up with how she was going to break the news to Andy and her family.

Her nan came straight to the point. 'Are ye planning on going home?'

Was she hinting that she should? How could Brenda go back to living under the same roof as Clare after everything she'd done? And even if she wanted to go home, hadn't her dad told her not to? Best to let things settle first, was how he'd put it. This latest news was hardly going to calm things down.

'I *can't* go back there.' It was the first time Brenda had voiced such feelings out loud to her nan. She glanced at her, seeking reassurance.

'We'll think of something,' was all she said.

Brenda got up to put more peat on the fire.

'Leave it, dear. It's spitting enough as it is and I'd like to keep what's left of my rug.' She motioned for Brenda to sit down. 'And what has Andy to say fer himself?'

'He doesn't know yet.'

THIRTY-NINE

Brenda's heartbeat quickened at the sound of the familiar English accent. Best to tell him about the baby straight away, she'd decided, before her courage failed her. Wait for his reaction and take it from there. Yet the moment she heard Andy speak, confusion took the place of anger.

'Brenda. Is that really you?'

He sounded so pleased to hear from her that she was almost prepared to forgive him everything.

'How are you?' he asked.

'Fine thanks.' Brenda took a deep breath. 'Actually, there's something I need to talk to you...'

'I was worried,' he said. 'I thought I might have scared you off for good.'

He didn't know how close to the truth that was. It ate away at Brenda that he'd cheated on his wife with *her*. And yet, if he truly believed the marriage was over, maybe she should give him a chance. She owed it to him. More importantly, she owed it to their child.

'I suppose Hazel's already filled you in?'

'Yeah. She told me everything.'

'I bet she did.'

His sudden sarcasm touched a nerve. Hazel had only done what any good friend would do.

'Jenny and I–'

'That would be your wife, would it?'

Mrs McDonald looked over, sensing trouble. She gave an embarrassed cough when she caught Brenda's eye.

Brenda's call to her family the day before had been every bit as awful as she'd imagined it would be. It had been made all the worse knowing Mrs McDonald was hanging on every word. Her mum was telling her about the new hairdresser she'd found – cheaper than Bernie and every bit as good – when Brenda cut in.

'Mum, there's something I need to tell you.' There was silence. 'I'm pregnant.' More silence. 'Did you hear me?'

'I heard you,' Her mum's sing-song tone had vanished. 'I take it that soldier you were seein' is the father?'

'Who else would it be?'

'What did she just say?' It was Clare's voice in the background. 'Don't tell me she's pregnant to him!'

'I thought you should know,' said Brenda.

'Well, now I do, and you won't be gettin' my blessing.'

'Now Bridie, don't be like that.' Her dad took the phone from her. 'It's the shock,' he said. 'She doesn't really mean it.'

She told her dad to leave it. She got the picture.

'Brenda. Are you still there?' It was Andy on the other end of the line.

'What? Yes.'

He was saying something about his wife making things

difficult for him, how she'd flipped when she found out about Brenda.

'You told her about us?'

'No. She found out from Paul. She cleared the house out and took off to her mother's. Took Stevie with her. That's why I had to go back.'

Brenda's stomach bunched into a tight knot. 'Andy, who's Stevie?'

Andy went quiet.

'Who's Stevie?' she repeated.

'He's my son.'

Tears pricked Brenda's eyes. 'You're fuckin' unbelievable. How old is this son of yours?'

'What does it matter?'

'Tell me!'

'He's 6 years.'

She wondered if the boy looked like his mum or his dad. She wondered what Jenny looked like.

'I know you're upset,' said Andy.

'You think?'

'I was in an impossible situation. I–'

'That wasn't my doing.'

'I didn't say it was.' Andy sighed. 'Look, I thought I was doing the right thing just now by coming clean with you.'

Brenda gave a derisory snort.

'Obviously I was wrong but if I hadn't told you about Stevie now, you'd have found out soon enough. Then what? You'd still be angry with me. Either way I couldn't win.'

'Poor you.'

All this crap about wanting to tell her but worrying how

she'd take it. Then when he did tell her, he tried to make it sound as if she was the unreasonable one.

'Save your breath. I've heard enough.' Brenda was about to hang up.

'Wait!' he said. 'At the start, you said you needed to talk about something.'

'Forget it. It doesn't matter now.'

She put the phone down and took a few moments to compose herself. Her head was thumping. It was still thumping when she arrived back at the cottage.

'Well, did ye speak with him?' asked her nan.

'Yes.'

'And?'

Brenda's insides shrivelled as her nan fixed her with one of her probing stares. It was pointless to hold anything back. Once her nan suspected she wasn't getting the full story she'd peck away until she did. Like a gull, picking at a shell until it succeeds in trailing out the spongy innards.

'He's married,' said Brenda, 'and ... he has a little boy. There. So now you know.'

'Indeed.'

'I didn't tell him about the baby in the end. And I'm not goin' to!'

Her nan said that was up to Brenda. She would support her decision.

'Really?' Brenda bit back tears. 'If I'd known he had a wife and kid I'd–'

'But you didn't. He's the one at fault here, not you.'

'I want to stay here with you, Nan. That's if, um, you'll still have me.'

Her nan squeezed Brenda's hand. 'You're not to worry

about that,' she said. 'Ye wouldn't be the first girl on the island to find herself pregnant when she hadn't planned it.' She thought for a moment. 'Mind you, usually the marriage follows soon after.'

'It's a bit different in my case,' said Brenda. 'I take it they don't go in for bigamy here?'

Her nan laughed. 'No.'

'What will you tell people?'

Her nan looked baffled. 'The truth of course. I'll say yer having a baby, the father let ye down and yer having to raise the bairn yerself.'

It sounded so simple when she put it like that. Brenda wished her mum could see it that way.

FORTY

Belfast

C lare lifted her feet but not quick enough to avoid the crack of hoover against ankle bone.

'No matter how many times I go over this,' her mum fumed, 'it still looks no better.'

The dark blue carpet had come with the new house and it wasn't to her taste. Clare's suggestion to buy a bright rug to add a splash of colour was met with short shrift. 'Money doesn't grow on trees.' Her mum unplugged the hoover and returned it to the cupboard under the stairs.

The crocheted cover, placed over the sofa back, had slipped down revealing the scorch marks it was meant to hide. Clare quickly repositioned it before her mum reappeared, a duster in one hand and a tin of Pledge in the other.

'Do you want some help?'

Her mum wiped her brow free of sweat. 'Nice of you to offer instead of sittin' on your backside watching me do everything.'

Clare had actually asked her, at the start of her cleaning blitz, if she wanted a hand. She'd received a curt 'No thanks'. Now, having worked herself up into a lather, her mum had changed her mind. 'Tell me what you need doin',' said Clare, 'and I'll do it.'

'I shouldn't have to tell you,' said her mum, handing over the duster.

Clare cast her eyes over what was left of their living-room furniture. The nest of mahogany-coloured tables, so lovingly cared for over the years, had perished in the fire. So too had her dad's armchair. Her mum had considered recovering it, but the smell of burnt foam was so bad that the only option, in the end, was to throw it out. Her dad had promised to replace the things they'd lost, but her mum knew it would take forever to save for them.

In the days following the petrol-bombing of the old house, her anger had been directed towards her husband. What was he thinking, getting into a fight with McManus of all people? Had he taken the head staggers? Now she was beginning to see things differently. She no longer blamed him for reacting to provocation. 'God forgive me.' She crossed herself as she said it. 'But if I was a man, I'd have had a go at him myself.'

The oval coffee table that matched the nest of tables had survived. Clare set to work on it, polishing the wood until it shone. 'What do you think?' She set a china basket of flowers in the centre of the table.

'Your father will have that knocked over in no time.' Her mum scooped it up and placed it on the mantlepiece. 'It goes here.' The mantelpiece wasn't as deep as the one in the old house. The ornament was too big. 'Oh, what's the point.' She

271

handed the basket of flowers back to Clare. 'Do what you want with it.'

'Come on now. Don't be like that.'

'How would you like me to be?' Her mum stood with hitched shoulders and upturned palms, as if open to suggestions.

Like your old self, she wanted to tell her. It was hard to get her mum to crack a smile these days. Or take herself out. If her mum had her way, she'd stay in her pink dressing gown all day if it wasn't for Clare nagging her to get dressed. She tried to get her to come to the shops with her. Her mum would take ages to get ready then change her mind at the last minute. 'Sure it'd be quicker if you went on your own.'

'Why don't you sit down for a bit?'

'I don't need to sit down. I'm not ill,' said her mum. She looked around the room taking in the peeling wallpaper and the blue-flecked carpet she despised. 'I don't know what your father was thinkin' of, bringing us here. We should have stayed put.'

'You know we couldn't.'

Her eyes lit on Clare. 'Whose fault was that?'

Clare bit her lip. She refused to be drawn into the same old merry-go-round with her mum endlessly debating which of her daughters had the most to answer for. At least Clare was here to contest the charges made against her. Brenda wasn't.

'We could play this blame game forever, Mum, but what's the point? What's happened has happened.' Clare looked cautiously at her fully expecting another outburst. Instead, she saw the first flicker of acceptance that their lives had changed. It was the encouragement she needed. 'Maybe we all need to move on,' she said.

'I'm not movin' again.' It was said with a half-smile.

'Make up your mind. A minute ago you couldn't stand this place.'

'It's all I've got,' she sniffed, 'so I'll have to make the best of it.'

'Dad says he'll decorate it any way you want.'

'Your father? I'm not lettin' him anywhere near a paintbrush.'

It was a sign that things were bad when Clare's dad turned his hand to DIY. Her mum had always been the decorator in the house. He'd taken a couple of days off work to 'tackle' the living room and asked her mum to pick some colours. At least if one room met with her approval it might help to lift her spirits. His too.

She let him make a start, all the while observing him with a critical eye. It wasn't long before she felt compelled to step in. 'Gimme that brush, Jimmy, because, honest to god, I've never seen anyone make such a pig's arse out of paintin' a skirting.'

He gave Clare a sly wink as he surrendered the brush to her mum. 'Show me.'

She had finished one length of skirting and was about to start another when he raised the idea of taking a trip to see Brenda and the baby.

'No.' Her mum's hand jumped. 'Damn it,' she said, grabbing a rag to dab the excess paint away.

'What if we all went? You, me, Clare?'

Clare's eyebrows shot up. It was the first time she'd heard any mention of her dad's plan.

'I said *no*.' She threw the brush down, spattering white gloss over the carpet.

He cast his eyes despairingly at the ceiling as she strode from the room. 'I don't know what to do or say anymore.'

'Did you mean it?' asked Clare.

'Sorry, what was that, love?'

The sudden tenderness brought a lump to her throat. 'About takin' me to Harris with you?'

The subject hadn't been mentioned since and the decorating had ground to a halt, but the idea of a trip together had been planted in Clare's head. It still horrified her to think of a soldier's child as one of the family, but it was a reality she had to accept. Denying the baby's existence wasn't going to make it go away. Maybe the trip was the way forward they all needed. She decided to broach it again with her mum.

'Do you ever wonder how Brenda's gettin' on?'

Her mum pretended not to hear and Clare wondered if she'd pushed things too far. 'I hope everything's alright, you know ... with the baby and everything.'

'You've changed your tune.'

'Brenda could have his baby any time now. I have to deal with that one way or the other. And so do you, Mum. All this talk about being ashamed...'

'I *am* ashamed.'

'Oh, come on. Brenda's hardly the first one, is she? Look at Teresa McCartney.'

Teresa had been in her final year at Clare's school when she became pregnant. The dad, no more than a lad himself, was all full of himself following the birth, like it was some big achievement on his part. He'd shown little interest since and it had been left to Teresa's mum to help raise the child.

Her mum gave a shudder of distaste. 'Teresa's a brazen hussy. Brenda's not like her.'

'No, but at least Mrs McCartney stood by her daughter.'

There was a flash of anger in her mum's eyes. 'I don't need lessons on mothering from you.'

Clare sighed. 'I wasn't gettin' at you, but–'

'It was Brenda's choice to stay on that awful island. If she thinks I'm traipsin' after her, she has another thing coming.'

Clare sat for a moment then tried again. 'So, what *are* you goin' to do?'

'Nothing. It's up to her to make the first move.'

'Maybe she's tried, but I've heard what you're like with her.'

The terse phone conversations between her mum and Brenda had grown shorter with each phone call. Brenda now bypassed her mum and spoke only to her dad.

Her mum bristled. 'What's that supposed to mean?'

'You can sometimes come across as ... a bit cold.'

'You think I don't care?'

'I wasn't sayin' that.'

'I do worry about her, all alone on that island with no-one to look after her.'

'But she's not alone,' said Clare. 'She's got Nan.'

'Yes, but she hasn't got *me*!'

She said it with such force of feeling that Clare was momentarily stunned. This was the root of it, she realised. Brenda had turned to 'that woman' for support and their mum couldn't handle it.

'I'm obviously not needed.'

'No-one's sayin' that.'

'Well, that's how it seems and it hurts.'

'Why don't you tell Brenda how you feel?'

Her mum turned her head away.

No, of course you won't. Too proud. Clare looked at her mum sitting there, all puffed up with righteous indignation, then thought of Brenda. They were cut from the same cloth, but couldn't see it.

'You're like two peas.'

'What did you say?'

'Forget it.'

Her mum was driving her own misery and only she could put a stop to it.

FORTY-ONE

Belfast

Things had escalated after Andy's unannounced appearance at Stevie's school. Jenny informed his teachers that the only people permitted to pick him up were Jenny or her mum.

He'd been straight on to the headmistress, Mrs Fulton, who sounded like a nice enough woman. 'I'm sorry about the misunderstanding. I hope I haven't landed you in my wife's bad books.' He wanted to be kept up to date on Stevie's progress, he explained. If she could send him copies of his son's school reports he'd really appreciate it.

'I'm not sure your wife would be too happy about that.'

'I'm not out to step on anyone's toes, but I am the lad's father,' he said. 'Doesn't that count for something?'

'Well...'

'I just want to know how he's getting on.'

Mrs Fulton considered for a moment. 'Leave it with me.'

When Jenny found out, she was furious.

'The school shouldn't have agreed anything without discussing it with me. My solicitor says...'

'Screw your solicitor. Are you seriously telling me I can't enquire about my son's education? Since when was that the law?'

'Andy, you're shouting again.'

'I'm not!'

'You are and I'm fed up with the way you go off on one every time we talk.'

It had been like that for the last year or so, she told him. Every time he came home she'd found herself picking over her words, worrying that the wrong comment from her would trigger another outburst. It wasn't just her; his moods affected their son too.

'What do you mean by that?'

'Oh, come on, Andy.'

'Give me an example.'

'I shouldn't have to spell it out but seeing as you've asked...' On his last leave, when he'd arrived at the house, he'd insisted on dragging Stevie out of bed in the middle of the night so that he could chat to him. It had to be right there and then; it couldn't wait until the morning. Stevie had been bewildered. Could Andy not see that? It had taken her ages to get him back to sleep. The next day – so typical of Andy – he'd reacted as if nothing had happened. 'The child was tired but you kept banging on about taking him to the park.'

'We had a great time.'

'He wanted to stay home. He only went because he didn't want to upset you. He was doing everything he could to keep you happy. He's just a kid, Andy. It should be the other way round.' She took a moment to gather her thoughts. 'And that scene you caused on Mum's doorstep? Stevie felt responsible. He kept saying if he hadn't gone with you, we wouldn't have had the huge row. I don't want our son carrying that guilt around.'

'Stop right there,' said Andy. 'If he was feeling any guilt, it's thanks to you.'

'What?'

'You made him think he'd let you down.' Stevie had been relaxed in his company that afternoon. They'd had a good time together. If Jenny hadn't overreacted, there wouldn't have been anything for Stevie to get upset about.

Another solicitor's letter swiftly followed this latest exchange with her. He was to have no contact with the boy until the custody case had gone to court. At least he knew where things were heading for him, Jenny and Stevie. The legal process would roll through to its inevitable conclusion and Andy would be frozen out of his son's life.

It was different with Brenda. Yes, he'd messed up. He accepted that. But it didn't feel like the end. He'd written to her several times telling her how much his son meant to him, how much she meant to him, and that he didn't want to lose either of them. He'd pleaded with her to get in touch but heard nothing. When he asked Paul what he should do, Paul told him to cut his losses.

'I can't.'

'That's up to you, mate but, if you ask me, it sounds as if Brenda already has.'

It was easy for Paul to talk about cutting losses. Paul didn't stand to lose *anything*. Andy did. His life was collapsing in on him. If he didn't do something about it, he'd suffocate under the weight of it.

FORTY-TWO

Isle of Harris, March 1973

The storm raged on. Howling winds drove cold, salty rain against the windows and whitewashed walls of the little cottage. Brenda felt another stab of pain. At the start there had been cramps and a tightening of her stomach. *This isn't too bad*, she'd thought. Now, hours later, it was as if her baby had a pitchfork and was raking and jabbing at her insides.

'Where *is* he?'

'He'll be here soon. I promise.' Her nan's voice was steady but she couldn't hide the concern on her face.

She'd made the call before they had been plunged into darkness then watched from the bedroom window as, one by one, every last pinprick of light on the surrounding hills blinked out.

A sudden gust blasted its way down the chimney, blowing soot into the room. The candle on the bedside table sputtered then flared again.

'Somethin's wrong.' Brenda squeezed the words from her throat. 'It's too soon.'

'Wisht now,' said her nan as she stroked Brenda's hand. The feel of her fingers, bony but strong, was strangely comforting. 'Everything will be fi–' Her nan jumped up at the flash of headlights.

There was the sound of a car door being slammed, men's voices. The light from a torch bounced off the walls as Brenda's grandfather climbed the stairs. He appeared with a bedraggled Doctor MacKay.

'That's a bit bracing out there!'

'It's a good deal more than bracing.' Brenda's nan hurried over to greet him. 'Thank you,' she said, pressing his arm.

'Right then, let's tak a look at you, young lady.' The doctor's bald head was wet from the rain, his jacket sleeves saturated as he bent forward to examine her.

Brenda started to panic. 'I'm goin' to lose it, aren't I?'

'No. The baby's decided to come a little early, that's all.'

He said it lightly but the brevity of his examination told Brenda everything she needed to know.

The doctor turned to her nan. 'We'll be needing to get her to the hospital in Stornoway.'

'What? How?' wailed Brenda.

The doctor turned back to her nan. 'She'll have to go in the back of my car.'

'I can't.' Brenda's mind raced back to the original journey she'd made from Tarbert to her nan's cottage, through the dark mountains and along the twisting, narrow road. And now they had to double that distance. Fear pressed on her chest. Were they mad? What if she didn't make it to the hospital? She'd be stuck in that desolate place with her baby on the way.

'That's enough now.' Her nan's voice had taken on a clipped no nonsense tone. 'If the doctor says ye need to have the baby in Stornoway then that's where we're going.' She began to issue instructions with the speed of a rapid-fire machine gun. 'James!'

Brenda's grandfather jumped to attention. 'Yes?'

'Grab the eiderdown and a pillow from our be–'

He shot off before she could finish.

'Tak them down to the car,' she shouted after him. 'And be sure to come straight back with that torch when yer done.' She flung the bedclothes back. 'Now get yerself up, Brenda. We've got te go.'

Brenda swung her legs out of the bed. The floorboards were freezing. She slid her feet into her slippers and wrapped a blanket round her shivering body.

Her grandfather returned with the torch. Brenda inched her way down the narrow stairs, the doctor in front and her nan following behind. She paused at the front door to catch her breath as the full force of the storm hit her. The sound of thunderous waves, crashing on the nearby shore, carried to her on a swirling gale that tore the blanket from around her shoulders. Brenda just managed to catch hold of it before it was whipped away. Needles of icy water penetrated her nightdress.

Her grandfather had layered the back seat of the car with the eiderdown and pillow.

'In ye go,' said her nan.

Brenda snatched at her arm. 'Don't leave me.'

'I'm right here. Now please, get in, Brenda.'

The car smelt of damp dog. Brenda eased herself on to the back seat and her nan slithered in next to her.

Her grandfather kissed her on the forehead then gruffly said, 'I'll see you and the bairn soon.' He shone the torch into the car one last time, closed the door and tapped the roof.

They rattled and bumped their way into the storm, the headlights almost useless at cutting through the spray and darkness. Brenda could see nothing through the windows. Only the glint of rivulets of water streaming down the panes of glass. The wind buffeted the car making it lurch to one side, then the other. She was convinced the vehicle would flip over at any moment. Her nan's soothing voice kept repeating everything would be alright.

She should never have come to this godforsaken place. 'Godforsaken', that was the word her mum had always used when she spoke of the island. She'd be sitting in front of the fire now back home, arguing with her dad about what to watch on television, unaware of what was happening to Brenda. She wished her mum was with her.

'How's my patient doing in the back?'

'I could do with a stiff drink,' she groaned.

'That's the spirit.' The doctor laughed at his own play on words.

'Oh fuck!' Another wave of pain swept over her. A gush of warm liquid soaked her legs.

'You'd best hurry, Donald. Her waters have broken.'

They sped on.

'Good girl,' said her nan. 'Yer doing fine.' The car skidded to a halt and she was thrown forward. 'In the name of fortune, Donald,' She rubbed her forehead, 'are ye trying te kill me?'

Doctor MacKay blasted the car horn. Even on this storm-drenched evening sheep lay by the roadside. Brenda had never understood why they chose tarmac over soft grass. Was it because the road held the heat of the day? Not much on an island like this but perhaps enough to a warm a sheep's underbelly. One sheep always got up and walked aimlessly towards the oncoming car. It would stare into the headlights, a look of eternal shock in its eyes, before skittering into the ditch.

'A few more miles and we'll be in Stornoway,' said her nan. 'If Donald manages to get us there in one piece,' she muttered.

'I'm doing my best, Moira, but it's pitch-black out there.' The doctor threw his hands up in exasperation. 'Yer welcome to tak a turn at the wheel yerself.'

Brenda's nan told him not to be silly. He knew fine well she couldn't drive.

A coil of wire was being dragged and twisted inside Brenda's stomach. She was vaguely aware the car had stopped and that her nan and the doctor were squabbling. All she could focus on was getting through the waves of pain. No time to gather her strength. As soon as one ended, another began. She wanted to run out of her body, away from the pain, but she was trapped. She felt a pulling, a tugging, a downward force. She had no control over it. She had to push. 'The baby's comin'!' Brenda felt between her legs. Her hand was wet and slimy. 'I can feel the head.'

'Donald, quick!' shouted her nan.

There was a sudden blast of cold air as Doctor MacKay opened the back door. The wind slammed it shut. He wrenched it open. 'Get out, Moira!'

Brenda looked down between her legs. A tiny head had appeared, followed by a shoulder.

'Stop pushing, Brenda,' said the doctor.

'I can't.'

'Brenda, listen to me.' Her nan was in the front of the car, twisted round in her seat, watching them both. Brenda reached up her hand. Her nan clasped it tight. 'Ye mustn't push. The cord's round the baby's neck. Doctor MacKay needs to free it.'

The urge was overwhelming. Brenda tried to breathe her way through the pain and remain still.

'That's my girl,' said the doctor. He eased the cord over the baby's head. 'Ok now push, Brenda. Hard.'

Brenda let out a banshee wail as she bore down one last time. The baby slithered into his hands. There was an iron-rich stench of blood which overpowered the smell of dog. The doctor cut the cord, patted the baby dry and gently rubbed his hands down the sides of its nose.

Brenda reached for the sticky bundle but the doctor didn't hand it to her. He began to rub the baby's back.

'Is it a girl or a...?' Brenda's voice tailed off as she realised she hadn't heard the baby cry. She raised herself up into a sitting position. The child's eyes were closed; its body was still. Brenda threw a frightened glance at her nan. Her nan's face was sombre.

'Come on, little one,' urged Doctor MacKay as he vigorously worked his hands up and down the baby's back.

Still no sound.

'Donald?' Her nan's voice was reed-thin.

An image of the tiny grave at Leverburgh church flew into Brenda's head. She should have had her baby in Belfast, in the Royal. They were good there. They knew how to take care of babies that came early. What did an island doctor know of such things?

A razor-sharp screech punctured Brenda's thoughts.

'That's more like it,' said Doctor MacKay. He turned to Brenda's nan and smiled. For a moment their eyes met.

'Thank you, Donald,' she said, with a gentle pat on his shoulder.

The doctor placed the tiny, naked bundle on Brenda's chest. 'It's a girl.'

Her nan wrapped the eiderdown close around Brenda and the baby. 'Ye must keep her warm.'

Brenda stroked her baby's head. How could something this light be a real person? Holding her was like cupping an injured bird –the same trembling body, the same rapid rise and fall of the tiny chest. Brenda's life was no longer her own. It had been taken away by her child's first cry. She surrendered completely.

FORTY-THREE

Belfast

Her dad tried his best. Sure it wouldn't be the same without her. Didn't she want to see her first grandchild? Brenda too? But no amount of cajoling on his part could persuade Clare's mum to join them. In the end they left without her.

They had made it all the way to the Scottish mainland and were waiting on the island ferry when her dad decided to make a quick call home. He returned looking agitated.

'I have to go back.'

'We're goin' home, after comin' all this way?'

'You can still go on without me.'

The thought of facing her sister and grandparents on her own filled Clare with dread. 'I'm not goin' if you're not.'

He told her not to be daft. He'd already paid good money for her fare.

'What about your own?'

'Never mind that.' Her dad unzipped his suitcase and

pulled out their travel documents. He handed Clare her ticket. 'Here,' he said, opening his wallet. He took out a wodge of notes. 'This'll get you started. I'll send some on when I'm back in Belfast.'

'What's goin' on? Is Mum alright?'

'She sounded very down.'

Lately her mum had seemed more positive. She'd started shopping by herself. She was attending Mass again. The new priest didn't give as good a service as her old one but seemed to be a decent enough man. She was sleeping better too. So, when she told them she'd be fine on her own for a short while, they'd both believed her.

'She needs to go to the doctor,' said Clare.

'So that they can dose her up on pills? I don't think so. We have to be patient with her. Once she's properly settled into her new surroundings she'll be back to her old self.'

He told her he'd find a bed and breakfast and set off in the morning. Then they sat together, sharing a cheese and pickle sandwich, and watched the ferry dock. 'Here. Take this will you, before I forget.' He opened his suitcase again and handed her a plastic carrier bag. 'It's somethin' for the wee one.'

Clare took a peek at the contents. Inside was what looked like a cot blanket and a pale pink matinee coat. Her eye was immediately drawn to the delicate scallop stitching on the tiny coat. 'This is lovely,' she said, lifting it out to take a closer look.

'For Isla. Your mum made it.'

Clare looked at him. 'I thought she said–?'

'Your mum's bark is worse than her bite. She's burstin' to see the baby.'

'Then why didn't she come with us?'

'You know why, and your sister hasn't helped the situation with all this talk about never coming home.'

He took out his pipe, turned it over and tapped. A few charred tobacco leaves landed on the matinee coat.

'Hey, watch what you're doin'.' Clare brushed the ashes off and put the coat back in the bag.

Her dad proceeded to refill his pipe, pressing down the tobacco with one large thumb. Clare stared at his hands. They were big and strong – welder's hands – yet dexterous too.

'I hope you make it up with your sister,' he said. 'I hate to see my girls pitted against each other.'

'I'll give it a go, Dad, but I wish you were comin' too.' Clare had taken heart knowing he would be there to step in if things got too heated. Without his calming presence any prospect of a reconciliation seemed more distant.

'It doesn't matter if I'm there or not. I can't speak for you.'

'Pity. It comes out better when you say it.'

Her dad studied her for a moment. 'Tell her you're sorry. The rest will take care of itself.'

She wanted to believe him but it would depend on whether Brenda was prepared to listen. So far she hadn't shown much willingness. 'At least she's ditched that English arsehole. Less to argue about there.'

'Mmm.'

'He was stringing her along the whole time. I can't believe Brenda couldn't see that.' She glanced at him, expecting him to agree.

'She didn't see it because she wasn't lookin' for it. She loved him, simple as that. Still does if you ask me.'

'Don't be sayin' that.'

Her dad took a few puffs of his newly lit pipe. Perfect little circles of white smoke drifted into the air and hung there for a moment before losing their shape. 'There's somethin' else I've been meanin' to say to you, Clare.'

Clare gave a nervous laugh. 'Uh oh. This sounds serious.'

'I want to thank you.'

She looked puzzled. 'For what?'

'Everything you've done for your mother recently. It hasn't gone unnoticed.'

'That's ok.'

A call went out for all foot passengers to proceed to embarkation. Clare gathered up her things ready to board. She looked at him and smiled. 'How do you do it?'

'Do what?'

'Put up with us.'

'I've had years of practice at treadin' carefully,' he said, returning her smile,' and when that doesn't work I take myself off to the pub.'

———

Isle of Harris

Clare would sleep on the sofa in the living room. It wasn't ideal but space was tight.

'I hope yer an early riser,' said her nan. 'I need to light the fire in here first thing in the morning.'

'Erm, yes.'

She gave Clare a quick tour of the upstairs. 'This is yer

sister's room. Excuse the mess. We were caught on the hop and I'm still trying to get everything together for the bairn.'

Clare took in the 'mess'. Nappies and blankets were stacked neatly in the corner next to – what *was* that? It looked like something from a nativity scene, the crib they placed the baby Jesus in. Nappy pins, bottles, teats and talcum powder were lined up in neat rows on top of the dressing table. Clare's own dressing table back home was a jumble of eyeshadows, lipsticks, Ann French make-up remover, cotton-wool balls, nail polish nicked from the Rimmel counter in Woolies. Her mum had given up complaining about the pigsty Clare called a bedroom. Her nan, by the looks of it, had higher expectations.

'That one is our bedroom,' she said, pointing to the one other door. 'The bathroom is downstairs off the kitchen.'

Downstairs was as well ordered as upstairs. The kitchen was immaculate, the living room freshly swept and mopped but every room was gloomy. Small windows, dark furniture. She could only imagine what it must be like when winter truly set in. And no television in the house. That was insane. What did Brenda do with herself? She cast her eye around the room searching for a radio but there was no sign of one. All in all, it was like stepping back into the Dark Ages.

'She got a few cards, I see.' Clare nodded to the mantlepiece where they sat. She checked for the one her mum had sent but it wasn't among them.

'There's one from her friend Hazel,' said her nan.

'Are they still in touch?'

'Oh yes. She seems like a nice girl from what Brenda says.'

'I wouldn't know. I've never met her.'

A loud tapping at the window made Clare jump. Her grandfather waved a muddy hand in greeting then went back to turning over the vegetable patch that took up half of the front garden.

'He's lifting potatoes. They've been good this year. Nice and floury.'

Clare hated floury potatoes, the way they disintegrated the moment she stuck her fork in no matter how much butter she put on.

A few minutes later her grandfather opened the door and set a hessian sack on the slate floor. 'Here you go, Moira. That's the last of them.' He was about to step into the hallway.

'Ah ah ah,' scolded her nan. 'Boots off.'

He left them at the door and made his way into the kitchen to wash the soil from his hands. 'It's good to have ye with us,' he said, glancing at Clare over his shoulder. He flicked the excess water from his hands and reached for a nearby tea towel.

It was whipped away from him.

'Don't be using that. Here, tak this.' Clare's nan handed him a proper towel.

'See what I have to put up with?' He pulled an aggrieved face.

Clare grinned. His teasing manner reminded her of her dad.

'I thought I'd make ye some champ,' said her nan.

'Lovely,' replied Clare.

She sat with her grandfather as her nan prepared the food. Healthy soil, he explained was the key to a good vegetable plot. Seaweed was the best compost. The biggest enemy was the wind.

'I've seen young cabbages spin round in circles then take off like a helicopter.'

Her nan peeled the freshly dug potatoes and placed them in a pot, ready for boiling. Spring onions were finely sliced and left to one side, ready to add to the potatoes once they were mashed. When she was done she wiped her hands on her pinny and joined them at the table.

'I must say we're looking forward to having Brenda and the baby home,' said her grandfather. He glanced over at his wife. 'Aren't we, Moira?'

'Aye. She's a lovely wee thing. The deepest brown eyes you've ever seen.'

'Not like anyone in our family,' said Clare. 'Must take after the father.'

Her grandparents looked uncomfortably at one another.

'Probably,' said her nan.

Her grandfather steered the conversation back into safer waters. 'Yer dad tells us yer learnin' to type? It's good to have a skill, something useful you can use.'

Clare smiled at him. 'I know. I thought that too.'

'I was hoping yer father would make it over,' he said.

'Me too, but Mum didn't want to be left on her own.'

Her nan harumphed. 'She's happy to leave her eldest daughter on her own at the most important time in her life.'

Clare had meant to put it the other way round – that it was her dad who didn't want to leave her mum alone. She looked at the white-haired woman sitting rigid in the chair beside her, casting judgement.

'I know yer mum disapproves of the situation Brenda's got herself into but–'

Clare's grandfather gave a warning shake of his head.

'It's the whole having a baby outside wedlock thing,' said Clare. 'In her eyes, Brenda's committed a sin.'

'For pity's sake.'

'Quiet now, Moira. Let the girl speak.'

'You don't understand. That's a big deal for Mum.'

Clare's mum had her beliefs and nothing could shake them. It's what made her the person she was. To compromise those beliefs was asking a lot of her. Why could her nan not see that?

'Of course it is,' said her grandfather. 'We didn't mean to offend you in any way.'

Clare's nan went to check on the potatoes.

Clare found herself speaking to her back. 'It's not just that. Mum thinks you don't want her here.'

'That's nonsense,' said her nan but it was a half-hearted refute.

As they ate their meal it was her grandfather who encouraged Clare to talk more. She explained the changes in her mum over the past few months. How her dad was trying his best to keep her spirits up. That she felt abandoned by her friends and neighbours and excluded from Brenda's life. Her nan listened intently to it all. Her only comment was the odd, 'I see'.

They finished their meal and her nan began to clear the table.

'Do you want a hand?' asked Clare.

'No, I'm fine.'

She left her to the dishes and followed her grandfather into the living room.

'Best to let her have a little think on things,' he said.

Clare couldn't work the woman out. One minute she was nothing but snippety comments, the next she was all quiet contemplation. Her grandfather was easier to read.

'I'm sorry yer mum is finding things hard.'

'It's almost destroyed her,' said Clare. She thought of the events that had brought her mum to her current state: Brenda's attack and the threats that followed; the cruel disappointment in both her daughters; her fury with Clare's dad. Her mum's view of all of them had shifted. Her love had been tested. 'I'm not sure things can ever be the same.'

Her grandfather considered for a moment. 'Maybe not, but ye can try to make them better than they are.'

'You sound like Dad. He's the eternal optimist too. Truth be told, he's the reason I'm here.'

'Ye don't strike me as the sort of girl who could be forced into doing something she didn't want to do.' Clare took it as a criticism and was about to defend herself until he added, 'I'd say yer here because deep down ye want to be.'

'I suppose.'

Her nan, having finished in the kitchen, had come to join them. 'Well, that's a start,' she said, catching the tail end of their conversation.

Clare wasn't sure what to make of the remark. She left it there.

By the time it had reached nine o'clock her grandparents were ready for bed.

Her nan raked the fire then fetched some bedclothes and a

pillow and set them on the sofa. 'There ye go. We'll talk more in the morning.'

'I was thinkin' of going to the hospital tomorrow,' said Clare, 'to see Brenda and the baby.'

'I'm sure something can be arranged. Let me run it by her first.'

With nothing to entertain her, Clare's only option was to go to bed too. She lay in the dark, watching the fire turn to ash. She imagined her nan having a word with Brenda, testing the waters. What if Brenda didn't want to see her? Then what?

FORTY-FOUR

Lewis Hospital

Her nan had been and gone leaving behind a couple of bruised bananas and a well-thumbed copy of *People's Friend*. Brenda had read it several times over. She looked at the empty bed next to hers. Maureen had left early this morning, all smiles, with her new son. She'd be home by now. Brenda lay back on her pillow and, for the hundredth time that day, her eyes followed the crack that ran the whole length of the ceiling. A trolley rattled as it was pushed down the corridor. Soon nurses would appear and begin to serve up afternoon tea and bone-dry Marie biscuits. Only one more day and she'd be out too.

Beside her, Isla lay sleeping. Brenda watched her stomach inflate like a balloon with each new intake of breath. Then, when it looked close to bursting, she'd let out a long, deep breath and her tiny stomach would sink flat again. Funny, wasn't it? All through her pregnancy Brenda's thoughts had been taken up with what she was going to *do* –

how she would break the news to her family, what she would say to Andy, where she would live, how she would care for her baby. She hadn't had time to think about how she'd *feel*. She hadn't expected to be swept away by this tidal wave of love.

She often found herself thinking back to the night of the birth – the storm and the blackout, the long bumpy ride to the hospital in Doctor MacKay's car, the whole time fearing she was about to lose her baby. She'd had no family to support her then. No partner either. Only her nan to help her through. Here, in the ward, the other women had each slipped into a routine of feeding their babies, changing them, putting them down to sleep. Brenda watched them, feeling useless. At night she'd cried silently.

She'd been scared to hold Isla at first, convinced she would crush her. Her daughter barely filled the space on her lap as she struggled to get her to drink from the bottle. Every time Brenda offered the teat up to her mouth Isla jerked her head away and milk dribbled down on to her neck. The nurses in the hospital told her not to worry, she'd get the hang of it but, in the end, it was her nan who had shown her what to do.

'Ye need to be firm with the bairn.'

Cupping her head to stop it rolling from side to side her nan pressed the teat to Isla's lips. She held it there despite the baby's protests, teasing her mouth open. Eventually Isla accepted it and drank hungrily. Even now, a couple of weeks after Isla's birth, Brenda still wasn't as confident as her nan when it came to handling a baby.

'Can I check your blood pressure?' It was Shona, the young nurse with the dimpled smile.

Brenda put her finger to her lip. 'Sshh.'

'Oh sorry,' said Shona in a low whisper. 'I'll try not to disturb you too much.'

Brenda offered up her left arm.

'Looking forward to getting out tomorrow?'

'I was. Now I'm not so sure.'

'It's natural to feel nervous with your first but you'll be fine.' She began packing her equipment away. 'All good. I'll leave you in peace.'

Brenda turned on her side and tried to block out the intrusive hospital sounds that dictated whether she'd get any rest or not. No sooner had she closed her eyes than there was a loud voice in her ear.

'Tea?'

She looked up to find the tea trolley stationed next to her bed. 'No thanks.'

The nurse in charge proceeded to work her way round the ward, asking the same question of each occupant. Somehow Isla slept through it all – the sound of the tea urn being lifted and set down, the clattering of side plates, cups and saucers, offers of milk, sugar and biscuits.

Afternoon rolled into visiting time and Brenda's stomach was in knots. Relatives came and went but there was no sign of Clare. The hum of voices grew lower; the number of visitors dwindled to a trickle and then there were none. Brenda got up and began emptying the contents of her bedside table. It would need sorting before she was discharged, may as well do it now. She pulled out boxes of tissues, her toiletries bag, hairbrush and comb, a bag of boiled sweets, the blackened bananas her nan had left earlier in the day.

'Sorry to interrupt.' The ward sister looked at the contents scattered across the floor.

Brenda scooped them up and shoved them back into the cupboard.

'There's someone asking about you. She says she's yer–'

Clare stepped from behind her.

'I thought I asked you to wait outside.' Sister Kelly scowled.

'It's alright,' said Brenda.

'This is my ward and I'll be the one to say if it's alright or not.' The sister turned to Clare. 'I'm afraid visiting time's over for the day.'

Clare gawped at her. 'You must be jokin'. I've just got here.'

Brenda knew the sister wasn't one for joking. 'Sorry,' she said, apologising on behalf of her sister. 'Maybe you could bend the rules a little? She's come a long way.'

Sister Kelly tapped her watch. 'Ten minutes and no longer.' She gave Clare a warning glance then walked briskly from the ward, her shoes squeaking on the freshly polished floor.

'A bit of a dragon.'

'She's been good to me.'

'I'll take your word for it.' Clare smiled. 'You're lookin' well.'

'So are you.'

'I brought you this.' Clare placed a copy of *Cosmopolitan* on the bed. 'Not sure if you've read it?'

Brenda looked at the glossy front cover. It was this month's edition. 'No, I haven't. Thanks.'

'Hot in here, isn't it?' Clare unbuttoned her coat. She

pulled a couple of bags of Tayto cheese and onion crisps from her handbag. 'Sorry, they're a bit crushed.'

Crushed or not, Brenda's mouth watered at the memory of the tangy taste.

'Dad had to go back.'

'Nan told me. Pity. I was really lookin' forward to seeing him.'

'You'll have to make do with me.'

Brenda gave a tight smile. 'How's Mum?'

'Better now that Dad's with her.' Clare walked over to Isla's cot. 'I think everything's finally getting on top of her.'

'Sorry to hear that.'

'Yeah ... well.'

The small bundle inside the cot began to stir.

'Ach look,' said Clare. 'Isn't she gorgeous?' She reached out her hand to touch Isla, hesitated then took her hand away.

'What were you expecting – cloven hooves?'

'What?'

'Nothin',' muttered Brenda. She lifted her daughter out of the cot. 'Don't tell me you're hungry again.' She nodded towards the bedside table. 'Reach me over that bottle, would you.'

'There's hardly anything left in it,' said Clare, handing it to her.

Isla gulped down the remains of the milk and began to cry for more.

'She's starvin'.'

'I know. The nurses said they'd bring a fresh one. That was ages ago.'

'I'll go and see what's keepin' them.'

'Clare, wait. Don't be causin' a fuss.'

'I'll check they haven't forgotten.' She walked off, ignoring Brenda's pleas and reappeared a few minutes later carrying a full bottle. 'Here you go.' Clare pulled the curtains around the bed. 'Let's give you some privacy.' One curtain snagged on the rail. She gave it a tug.

'Leave that, Clare.'

Clare gave it another tug. The curtain rings started to detach from the rail. She tried to hang the curtain back.

'Leave it alone, will you.'

'Sorry.' She looked around for somewhere to sit. 'Is there a chair I can use?'

'Over there.' Brenda nodded at the bed opposite them.

'Mind if I borrow this?' Clare asked the expectant mother, removing the grey plastic chair before she had a chance to reply. She set it close to Brenda's bed. 'That's better. Now we can have a proper chat.'

'Oh, cut it out Clare. You can drop the act.'

'Huh?'

'The considerate sister. We both know that's not you.'

'Brenda, don't.'

'I'm surprised you can even bear to look at Andy's bastard.'

'Please, Brenda. I haven't come here to fight with you.'

The more her sister backed off, the angrier Brenda felt. 'Did you think you could waltz in here and act as if nothing has happened? Say a few nice things about Isla and all would be forgiven? Well, you can't!'

Clare got up.' 'I can see this was a mistake.' As she turned to go she bumped straight into Sister Kelly.

'The sister took in the torn curtain and Brenda's flushed face. 'Time for you to go.'

'I was about to.' Clare stood for a moment, shifting her weight from one foot to the other. She looked at Brenda. 'I know this isn't the best place to talk about all of this but...'

'*Now!*' ordered Sister Kelly.

Brenda watched them leave, then lay down and closed her eyes. She tried to calm herself but the blood was pumping inside her head. She'd promised herself she wouldn't get angry. Clare could have her say. Brenda would simply hear her out, keeping her own feelings in check. It had all gone out the window the moment her sister stood in front of her with her fake pious face.

Brenda's eyes flew open. She looked down at her daughter. 'Oh Isla. I promise I won't *ever* call you that again.'

FORTY-FIVE

Isla was a beautiful child, all big eyes and rosebud lips. The first time Clare held her she'd stared into those big eyes and Isla had stared back, never taking her gaze from her.

'She's givin' you the right once-over,' said Brenda.

And much to Clare's delight she was.

Since the flare-up in the hospital she'd been careful not to touch on the events that had taken place back home. She kept her conversations with Brenda neutral and centred on the baby. The constant tiptoeing around her sister was unnatural. 'If you want me to go, I'll go,' she offered at one point, but her grandparents talked her out of it. So, Clare stayed on and slipped into a routine of sorts – giving Brenda a break from changing nappies, helping her nan out around the house, if she'd let her.

Today was ironing day. Her nan had placed a thick woollen blanket on top of the kitchen table and covered it with a white cloth. A bowl of water sat nearby. Clare watched her lay one of her grandfather's white shirts flat, dip her hands into the bowl and sprinkle the shirt lightly with water.

Steam rose as she pressed down on the cotton. When she was done she hung it on a wire hanger and draped a black tie around the collar. From the corner of her eye she caught Clare observing her.

'Funeral,' she said.

Brenda glanced over, a look of concern on her face. 'Who is it, Nan?'

'An old friend of yer grandfather. Ye wouldn't know of him.' She ironed one white cotton handkerchief then another and folded each into a tidy square. 'He'll be missed.' She paused for a moment to reflect. 'But he had a good life.'

Clare turned to her sister. 'That reminds me. You'll never guess who else is dead.'

Brenda was stroking the corners of Isla's mouth, trying to make her smile. 'Who?' she asked in a distracted way.

'Peter's uncle. Remember him?'

'Sort of.'

'He was shot comin' out of the garage. Peter said the UDA deliberately singled him out.'

Brenda's head jerked up and immediately Clare knew she'd said the wrong thing.

'Please don't tell me you're still in contact with *him*.'

'What if I am?'

'Fuck's sake, Clare.'

Their nan set the iron down with a thump. 'I don't know who this Peter is–'

'He's an idiot and so was his uncle. He–'

'We don't speak ill of the dead in this house,' she said, cutting Brenda short. 'Here.' She handed Clare her grandfather's pressed shirt. 'Tak that upstairs for me.'

'I thought you'd like to know,' muttered Clare. She cast

her eyes towards her sister, but Brenda had already turned her attention back to her child.

Clare had always thought Peter's uncle was a bit of an arsehole but no-one deserved to be gunned down like that in broad daylight. His killing had shocked her. She'd thought it would shock Brenda too. Instead, she'd gone off on one at the mere mention of Peter's name.

Her nan was gone by the time Clare returned to the kitchen. Off to pay her respects to the man's family, said Brenda. The table had been cleared, the iron left to cool on the draining board.

'I could have done a bit more for her.'

'She said to leave it. She'll finish it when she gets back.'

Isla had fallen asleep in Brenda's arms and the two sisters, having no chores to do and no baby to fuss over, found themselves with little to say to each other. The clock on the mantelpiece, the same one that kept Clare awake at night, filled the space between them with its loud ticking.

Through the window Clare caught sight of the top of her grandfather's head and went to take a closer look. He was stooped over the vegetable plot, digging out weeds with a small trowel. Every so often he stopped, pulled himself upright and rubbed his back. It struck her that their grandparents were as old as the friend soon to be buried. 'How long do you think you'll stay here, Brenda?'

Brenda glanced up. 'As long as they'll have me. Why?'

'Just wondered, that's all.'

Brenda eased herself off the sofa, trying not to disturb her sleeping baby. Her footsteps were slow and careful as she mounted the narrow staircase. Clare heard her settle Isla into the cot. There was a soft click of the bedroom door followed by her sister's footsteps, faster and lighter, on the wooden stairs.

'Has Nan said somethin' to you?' she said the moment she reappeared.

'No.'

'Then why did you ask me that? Did Dad put you up to it? Mum?'

'No, although you know Mum would have you back in a flash, don't you?'

'I thought she was too ashamed to have me anywhere near her.'

'That's all talk. She doesn't really mean it. Well, she did, but now she's...'

'Seen the light?'

'I wouldn't go that far,' said Clare, 'but you know what? I think it would do her good to have a little one to fuss over.'

Her sister appeared to consider the possibility. Then her face clouded. 'That's all very well for Mum, but I've got Isla to think about too. I don't want her caught up in all that madness. She's better off here where it's quiet.'

'Quiet? You're tellin' me!'

'It's safe too. This is a great place to bring up a child.'

'Listen, Brenda. I know you think it's ideal here, but give yourself another year and you'll be goin' round the bend.'

'Why the big interest in me movin' back home? I thought you were only too glad to see the back of me.'

True, thought Clare, but then a year ago neither the pair of them could stand the sight of one another. A lot had changed since then. They had changed. Clare gave a casual shrug. 'I was thinkin' new house, new start?

'You do realise it means I'd be movin' back in with you too? Have you thought of that?'

'Not until today but...'

'I have.'

An uneasy silence settled between them.

Her sister's words were laden with a meaning Clare didn't want to explore. She turned away and looking for something to do, began sorting her nan's pile of freshly ironed laundry.

'You wanna know the real reason I don't want to go home?'

Clare set the bed sheets to one side, ready to place in the airing cupboard. She kept her back turned, ignoring the question but Brenda wasn't about to let go.

'Because *you're* there.'

'I think you should stop now.'

'And every time you go near Isla, my skin crawls.'

Clare whipped round, knocking the pile of sheets and pillowcases to the floor. 'Don't say that!' She thought of the times she'd helped feed her, bathe her, dress her, thinking she was doing Brenda a favour. Her sister hadn't stopped her.

'You might be puttin' on a good show, convincing everyone you've changed,' said Brenda, 'but I know you better than that. You're full of hate.'

'Now it's all comin' out.'

'You ruined my life with your hatred. I won't let you ruin Isla's too.'

'You think you're the only one whose life has been affected? Do you know what Mum and Dad have gone through? Do you even care?'

'That's not fair and you know it.'

'Oh yeah, I forgot. Nothin's ever your fault. Tell me this, Brenda – how long do you plan to live off what Dad sends you and let two old people run after you? You're selfish and always have been.'

'And you're one evil bitch! The only reason I'm here in the first place is because of you.'

'Hey!' Their grandfather rapped the window. 'I can hear ye from the garden. I'm sure half the island can too.' He threw down his trowel and marched inside, muddy boots still on his feet.

'Get her away from me,' Brenda's face was red and blotched, 'before I do somethin' I'll regret.'

'Don't worry, I'm out of here'.

'Just a minute,' their grandfather called, following Clare into the hallway.

Clare's eyes glistened with pent up tears. 'You don't have to come with me.'

'I was about to head out any way. I told yer grandmother I'd join her once I was done here. Give me a moment to get ready.' He replaced his boots with walking shoes and dusted the soil from his trousers. 'Yer sister and I are going to tak a walk,' he shouted back to Brenda.

'Fine!'

Clare had stormed ahead. Her grandfather was out of breath when he caught up with her. 'Would ye care to tell me what all that was about?'

'She hates me!'

'I'm sure she doesn't.'

'Apparently I...' Clare swallowed. 'I make her skin crawl.'

Her grandfather gave a little 'oh' of surprise. 'I can see

why ye'd be upset.' They walked on, at a slower pace. 'The thing about arguments,' he said after a while, 'is that a lot of hurtful things get said in the heat of the moment.'

Clare stared at him. 'Why are you makin' up excuses for her? You're as bad as the rest.'

Her grandfather knitted his brow. 'I'm afraid you'll have to explain that one to me.'

That was all it took for the dam to burst. Resentments Clare had stored up over the years came spilling out. He had no idea what it was like living in someone's shadow, she raged at him. All her life it had been Brenda this and Brenda that. He took a slight step back from her. She saw the startled look on his face but couldn't stop herself. 'Everyone treats me as second best and I'm sick of it!'

'Second best? Where are ye getting that from?'

'Dad for starters. The way he talks about Brenda, like she can do no wrong. The way he takes her word over mine. She's always been his blue-eyed girl.'

'I'd have te disagree with you on that score. He loves you every bit as much as Brenda.'

'You say that but–'

'He's always spoken fondly of ye.'

'He has? When?'

'In every card we got from him, every letter he sent, every phone call he made. He thinks the world of ye.'

'It's never seemed that way to me. For a while it felt as if he'd given up on me.'

Her grandfather stopped and placed a hand on her arm. 'He would never do that.'

She looked at his earnest face and realised he meant every

word. 'Maybe Dad hasn't,' she said, 'but Brenda has. She made that very clear to me.'

Her grandfather nodded towards a narrow track leading to a small cluster of buildings in the distance. 'I'm headed there,' he said. He suggested she walk a bit more to cool down before she went back to the house. 'I know you and Brenda have your differences,' he said, 'but you need to talk about them. Nothing gets resolved through shouting.'

'She won't listen to me. She...'

'Try her. Wasn't that the whole reason ye came here? To put things right?'

It was but Clare had no idea how to do it when she first arrived and had even less now. Brenda, it seemed, was closing the door on her for good.

———

Her cooling-down walk took Clare past the post office. She had smoked her last cigarette and went in to buy some more.

Mrs McDonald's eyes glistened with barely concealed excitement when she saw her.

'I'm glad you stopped by!' She looked past Clare towards the door. 'Is yer nan not with you?'

'I'm on my own.'

There was a look of disappointment on Mrs McDonald's face. 'Ah well, I'd best tell you I suppose.'

'Tell me what?'

'Someone was in asking for Brenda. A good-looking lad.'

Clare gave a wry smile. Even on a tiny island her sister still managed to reel in the talent. 'Lucky Brenda.'

'An Englishman, had a nice way with him.' Mrs

McDonald thought for a moment. 'Now what did he say his name was?' She snapped her fingers. 'Andy, that's it!'

Clare's smile slid from her face. 'Did you say Andy?'

'That's right. He said he was staying in a bed and breakfast in Tarbert. Maggie Branagh's place, I wouldn't doubt from the way he described it.' Mrs McDonald leant across the counter, a hand shielding her mouth, even though there was no-one in the shop. 'And the ridiculous price she's chargin' him.' She straightened herself up. 'I wonder what he wants with Brenda?'

'I don't know, but he can fuck right off.'

Mrs McDonald looked horrified her news had caused such an outburst. 'Well, it's just…' she blustered. 'I thought you'd want to know. He was looking for directions to the cottage and I–'

'I hope you didn't give them to him.'

'He told me he was a friend of the family. Said he wanted to keep his visit a surprise.' Mrs McDonald had an anxious look on her face. 'I do hope I did the right thing.'

'Actually, no you didn't.'

What was that twat playing at? Pretending to be Brenda's friend. Saying he wanted to surprise her. It was supposed to be over between him and Brenda. Or so she'd said. Clare left the shop abruptly, forgetting the cigarettes she'd come in to buy. She looked up at the darkening sky then took off at a brisk pace. There was only one way to find out.

———

This had to be the place – the whitewashed cottage fitted the description the woman in the post office had given.

'And you'll get the chance to see her lovely baby too,' she said when Andy told her of his plans.

His stomach had dropped to the floor.

'Brenda's little girl,' she added.

She told him to take it easy. It had been stormy and wet; there was no telling what state the road would be in.

The car had skidded and stopped short of a ditch. Surface water, just as the woman had warned. He looked in his mirror out of habit, checking for traffic but on the drive from Tarbert he hadn't met another car or seen a single person, only a few sheep struggling to stand up in the mud-churned grass by the roadside. As far as he could tell there was nothing but dark rock, grey moors and black-water lochs. Here there were more signs of life. A smattering of houses with smoke curling from their chimneys.

Andy drummed the steering wheel with his fingers and considered his next steps. Paul had thought he was mad to travel all the way to Harris to seek her out but here he was. And now the baby changed everything. What he couldn't understand was why Brenda had kept it from him. She wasn't a vindictive person. The Brenda he knew was warm and forgiving. She was in a peace group, for Christ's sake. Yet he'd only found out about the baby – his baby, he was sure of it – by chance, from some woman he'd never set eyes on until today.

It was one thing for him not to confide in Brenda about his ailing marriage. He'd always intended to put that right. It was an entirely different thing for her to choose not to tell him he was going to be a father. That was unforgivable. He sat for a while as dark clouds scudded across the sky and the car slowly turned to a fridge.

The cottage appeared empty but something told him they were in there. Andy had read somewhere – or maybe Brenda had mentioned it after one of her psychology classes – that the first few weeks of a baby's life were the most important. Something to do with facial recognition and attachment. Why waste time in a bollock-cold car, when he could be with his daughter?

A light went on and a figure appeared in an upstairs window. He glimpsed a beautiful face framed with russet-coloured hair. Andy sprang from the car. The door to this small cottage was all that was keeping him from her.

FORTY-SIX

B renda went over the argument again and again. What was it with Clare? How come she always had the knack to set her off? Driving her to voice her ugliest thoughts then walking away leaving Brenda feeling the worse for it.

She looked at her daughter, asleep in her cot, oblivious to the drama that had just played out downstairs. The wooden cot, borrowed from neighbours, was too big for her. At times you'd hardly know she was in there until she let out a scream. She smiled at the thought. Isla might be tiny but she had a right pair of lungs on her.

Brenda remembered her own first sleeps in the cottage, the eerie silence and the pitch blackness. She switched the bedside light on so her daughter wouldn't wake and find herself alone in the dark. She was debating whether to draw the curtains or leave them open when there was a loud hammering on the front door. Brenda jumped, almost knocking the lamp over.

She hurried down the stairs.

'Coming,' she called before whoever it was had the

chance to hammer again. 'Quiet,' she said, putting a finger to her lips as she opened the door.

'Hi, Brenda.'

'Andy?' She gawped at the man standing in front of her, not trusting her own eyes. 'What are you doin' here? How did you–?'

'Nice to see you too.' Large droplets of rain began to fall. He glanced up at the dark sky and grimaced. 'Can I at least come in?'

Brenda hesitated.

'Please,' he said, taking a step forward. 'We need to talk.' Before she knew it, he was over the threshold. He followed her into the living room and sat next to her on the sofa. 'You're looking good.'

This morning, as with most mornings, she'd thrown on the first top that came to hand and clipped her fringe out of her eyes. She looked a mess. Andy leant forward and kissed her lightly on the cheek.

'Whoa.' Brenda pushed him away. 'Stop.'

'Sorry. I couldn't help myself.'

The rain had left dark marks on his leather jacket. Brenda had always liked the way Andy dressed, that he took care over his appearance. Yet he looked out of place in his smart casual clothes. On Harris you dressed for the elements.

'Why are you here, Andy?'

'I had to come. I couldn't stop thinking about you.'

She felt a tingle in her spine. Part of her still wanted him to desire her.

Brenda took in his exhausted face. She knew that face well – the dark circles under his eyes and the muscle in his left cheek that twitched when he'd had no sleep. In Belfast, long nights on duty had often left him looking like this. She used to rub his cheek with her fingers as if by doing so she could melt the tension away.

'Why didn't you answer my letters?'

He said it so quietly and so suddenly it threw her. 'I um,' she stuttered.

'Did you even bother to read them?'

Brenda was conscious of his eyes upon her, his closeness to her. 'I did read some.'

'That was good of you.'

He'd sent lots of letters but she hadn't answered them. The first had been full of apologies and details of his divorce. She'd wondered if she was being too harsh with him, almost wavered, but the tone quickly changed. Andy became more insistent. He accused her of being bloody-minded, kept asking her to get in touch with him. It sounded more of a command than a request. After a while they stopped coming.

'All I wanted was the chance to explain.'

'That you'd been hiding things from me?'

'That's good coming from you.'

Brenda darted a look at him. *Does he know?*

Her gut churned as she waited for him to reveal more. Instead ,he watched her, basking in her discomfort. She got up and went to the fire. 'It's nearly out,' she said, prodding it with the poker. A few embers sparked then died away. 'Too late to rescue.'

Suddenly he was at her side. He reached past her and lifted a card from the mantlepiece. The card was from Hazel. *Congratulations on your new baby* was scrolled on the front in pink lettering.

'Who's the lucky father?'

Her eyes met his. 'You know it's you.'

He returned the card to its resting place, scattering the others in the process. A couple fluttered down towards the dying fire. 'Why didn't you tell me?' His eyes took on a cold stillness. 'Was it your way of getting back at me?'

'What? No.' He was twisting things, making her out to be the one who was in the wrong. 'You've got a cheek, preachin' to me,' she said. 'You didn't exactly rush to tell me about your own kid.'

'Keep Stevie out of it.'

'Well, you certainly did. You never mentioned him once the whole time we were together. What sort of a father does that?'

'Don't *ever* say I'm a bad father,' he said, stabbing the air with a finger that matched the staccato timing of each word.

She knocked his hand away. 'Get your finger out of my face.'

Brenda heard it first. Quiet sobs that sounded more like hiccups. Soon the sobbing turned to loud wails as Isla woke from her sleep. 'I have to go to her,' she said. As she made her way upstairs he was close behind her. Brenda lifted Isla from the cot and rocked her in her arms, trying to soothe her. Andy stood in the doorway observing them. Then he entered the bedroom and shut the door. 'Let me have a try.' He held his arms outstretched, waiting for Brenda to hand the baby to him.

Instinctively Brenda recoiled.

'I won't drop her, if that's what you're worried about. I have done this before you know.'

She pulled Isla closer, shielding her from him. Andy

318

filled the space in front of her. 'Please, let me past. She's hungry.'

He watched her struggle in vain to calm Isla's crying. 'Oh, Brenda,' he said, with a slow shake of his head, 'you haven't really thought how you're going to do this, have you?'

'What do you mean?'

'Raise a child on your own. Think about it. You've got no money coming in, not even a student grant. No job.' He cast his eyes over the cramped bedroom, taking in the cot and the baby paraphernalia stacked everywhere next to Brenda's books and personal belongings. 'No real home. Unless you think this is a suitable place to bring up a child.' Andy frowned. 'I don't.'

She couldn't tell if he meant her grandparents' cottage or the island. Either way, Brenda felt self-conscious. He'd also managed to cast fresh doubts in her mind. The panic began to creep back. Brenda knew she couldn't stay here forever. She didn't need Clare or him to point that out to her.

'Of course, you know it's down to me to decide what's best for her. Legally that is.'

'What?'

'The rules are different with an illegitimate child. The father has more rights. Didn't you know that?'

Brenda's stomach clenched. He seemed so sure of himself and she knew nothing about the law. It might be different in Scotland.

'The sensible thing,' Andy paused, allowing the full weight of the word to make its impact, 'would be for us to somehow deal with this together.' He was being posted to Germany. She could come with him. They both could – her and the baby. He was offering her the chance of a family life, a new start.

'You're already married, Andy, in case that slipped your mind.'

'Not for much longer. Then you and me can be together.'

He seemed to think they could magically rekindle what they'd once had.

'That's crazy talk.'

He looked at her as if she was the crazy one.

'What about your son? How will that work?'

'I don't know. I'll sort something out.'

'Like what?'

Stevie could stay with them, he suggested, when Andy was on leave.

'With you, me and the baby? The whole time you're on leave?'

'Maybe not the whole time.'

Brenda looked horrified. 'I've never met your son.'

'I can't just walk away from him even if that's what they'd like me to do.'

'They?'

'Jenny and her mum.'

Brenda's arms ached from holding Isla. 'I don't know what's goin' on with you and your wife, or your mother-in-law for that matter. All I know is that you're not making sense and I don't want to be dragged into it. *Please,* Andy,' she said. 'I want you to go.'

His face hardened. 'Oh no. You're not keeping me from my own child. It happened once. I won't let it happen again.'

FORTY-SEVEN

A ndy was frightening her now. He talked of Isla as if she was his to claim. She had to do something, but what? Play along? Say she'd think about his suggestion? Would that reassure him enough to get him to leave? Or would it do the opposite: feed the fantasy going on in his head and make things worse? Brenda was frantically working out how to make her move when there was a slamming of the front door, followed by Clare's voice.

'Brenda, you won't believe who's showed up.' Her sister checked the living room then the kitchen.

'I'm up here,' yelled Brenda.

Clare bounded up the stairs. 'That wanker, Andy!' She threw the door open almost catching the side of his skull. There was a sharp intake of breath as she took in the scene. 'What the–?'

'Who are you?'

'Never you mind who I am.'

Isla's back arched; her body stiffened in Brenda's hold.

'Now see what you've done.' Andy went to Brenda and the baby. 'You've frightened her.'

'Oh, it's like that, is it? Playin' happy families.'

'No, we are *not*.' A moment earlier, when Clare burst into the room, Brenda could have kissed her. She'd never been so glad to see her younger sister but, as usual, Clare had got it all wrong.

'This is between us,' said Andy. 'It's got nothing to do with you.'

Clare screwed up her face. 'Tell him to fuck off, Brenda.'

'It's alright,' said Brenda, trying to signal with her eyes that things were far from alright and her sister wasn't helping matters.

Andy remained close by Brenda's side. 'Actually, we were just finishing off our chat when you bowled in.' He glanced up at Brenda. 'Weren't we?'

'Go ahead.' Clare folded her arms and cocked her head to one side. 'Don't let me stop you.'

'Thanks. Nice of you to let me talk to her this time.'

Brenda's eyes darted to her sister. 'This time?'

'You didn't tell her, did you?'

A sick feeling began to build in the pit of Brenda's stomach. 'Tell me what?'

'I phoned your parents' house a couple of days after they attacked you. Your sister here,' he jerked his head towards Clare, 'took the call.'

'Don't listen to him,' said Clare, drawing her arms into her chest. 'He's tryin' to stir things up.'

'She refused to fetch you. Threatened to report me if I tried to contact you again.'

'Is it true?

'It didn't happen the way he–'

'Did Andy phone me? Yes or no, Clare?'

'Yes.'

In the days following the attack Clare had taunted her mercilessly, asking constantly if she'd heard anything from him, making jibes about Andy doing a runner. Brenda hadn't known what to think. Was he injured and lying in a hospital bed somewhere, unable to get in touch with her? Or was it as Clare said: he'd realised he was in over his head and had decided to bale out? If she'd known what had really happened, she might have made different choices but her sister had stolen those choices from her.

'All that time you let me think he didn't care. What's wrong with you?' Brenda curled her lip. 'You're twisted, Clare.'

'Don't forget bitter,' said Andy. 'Bitter *and* twisted.'

'Happy?' Clare gave Andy a glare that could cut through plate steel. 'Screwin' up a country isn't enough for you? Now you have to screw up my relationship with my sister.'

'I'd say you've done a pretty good job of that all by yourself.'

'Shut up you Brit bastard.'

'Is that the best you can come up with after everything you've done?'

Clare raised her hand to strike him.

'I wouldn't if I were you.'

She tried to follow through but he grabbed hold of her arm mid-swing. Clare swiped at him with her free hand. 'Think you're so clever, don't you?' She lashed out with her feet.

Andy spun her round and pinned her arm behind her back. He pushed her against the wardrobe.

'Let go of me!'

'Not until you calm down.'

'Andy, stop it,' yelled Brenda. 'Stop it the pair of you!'

The wardrobe wobbled under their combined weight. A large metal key fell to the floor. Andy pushed Clare's arm higher up her back.

Clare howled. 'What are you goin' to do? Finger-fuck me like your other mates did?'

Andy dropped her arm and sprang back. 'What? No!'

Clare's eyes filled with rage. 'You're all the same. You think you can do anything to us and get away with it.'

'I've no idea what she's talking about.'

Clare turned to Brenda. 'Do you know what it's like to be pawed over by one of his lot, to beg them to stop but they won't? Oh, wait a minute, of course you don't. Lover boy here gets to ask you first.'

With creeping horror, her sister's meaning began to sink in. 'What happened, Clare?'

'Remember that night you said I was drunk?'

Brenda floundered.

'The night I went to Lavery's!'

'Yes, I remember.'

'They stopped me on my way home. Said they had to search me.' Clare paused, her mouth taking on a bitter twist. 'Let's just say they got carried away.'

Brenda recalled her sister's ripped tights and the cut on her cheek. She'd been so ready to believe her when she said she'd fallen. Too quick to judge. 'Did the soldiers hurt you?

If they did, you need to tell me.' Fear flooded Brenda. 'Oh my god, were you...?

'No, I wasn't raped.'

'Of course she bloody wasn't. We're not animals.'

'Not in the way you think but they did things.'

'What kind of things?'

'Just things. That's all you need to know.'

'She's making it up. We'd have got a woman to search her. That's what the WRAC are for.'

Clare gave Andy a swift, angry glance. 'Yeah well, they didn't.' She turned her gaze back to Brenda. 'You really think they have Army women to call upon,' she clicked her fingers, 'just like that, for every checkpoint? Think again. Dark streets. No witnesses.'

'You should have reported it. We stamp hard on that sort of thing.'

'You have no idea, have you? The word of one little Catholic girl against two upstanding British soldiers. How do you think that would finish?'

The silence in the room answered her question. If it came to her sister's word against theirs, the outcome was inevitable. Brenda knew it. So did Andy.

He stood quietly appearing to absorb what he'd heard. He was slow to offer his response and when he did speak it was only to Brenda. 'I'm sorry for what happened but you can't lump us all together. What I said before, I meant every word. My offer's still open.'

'What offer? Don't tell me you're–'

'I sprang things on you. Maybe when you've had a chance to think?'

For the first time since he'd arrived at the cottage he sounded apprehensive and Brenda seized upon it.

'Maybe I do need some time,' she lied. 'Why don't you leave me to think it over.'

He seemed not to trust what he'd heard. Brenda held his gaze.

'Ok,' he said. 'But we're not finished here. You and me still have things to sort.'

Brenda nodded. 'I know we do.'

She listened as he made his way down the stairs. He paused at the bottom and her chest tightened. Then he opened the front door. Through the sheeting rain she thought she heard a car start. 'Is he gone?'

Clare went to the window and glimpsed out. 'Looks like it.'

Relief flooded Brenda's face.

Clare saw she was trembling. 'Are you ok?'

'Not really.'

'I'm sorry,' said Clare. 'I didn't mean to set him off like that but when I first walked in on you two, I thought you were makin' up for lost time.'

'Wrong end of the stick.'

'So, what *is* goin' on?'

'He was freakin' me out the way he was talking. He said he had more rights than me when it came to Isla.'

'That's bollocks.'

'Of course it is, but he rattled me, turning up out of the blue like that. One minute he was all threats, the next he was askin' me to go to Germany with him.'

'Don't even think about it.'

'I'm not. Something's changed in him. It's like I don't

recognise him anymore.'

Clare rubbed her twisted arm. 'Maybe you're seein' him for what he is.'

Everything was so black and white with her sister. People were either good or bad, right or wrong, with nothing in between. It was never as simple as that.

'Why didn't you tell me?'

'About my little run-in with the soldiers?' Clare gave a deep sigh. 'I wanted to but then I heard you tellin' Mum I was drunk. You both assumed it but I wasn't. Not that night.'

'Does Dad know?'

'No and don't you ever tell him!'

'But–'

'I mean it! Promise me you won't say anything.'

Brenda thought of her father and how he would react. She couldn't do that to him. 'I can keep a secret.'

'Yeah.' Clare gave her a wan smile. 'When it comes to soldiers, we both can.'

Their attention was drawn to Isla who was making loud sucking sounds and gulping in air through pursed lips.

'She's famished,' said Brenda. 'Keep an eye on her, will you, and I'll go and make up her bottle.'

'Am I allowed to touch her?'

Brenda baulked. 'What I said earlier... I...'

'Give her here.'

In the kitchen, waiting for the kettle to boil, Brenda's thoughts returned to Andy. She might have won herself some breathing space but there was still the issue of his presence on the island to deal with. She didn't want to meet with him again, but she would. This time it would be on her terms and in a setting of her choice. And Isla definitely wouldn't be there.

She was about to head back to the bedroom when there was a scream from Clare. The bottle dropped, smashing glass over the slate floor. She ran to the stairs but she was too late. Andy was already past her and out the door. She raced after him then stopped dead. Behind her, she heard Clare gasp.

FORTY-EIGHT

Andy held Isla tight to his chest, his jacket wrapped round her, swallowing up her tiny frame. Only her head was visible. The rain beat down on it. A red, mud-streaked car sat in the road; the driver's door lay open. Fear pulsed through Brenda. Even if she made a sprint for it, he'd be inside before she could reach it.

Clare was coiled taut, ready to make her move. 'For god's sake, get her off him before he suffocates her.'

Brenda held her back. 'Stay where you are,' she hissed. 'Let me talk to him.'

'What?'

'He's not thinkin' straight.' She glanced at her sister. 'We need to go easy.'

Clare stopped straining against her, gave a small nod of her head. 'Ok.'

Brenda took a couple of tentative steps towards him. 'Andy?'

He glanced up.

'Why don't you give her to me?'

329

Andy stared at her unblinking.

'She's getting wet.'

He ran his hand over Isla's head and wiped the wetness away. Brenda felt sick. She swallowed, tried again. 'Let's bring her inside and dry her off properly.'

'You'd like that, wouldn't you? So you can have her all to yourself.'

Brenda raised her arms, her palms open, in a surrendering gesture. 'That's not what I'm saying.'

From the corner of her eye she caught the shadowy movement of her sister and prayed Andy hadn't noticed. She focused on keeping him in her sights as her mind scrabbled for the right words to say to him. He opened his jacket and turned Isla to lie flat in his arms. She kicked her legs and punched her fists in the air.

'Careful. She–'

'Your mum must take me for a mug,' he said, gazing down at her as she thrashed about in his hold. 'She had no intention of thinking things through.'

'Andy, *please*.' Brenda choked back tears. 'Give her to me.'

He glanced at the waiting car. Brenda froze.

Beyond them lay the sandy beach fringed with dark mountains. Where did he think he could go? This was an island. There was no way off other than the ferry and that didn't sail until tomorrow morning. Unless he had no intention of leaving the island. Unless ... Her mind swirled with possible scenarios, each one more terrifying than the other. She wanted to charge at him and snatch her baby from his arms. *Don't do that. Think, Brenda, think*! But she couldn't still her mind long enough to work out what to do.

'You haven't lost her,' rang out a voice next to her. 'You'll always be part of her life. That's right, Brenda, isn't it?'

Panic gripped her throat. The words wouldn't come.

Clare gave her a nudge. 'Tell him.'

'Yes,' blurted Brenda. 'I won't keep you from her.'

'You see,' said Clare. 'No-one's shuttin' you out.'

'Why should I believe anything you say?'

'I know you don't trust me, but at least talk to Brenda.' Clare half-turned her back on him. 'I promise to keep well out of things this time.' She opened the palm of her hand revealing a bunch of car keys then snapped it shut. 'Don't worry,' she whispered. 'Soldier boy's goin' nowhere.'

With a silent meeting of eyes the sisters showed they understood the stakes had shifted.

Brenda conjured up a ghost of a smile. 'She's right, Andy. We do need to talk. You said so yourself.' She took a shaky step closer. When he didn't move she took one more, then another until at last she reached him.

The last band of rain had passed over but the air was damp and chill. Her baby's legs were bare. Brenda reached out to touch them, her face creased with concern. 'They're freezin'.' She lifted the sodden matinee coat and felt the vest underneath. It clung to Isla's skin. 'She's soaked through.'

Andy ran his eyes along the length of Isla's body. 'Christ!'

Brenda offered up her arms. 'Can I?'

Isla gave a soft whimper as he handed her over. 'Go,' he said, jerking his head in the direction of the cottage.

Brenda turned and ran.

Clare was waiting at the door. 'Quick. Get in.'

Brenda glimpsed back. Andy was on his knees, bent over, his head in his hands.

'Come on, never mind him.' Clare pulled her in and bolted the door shut.

Brenda began to strip Isla of her clothes. 'Check the back door too.'

Clare was already on her way to the kitchen. 'It's locked,' she shouted, lifting a towel from their nan's pile of laundry and bringing it to her.

Brenda patted Isla dry. 'I need a blanket.'

'I'll get it.' Clare dashed upstairs and returned with one stripped from Brenda's bed.

Brenda wrapped her daughter in it and sat with her next to the fire.

'Is she ok?'

Isla let out one of her piercing cries.

Brenda gave a brittle smile. 'I'll take that as a good sign.'

'I'm sorry.' Clare spoke in short bursts. 'I tried to stop him. He was too strong. Too fast. He was out the door before…'

'Hey, it wasn't your fault.'

'You see if he'd hurt her, I swear to god, I…'

The spikey, combative Clare briefly flared but quickly died away leaving a frightened, tear-stained version of her younger sister Brenda had never seen.

'What's wrong with him? Has he completely lost the plot or what?'

Brenda's mind was on her child. She hadn't thought to check on Andy. 'Where is he now?'

Clare went to the window. 'Still kneelin' in front of the gate where you left him.'

Brenda took a look for herself. 'Give me the car keys.'

'Why?'

The keys lay on the floor where her sister had dropped them. Brenda scooped them up. 'I can't leave him like that.'

'What are you doin'? Come back!'

'I won't be long.'

A loud guttural sob rent the air as she stepped outside. An animal sound, wrenched from somewhere deep inside him. She'd never heard a man cry like this. It was awful to hear.

He looked up as she approached. 'I don't know what I'm doing anymore.'

Brenda knelt in front of him.

'This isn't me,' he said. 'I ... I can't think straight anymore, can't focus. Everything is twisted in my head. It's one big tangled knot – you, Belfast, Stevie.'

The surrounding hills had taken on a sharply defined silhouette. They crouched in the growing gloom as if listening to every word they said.

'You've had a lot on your plate.' Brenda spoke slowly as if to a child. 'Your job, your divorce, us. It's a lot to take in.'

'I keep messing up. Why can't I hold on to the people I care about?'

'Sshh now.' She placed her hand on his cheek and gently rubbed it. 'Don't talk like that.'

Andy closed his eyes. 'I love you,' he said.

'I love you too.'

She stayed with him, his head resting on her shoulder, until he grew calmer. 'You know I can't let you back in the cottage. My grandparents will be back soon and I don't want them involved. You should go, get some sleep. Everything will seem clearer in the morning.'

'Yes,' he said, pulling himself up to standing. He swayed for a moment before steadying himself.

'Are you alright?'

He brusquely wiped away his tears. 'I'm fine.'

She handed over the keys.

Andy took them mechanically from her then looked towards the cottage. 'You better get back to her.'

Brenda was almost at the door when she stopped. She turned, seeking him out one last time, but he was already gone.

'What did you say to him?' asked Clare once she was back inside.

'I told him what he needed to hear.'

EPILOGUE

S unday's paper lay on the kitchen table, covered in a fine dusting of cocoa powder. Brenda wiped it off and cast her eyes over the picture on the front page. It was of a large crowd, mostly women, gathered in a Belfast park. Hazel was somewhere among them, so too was big Patsy.

'Mummy!' Isla bounded into the kitchen, closely followed by Brenda's nan.

'She's like a whippet. I can't keep up with her.'

Isla stuck a podgy finger into the icing bowl.

Brenda lifted her hand out. 'That's to go on the cake.'

Their summer stay was almost at an end and the chocolate sponge was her parting treat. It had sunk in the middle. Her nan eyed the collapsed disaster and stifled a laugh.

'Have you seen this?' Brenda pushed the paper towards her. 'Fifty thousand, they reckon. It's incredible.'

'Aye, I've seen it.' Her forehead creased. 'The pity is it took the death of three innocent bairns to bring it about.'

The children had been walking with their mother when a speeding car, driven by an IRA gunman, lost control and ploughed into them. He had been shot and killed moments before by a chasing Army patrol. People were sickened by what happened, her mum told her. They were angry with the Provos. Clare was angry too. She blamed the British soldiers.

'If they hadn't shot at the car it wouldn't have gone out of control.'

'Didn't the driver's mate aim a rifle at them?' Brenda asked her. 'Or at least that's what I read.'

'The point is he didn't actually fire any shots from the car. The soldiers fired first.'

'Does it matter? Children died.'

Putting the blame on one side or the other wouldn't undo the tragedy, but Clare was latched on to a matter of principle. She was determined to push her case.

'It matters when they don't get the facts right.'

Where did Clare get *her* facts from? she wanted to ask. Instead, she backed off and cut their phone call short.

Yet again a conversation with her sister had left Brenda dismayed at the inevitability of their differences. Over the last couple of years, they had tried hard to contain those differences, but they simmered and stewed, waiting to surface.

Brenda had ventured back into her peace campaigning, whereas Clare fluttered around the fringes of her old haunts. Neither probed too deeply into each other's thoughts. They still clashed and, when it happened, it was as if the earth had cracked open and each sister stood on opposite sides of the fault line.

Her mum had made the first move, in the end, surprising

everyone. Things had settled, she'd said. McManus had risen further through the ranks. He was done with Brenda and had bigger things to worry about, like watching his own back. She should come home.

Isla was the common love that helped bring them closer. Brenda worried about using her in this way but her daughter was the glue that kept them all together as a family. They loved her unconditionally – her sister, mother, father – and it was more than Brenda hoped for. She couldn't have picked up the pieces of her life without them.

Brenda felt a tugging at her sleeve. Isla was impatient to get back outside.

'You go on,' said her nan. 'I'll see to the cake.'

Brenda left her to it. 'See you later,' she yelled as she headed out the door with her daughter in tow.

The afternoon walk along the beach was their special time together. A vast, beautiful expanse they claimed for themselves. It was also Brenda's thinking space. She had one more year of her university course and then it would be time to carve her own future. She wasn't yet sure what that might be. She still dreamed of a life beyond Belfast but perhaps it could be a life in Belfast, if the tide changed.

Isla took off at full pelt the moment they reached the sands. Then, spotting a shell, she stopped abruptly. She brought it back to Brenda, all smiles. Most of the shells she found were bird-pecked, jagged and broken. Brenda would say they were lovely and drop them back in the sand. This one was perfect.

She slipped it into her coat pocket. As she did so she felt the letter she'd picked up from the post office earlier that morning. In his unmistakable looped handwriting, it was addressed to Isla. She'd save it, along with the others, for when the time was right.

Isla stood gazing up at her, looking pleased with herself. She was so pretty with her big brown eyes. It was hard not to look at her eyes without seeing his. Tomorrow, she'd send that photograph he'd been asking for.

THANK YOU

So many people have helped me along the way. I am indebted to each and every one of you.

Let me start with you, mum. This is a huge, heartfelt thanks for sharing your love of books with me, and for your steadfast belief that I would become a published author. I miss you.

Thank you to my dear friends, Gill and Elaine, for always believing in me and in the book you hadn't yet seen. Sorry it's taken so long. Also to Liza for your boundless positivity … and your wonderful home-baked cakes.

Paul and Emma, my earliest writing buddies, your feedback was invaluable and helped turn a germ of an idea into a fully-fledged story. Gina, thanks for being such a great sounding board.

To my book-loving Northern friends - the three Janes, Anne, Gillian, Karen and Clare - I offer my appreciation for your unflagging enthusiasm and for collectively nudging me closer to publication.

And finally, my biggest thanks is reserved for you, Robert, my endlessly patient husband. You have lived and breathed every page of this book alongside me. You have put up with the surly pouts when things won't come together and the writer's version of a sugar rush (scary) when the words flow. I owe you everything!

ABOUT THE AUTHOR

Karen McKibbin grew up in Northern Ireland during The Troubles. After graduating in English from Queen's University of Belfast, she moved to London and embarked on an eventful career in retail and people development. Throughout this time she carried a story around in her head, a part of Irish history seldom told. *Soldier Doll,* her debut novel, is that story. She now lives, with her husband, on the Northumberland coast and writes historical fiction.

For more information visit:

facebook.com/KarenLMcKibbin

twitter.com/vanityfizz

instagram.com/karenmckibbinwriter